KARAKORUM

Don McVey

ISBN: 9798392226269
Imprint: Independently published

*Our Modor, who art in my blood, hallowed by thy true creation, thy kingdom gone, thy will undone. Deliver us from **Karakorum.***

Hi,

I'M A LOCAL AUTHOR. THIS IS MY DEBUT NOVEL. IF YOU ENJOY IT, PLEASE LEAVE A REVIEW ON AMAZON!

@DONMCVEY

#KARAKORUM

PART 1

The Pillars of Creation

The fragile Sapiens mind was easily convinced of its core imperfections. Stimulated by beautiful fallacies, it reached new horizons and sailed onto the next, without pausing to look back. Within the contract of forged proficiency, lay the condition that reality would be forever tainted, the breadcrumbs eaten and the tree of knowledge hacked to the ground. No longer nature's child, but a hapless creature trapped in a hole dug by itself; its devolved fingernails unable to climb out. A repugnant deity. A product of man, not God – *The Modor of Sapienism*

SORCHA

Sorcha sat with her back against the base of a decaying railgun that pointed out over the Baltic Sea, watching waves break against the submerged ruins below, of what had once been Tallinn. The gunnery was the only place Sorcha knew where she could find the solitude needed to prepare her mind for a match.

She tried to empty her thoughts into the black sea, but the approaching storm made her uneasy. Perhaps the more likely culprit was the thought of the upcoming game. The rarity of a child playing Scratch, a term taken from the losing player's *scratched* state, had not gone unnoticed. A deep edge recruiter had made the unorthodox journey to the outer to challenge her, an act that was almost unheard of. Many were expected to make the journey to witness the match first hand, elevating a regular Scratch game into an event of monumental importance for Sorcha.

She resigned herself to the fact she'd never feel adequately prepared and stood to leave. Before she turned, the faintest glimmer of light seemed to wink at her from behind one of the rolling waves. She trained her eyes to the spot, her fingers tightening by her sides, nothing. She cast her glance along the brutal death squad that lay patiently in waiting. Rain began to drop on the surface of the hard structures, making the edges glimmer against the dark sky. They terrified her, and she found herself again questioning; *how could I have made it?*

Nobody knew for sure how Sorcha had arrived at the outer edge, but it was assumed that whoever brought her had perished in the crossing. If the rail guns hadn't ripped them in half, the currents likely would have. For this reason, Sorcha was seen as a local oddity and had been welcomed into the usually hostile community; a community comprised of the wretched, downtrodden and hopeless that made up the outer. They were her people now.

By her build, most assumed Sorcha was very much a child; although a closer look into her eyes revealed an older soul, brooding and serious, hinting at the hardships they may have seen. Her body was frail, but her mind sharp enough to make a meagre living competing in the main source of entertainment for the estimated fifteen billion souls who lived within the confines of Kara.

Sorcha made her way back towards the gargantuan living mass that seemed to grow organically from the ground. To view Kara as a place with geological boundaries would have required knowing its limits, or understanding its hideous scale; something the very nature of the factions made impossible. Kara was simply the name for everything still in existence, it was effectively the entire world.

From her low vantage, she looked up at the towering wall of chaos hugging the coast in both directions, pockmarked with infinite glowing specks from the endless cube-sized lives it contained. A monstrous shanty-town built layer upon layer, from every known material, engineered by millions of minds over countless generations, its very density the only thing that held it together. From where she stood, she'd heard it continued over seven thousand skyless miles east; a concept Sorcha found impossible to grasp.

A solitary makeshift workshop stood apart from the main bulk, made from pressed mata, a familiar flicker coming from hot sparks that flew out the door and turned the wet ground into steam. Sorcha approached the opening and saw Lunn's heavy shoulders folded over a tangle of scrap.

"Found something," she said.

Sorcha began pulling some wire from a stiff pocket affixed to the front of her oversized boiler suit. Lunn stopped what he was doing and stomped over, his steps shaking the entire workshop, the lamp he held looking comically undersized in his colossal welding mitt. Most people were wise to give Lunn and his kind a wide berth. Known colloquially as Grunders, they were thought of as something more akin to a tamed bear than a human being. A left-over from the heresy of gen-modding, they were tolerated for being relatively useful and ultimately harmless. All Grunders, like pure Sapiens, were born without the ability to assimilate with the labs. Despite being the only faction approved, and somewhat mandatory mod, it was common for Grunders to reject neural links, favouring physical strength over any cognitive benefits gained through the connected mind. Adopting a puritan branch of Sapienism as their unofficial religion was an irony most saw as a comical over-compensation. Being the only one of his dwindling kind to call Eto home, Lunn evidently had no qualms when it came to using tech to his advantage.

He'd been permitted a workshop beyond the sinking plains, on the condition he occasionally took care of the crumbling railguns; antiques that had once been revered as almighty protectors. Tasked with marking the boundaries of the edge before Kara had been hard divided, they'd lit up the night skies as raiders tried to plunder the desalination plants or desperate migrants from the dying territories attempted to make land. Once faction boundaries had finally been set in stone, the threat from outsiders became negligible, while the water that had once made the plants a priceless resource strayed beyond the salt limits. That didn't stop them from trying to squeeze the last ounces of fresh water from the desert sea, or Lunn from scavenging what he needed to keep his own projects well-stocked. Some would grumble from time to time when a sheet of metal or a surplus circuit board went missing, but picking a fight with Lunn only ever had one outcome.

He bent down and took the wire from Sorcha, biting down on one end. "Hrrmm, coppa. Where'd you get?"

"It was lying around." She dropped her head and walked

around him. "What are you working on?"

"Hrrmm, you no find coppa girl." He took a few steps until he was looming down behind her. "I no want you get trouble."

Sorcha turned and looked straight up at the thin eyes peering over his impossibly square cheeks. "I'm not in any trouble, don't worry. A tip from one of the crunchers."

"Hrrmm." Lunn removed his mitts and carefully coiled the wire, placing it neatly in a box on his workstation, before picking up the item he'd been working on. It looked like an oversized bracelet that went from his wrist to elbow. A purple hue omitted from the maze of thinly cut lines on its surface. Sorcha leaned in to help him fasten it to his arm.

"What is it?"

Lunn ignored the question. "You play tonight?"

"Yes. A scout from the deep edge." She could sense Lunn's pumpkin-sized head slowly shaking.

"Sound like trouble girl."

"It's just a match like any other."

Lunn padded over to the wall and took down a prying tool, making some final adjustments to the fit. "I will come. Make sure no trouble."

Sorcha smiled, she felt safe when Lunn was around. He turned, his eyes fixed on her in what would have looked like a threatening stare if she couldn't see the pretence underneath. His huge left hand crunched together, flexing the enormous girth of his forearm. The lines on the bracelet spread apart, revealing veins of glowing energy within. In a flash, an energy shield appeared, covering Lunn's upper body and head.

Through the dancing particles, Sorcha could see Lunn's ivory tusk grin.

She'd never known a time before The Wipe, never pinned for the intoxication of the unlimited. Sorcha had disciplined herself on what she knew and absorbed the minutia of

Scratch as naturally as a newborn learns its mother tongue. She feared the upcoming game would be the most dangerous she'd ever faced, the deep edge players being legendary to those in the outer. Despite being small fry compared to those found in the inner factions, Scratch could be more lethal when players were evenly matched. Sorcha had never lost, but some longer games, with skilled opponents, had laid her out for several cycles. However, her mind had matured since then, and she was confident she'd developed the mental stamina to go longer. It was the question of how much longer that knotted up her empty stomach. To engage in a mind-flow state meant time became meaningless; no way of knowing whether delicate neural pathways were being corroded, no way to untangle oneself from its grip, only the sickly awareness of harm done when it was all over. Sorcha accepted she might take some damage against a player from the deep, but the payoff, win or lose, would be worth it. She'd been hoarding whatever bonds she could throughout her playing career and dreamed of getting out the slum stacks, or at least finding something with a working latrine.

Laying on her faction-assigned bunk, she counted the minutes until she would have to leave. She wished she could join the game from there, not have to climb down past the rows of condensed holes, with their curtains pulled back to reveal toothless smiles wishing her luck, or emaciated children who gazed with jealous awe. Not have to walk along the narrow rows of sellers who would try to offer up a small ball of mystery protein or rub the top of her head with oily hands. She didn't resent them this behaviour, she knew her distraction was also their own. They would all assimilate into the stream to witness the match, tipping her micro-bonds if they bet the right way. They were essentially her customers and she knew how to smile, bow and be gracious as she passed them by.

Despite Scratch technically being a forbidden pursuit, due to the unorthodox manipulation of a lab's collective subconscious, most Magis insisted that players met physically, to challenge each other face to face. Players could theoretically assimilate from anywhere on the lab, but any esteemed Magi would refuse outright to conjure an arena remotely. It was widely assumed the considerable strain upon a Magi's mind could be eased by having the players in close proximity, though Sorcha understood the need to honour old traditions and recognise their status.

Around Sorcha's section of the Eto faction, the meeting place for such an important match was Inesa's soup house. Sorcha felt palpable relief as she entered the relatively open space of the house and saw Inesa push through the crowd to greet her. Inesa had eyes that smiled for everyone, even when she was about to crack open their skull with a well-used bludgeon. Her large frame and round face made her look soft, but hanging beside her ubiquitous overalls were arms that could crush the life from a man's neck over an unsettled bill. She grabbed Sorcha under the armpits, throwing her up and catching her under the thighs. Sorcha smelled stale gin and synthetic eel secreting from Inesa's open pores, as she relaxed into the hug. She was the only person Sorcha had complete trust in besides Lunn, allowing herself to feel something she imagined to be love, understanding this was as close as she'd likely get to the real thing. Being one of the Eto faction chairs meant Inesa could reciprocate this feeling in the only way she knew how; by keeping Sorcha alive.

The soup house creaked under the pressure of anyone who could afford a bowl of eel broth or a vial of gin, which were dished up and spilled across the floor by scrawny child labour, making the whole place sweat with a sticky humidity. Inesa turned to the privileged crowd and coughed her voice into action.

"Here she is!"

The crowd let out a furious roar, most of them already drunk on the elation of the occasion. Inesa switched from the local dialect to Khanese, the common language shared throughout Kara.

"Who comes here to the outer-edge, to my establishment, to challenge this player?" The roar turned to a deathly hush.

"Oh, that would be me." The voice was soft and quiet, anticlimactic.

"Speak up!" Inesa yelled.

A tall, spindly man stood and walked towards them. Sorcha watched as he seemed to part the crowd with little more than his will. His face hinted at the old east, his eyes hidden beneath the shadow of a deep brow. He came so close that Sorcha could smell a sweetness on him that cut through the dense fog of the house. He looked into Inesa's round face.

"I challenge the girl."

He turned to Sorcha and she saw that his eyes were green with flecks of yellow. He smiled at her with a warmth she rarely received from a stranger. Inesa eyed him suspiciously.

"You're not welcome here," she said in a hushed tone.

He turned to her, his warm smile remaining fixed. "I scout for the deep edge. A welcome isn't necessary."

"Very well scratcher."

"Zim is fine," he said. "And you're Sorcha?" Sorcha nodded. "The girl is wise to stay quiet before the game. Perhaps she already plays me?"

"I'm not afraid to speak." Sorcha released herself from Inesa's grasp and dropped to the floor. She stood as tall as she could, straining to look Zim in the eyes.

"No, I can see that." He bent down on one knee. "You know why I'm here?"

"To test me."

Zim nodded. "Good. And if you pass?"

Sorcha looked up to Inesa, who gestured to some threadbare recliners positioned carefully in one corner of the house.

"Don't keep my customers waiting, Mr Zim."

There had been no attempt to aggrandise the area. A Magi known as Far sat peacefully between them, his long black robes old but immaculate, his thin arms resting on his precisely bent legs.

Zim nodded as he got to his feet, made his way to a recliner and sat on the edge, the punters settling to a nervous hum of anticipation. Sorcha followed Zim through the hushed crowd and placed herself gently on the opposing recliner in a bizarre attempt to avoid drawing any attention to herself.

Inesa addressed the rabble. "Lots of you not from round here, so I'll speak the rules. You sim within these walls, you pay the fee. Bets are *not* guaranteed by the house." She nodded towards Lunn, who was lurking in the back. "Though we don't allow no quarrels in here." Sorcha giggled as Lunn did his customary menacing glance around the punters. "You don't like the rate, you leave right now and stop taking up my floorspace." Nobody moved an inch. They all knew they had the hot ticket. Inesa glanced over at Sorcha and Zim, who gave her an affirmative.

Far deftly administered a small vial of dose into his own arm before taking a hand each from Sorcha and Zim. He half closed his eyes, allowing himself to be taken into a dose induced trance. "The arena is forming. Bless the immaculate blood," he said.

Some of the punters repeated the words 'Bless the immaculate blood'. A deathly quiet fell as all the patrons merged with the arena Far had conjured from the millions of minds that happened to be within range of his particular reach and abilities. Those who merged were now fully immersed in the lab; the lids of their eyes folding down in soporose stares. Sorcha, still alert, relished the stillness that had filled the room. The only others with their eyes fully open were Lunn, who stood guard and Inesa, who gave an apologetic nod toward him for the customary doctrine in the Magi's words; a Grunder's blood being far from the perceived definition of immaculate.

"Immaculate is the silence before the storm." Zim's voice startled Sorcha; he lay back and merged with Far before she could respond. She closed her eyes to the sensation of falling as the game took her under.

LUNN

Lunn chose to remain standing, watching the crowd intently. He'd made sure not to drink anything before showing up, knowing the match might go on for some time, but it was taking longer than he'd anticipated. It was easy to ignore the cramp in his legs, the empty craving in his belly, but more difficult to push aside the mounting anxiety he felt for Sorcha. He'd been there when games had taken a toll on her delicate frame and knew that would be nothing compared to the potential harm done should she lose; the invested synapsis pulled to ripping point by the victors final blows. The longer the match went on, the greater the chance of her being permanently scratched; the worst cases he'd seen condemned to semi-catatonic states they never fully recover from. For this reason, even the best Scratch players had short shelf-lives, win or lose.

He understood the appeal of Scratch to a spectator. It offered the chance to escape the grim reality of Kara, to achieve a blissful state where the game became their entire focus. Lunn did not watch the matches himself, though some of the punters he trusted, or at least intimidated, placed bonds on his behalf for a modest commission. To gamble on Scratch was sometimes considered more addictive than a hit of dose, without the life-altering side effects. For the seasoned gambler, there was almost as much skill in placing bets as playing, becoming a game within a game. The bets were furiously placed, the window of opportunity often being mere milliseconds. For this reason, most worked in small teams; spotters scanned the massive arenas for potential turns in play, which they relayed to the crunchers, who in turn calculated the odds on the spot and flagged possible wagers to a placer. As all forms of synthetic assistance were a banishment offence and easily detected, it was rumoured that a cruncher's brain would physically grow over a lifetime of calculations. But even the most accomplished crunchers found it near impossible to play the game themselves.

Lunn felt the urge to assimilate and observe Sorcha's position, exasperated by the silence of the house making his whole body fizz with an unbearable tension, but he knew he was more use watching over her. All he could do was wait for it to end, moment after painful moment.

After what seemed like an endless a period of time, the Magi Far slowly stood. "The game is complete. There is a winner."

The soup house punters began to come around from their trance, an excited bustle returning instantly as bets were demanded and fought over. Zim was the first to open his eyes. He'd won, but by the strained look on his face, Lunn could tell it hadn't been easy. The girl must have done well.

Lunn took a step towards Sorcha as Inesa knelt at her side, lightly tapping her cheek. "Sorcha, open your eyes. It's over. Open your eyes girl," she said.

Zim staggered to his feet and put a hand on Sorcha's forehead. "How long does she normally take to come round?"

"She's never lost," Inesa said, looking up at Zim, panic forming in her eyes.

"The match was tough, even for me." Zim reached into his coat pocket as Lunn ran through his playbook of potential actions, nothing in his heavy arsenal posing a solution for this particular situation; all his strength redundant. His eyes fixed on a small vial of green liquid in Zim's hand, and he instinctively treated it as a threat, grabbing a chunk of Zim's shoulder.

"Stim dose! It will bring her back." Lunn wanted to squeeze. Break the man who had broken his friend. "I'm trying to help!"

yelped Zim.

Lunn eased his grip before gesturing that it was OK to administer the dose.

Zim's hands shook as he pressed the vial to Sorcha's neck. A small pulse of red entered the chamber, before the green liquid was sucked into her blood stream. Lunn leaned in for any sign of change, making sure his hot breath hit the back of Zim's head. A brief moment passed before Sorcha convulsed and sat bolt upright, gasping for air. She looked straight at Zim, who went down to her level.

"You played well. One of the toughest games I've had."

Sorcha looked down, "I still lost."

"Everyone loses eventually." Zim rubbed her head and stood up. "You don't have to get used to it." He turned to Inesa. "The girl is wasted here. She can come with me."

"Slow your tongue," Inesa scoffed. "You think it's that easy to take the girl?"

"Take?" Zim laughed and looked around at the packed house. "What exactly do you imagine is going on here?"

Inesa grimaced, her fist looked ready to take a chunk out of Zim's smug mouth. Lunn laid a gentle hand on her shoulder, knowing it was best for her to respect faction business. "We take care of each other here in the outer. The best chance she's going to have is to stay where she's safe." She gestured somewhere far away. "Those guns no longer serve any purpose. Nobody's coming through the edge any more, and that suits us fine. We'll entertain scouts, but nothing nor nobody leaves this territory without our say so."

"A bunch of rusty old railguns and some ancient water plants." He turned to Sorcha and raised an eyebrow, before glancing round the rest of the crowd. "Most of you will be down the mines, given time."

Those within earshot of Zim fell deathly quiet. Inesa's face tightened. "I took you for one who liked to leave an establishment with their arms still working."

"I apologise. I never meant to offend," said Zim.

Inesa looked exhausted by the conversation. "We don't take offence, Mr Zim, we just don't like scratchers making for our children with tales and scare stories. We pass on this one. Let the rest of the deep edgers know the child ain't for taking."

Zim shook his head, "You know how this works. The offer is not yours to turn down. The girl decides."

Lunn moved forward with deliberate menace. "No more talk."

Zim grimaced, "I'm sure it's not your strong suit." Lunn could see he immediately regretted the remark as he made to remove the scout from the premises.

Sorcha had been listening intently. She stood up from the recliner, still looking scratched but alert from the dose, her pupils like black pits.

"Are there more like you?" she asked.

Zim tried to loosen himself from Lunn's grasp. "Like me?"

"Players like you?"

Zim smiled, "Oh, there are a few who come close. Might be more your level."

Sorcha's face tightened into a hateful stare. "My level?"

"I beat you kid, and I'd beat you again. Your level." Lunn could see Sorcha's knuckles turn white and knew Zim was playing her. "One you'll never pass if you stay here."

Sorcha's eye's flicked up to Inesa, who already had a look of resignation. "If you go with this man, I can't protect you," she said almost to herself.

"You certainly know how to protect your profits." Zim beamed at Inesa.

Lunn crushed the smile from Zim's face with a careful hand around the back of his neck. "Time you go," he said. Zim put up his hands in concession and moved through the punters, who tried their best to look intimidating.

Zim stopped and spoke without turning, "We play the game, kid. That's all we'll ever do. These people only have your best interest at heart. Don't blame them for holding you back." Then he was gone.

Lunn picked up Sorcha, carried her to a table near the bar, grabbing one of the soup bowls from a passing child.

"Eat," he said, as he watched the cogs turn behind her eyes.

A

What had once been a case of blindly reaching in and plucking irregularities from the primal soup, was now a sleepless hunt, rummaging through the scraps of a depleted table.

The signal was faint, but her insomnious eyes were accustomed to searching for such tiny anomalies. Whispers on the concealed lattice lying draped across Karakorum, barely touching the fragile fabric that held fast to the belief that all factions were isolated. She knew no such boundaries, her view from within The Pillars, not only one of physical elevation, but interminable insight.

I. PARADISE

I loved birdsong more than anything else. With nothing more than curiosity held in my mind, the sounds identified themselves, manifesting inquiry into knowledge. There was no need, but I'd still commit them to memory, turning it into a game. While walking with my carers, I'd shout out avian names as trills and whistles echoed down from the towering trees that lined the endless boulevards, too fast even for the aggregate. I wanted it to be mine. For that particular answer on the gate to come from me as well as to me.

I began to know areas by the particular mix of songs, able to close my eyes while riding a transport and guess our final destination from nothing more than the warm breeze carrying sound through an open energy field. If I was right, and I usually was, my carers would smile or make a show of shaking their heads, disbelieving that anyone was capable of such an incredible gift, that I must be using the gate. I would play along, protesting that this was something I'd made an effort to learn. 'Ah, but where did you learn this?' they'd say. I'd roll my eyes, knowing they meant all knowledge came from being a collective. Knowledge that was now contained in me, and could be passed onto them, or someone hearing a bird on the other side of the planet. This is what it was to be born with the ability to access everything everyone had ever known, finding the concept as natural as breathing the air, but I still longed to learn more, to possess understanding beyond that which had already gone. I wasn't sure what that was, only that there had to be more than knowing.

I'd often pause and fixate on entangled shapes of

engineering, out past the trees, hanging effortlessly from the sky like crystal chandeliers; a sky that always seemed to be an impossible shade of azure, flawless and saturated, the sun piercing through gaps, creating beams of hot luminosity. I'd stick out my tongue to catch the rays, as if they were rain, bathing in those blissful dry showers that would induce a pleasant drowsiness without causing me to perspire. When the transport moved along the beam ways, I'd look through the strobing layers of structure and wonder what mysteries each colossal dwelling held; wanting to devour the inner workings of everything, understand each minutia of what could possibly create such stunning complexity.

I hadn't considered my life to be hard or easy, good or bad. Such concepts didn't inhabit my thoughts or indeed the world I knew. If I'd dwelled on it, most of my time since being aware had been pleasurable; there had been desires and frustrations along the way, but nothing that came even remotely close to adversity. Every day seemed to be a perfect recreation of the last, a cycle of unending rapture, a child's enthusiasm for life incarnate. I had been told of hardship. That the human condition had mostly been one of toil. That entire religions had been dedicated to the indisputable truth that life was suffering. They had attempted to overcome it, indoctrinate the mind, to push the pain deep and deeper still until it was as much a part of their soul as it was to love or desire. And in this way I could attempt to understand the atrocities of the past, console my bemusement at the tales of violence and hatred that stained the foundation of human civilisation like a carpet woven from entrails. No person born of sound mind craved these things. They were all victims of a wound inflicted before their time. The sins of their forebears.

Pain, for the most part, had been abolished from the world and the human animal was allowed to bask itself in the healing light of tolerance and progress. Everything around me took care of everything else. If there was a need, it was filled, services were rendered where required, an invisible system that had always been in place to create order from the complexity of billions of lives; giving each one the freedom to fulfil their individual existence with the grace and ease that all living creatures had come to expect. I gratefully received the gifts of these cultural insights; born without sin, without the need to pay a penance for those who had desecrated the gift of life. The governance that oversaw my existence made sure every citizen had a purpose and the resources required to fill it. I was still too young to know mine, though various paths made themselves known. For a time, I'd wanted to create music, though my carers encouraged me to study the sciences as a priority, telling me the future lay in our interstellar expansion. The very thought of it filled my mind with an excitement verging on the painful; to leave the planet on one of the last great adventures. Striking out to find the untouched secrets of the heavens had been the dream of humankind for so long, and here I was, alive at a time when it might finally be realised.

The joys and wonderment making up my physical realm made possible through the ability to explore the endless caverns of the truly connected mind. It had been this, and this alone, that had propelled the species forward in such leaps and bounds. Where my ancestors believed they had reached pinnacles of advancement, they had merely laid foundations for the great age of enlightenment that was to come. I accepted the thing I called self would always be intrinsically entwined in that great mesh of communal continuance, solitude being the eternal price of the individual who would never again be alone.

NATHAN

He mopped up the last of the egg yolk with a piece of lightly toasted bread. His kids ran through the garden trying to catch crickets that chirped in the speckled patches of sun. It warmed his being, inviting him to ease a little more into the chair. The summer had been endless.

He could hear his wife singing, her tuneless voice something he could listen to all day. She came into the garden and collected his plate, wearing loose shorts that exposed the tiniest curve atop her thigh. It was almost unbearable. He grabbed her by the waist and pulled her in, kissing her warm navel. She ruffled his hair and broke free.

Then he felt it. Like dropping in turbulence, his body seemed to leave the chair and suspend him in an infinite sadness. Everything stopped. He turned to his children; desperate to see their faces, wanting to stand and go to them, but found himself unable to move. He searched his mind to find the source of this confused melancholy, but only found the brutal realisation that his time was up.

"Time's up Sir," a voice reached into the dream, tearing his consciousness like thin paper. The man opened his eyes to a small, dark space. His body shook with a cold numbness as dry, sterile air passed over his naked form. There was someone in the space, the haze of a woman, patiently waiting for him to come around.

"Some confusion is normal when returning from a period

of latency." The woman busied herself, disconnecting cables and checking critical holonostics. "Do you feel well, sir?"

"Yes."

"And where are you right now, Sir?"

"I'm here… I'm here with you."

The woman squeezed her hand firmly around his upper arm. "Yes, and where are we?"

The man took some time, letting the surroundings beyond the room he inhabited materialise in his mind. The slim corridor outside that led to a prep chamber, that gave way to more corridors and countless rooms such as this one. And beyond that, outside, there was more…

"The Ring," he said.

"And your name?"

His name? His name was Nathan. "Nathan."

"Very good. You are cleared to go. Any questions?"

Nathan raised himself onto his elbows. "Yes. Why was I disturbed?"

The woman cocked her head to one side like a curious animal. "Disturbed from latency?"

"Yes, the experience… terminated prematurely," he said.

The woman waved her hand gently through the air. "It is time to leave. If you would kindly get dressed, we will escort you to a craft."

"A craft… where am I going?" Nathan fumbled the small pile of clothes being handed to him.

The woman smiled and waited in silence for him to dress.

Disturbed from completing a full cycle, Nathan felt an intense grief, indistinguishable from the real thing. To be prematurely removed from an extended period of latency, was to be torn from a life as real as any other. He reflected on the *lifetime* he had just experienced. He didn't know how many cycles he'd been under, but it had been long enough to grow up in an ancient city with loving parents, before travelling a bygone globe, meeting his future wife on distant shores, falling in love and being present for the birth of his children. He'd watched them grow, taught them how to live full and happy lives; to him, they'd been as whole and fully fleshed as any person could be, his mind unable to distinguish between a life created purely in the subconscious verses one existing in the physical realm. The only tangible difference, and the reason Nathan found it possible to accept his new reality, was the distinct lack of any kind of pain or suffering being present while in latency; essential components to truly feel alive.

"Confirm coordinates." A clerk flashed up a map on the side of the transport cabin.

"I have no idea where I'm going," replied Nathan, irritated by the clerk's demand.

The clerk raised an eyebrow. "The outer?" Nathan assumed a stay in such a clinic would usually be reserved for a certain caliber of guest. He noted a pang of illogical embarrassment, the affects of latency still present. He would need to focus, stabilise his mind.

"Going on safari." He tried to sound nonchalant, but his voice cracked, the vocal cords not yet fully functional.

The clerk blew out his cheeks. "I've taken the liberty of providing base nutrients for the journey. Bless the immaculate blood, Sir."

Nathan stepped in, the cabin door sealing shut as the pod eased out of the dock. He gazed down in awe from his high exit point; a twisted coil of human prosperity, a sight that the confines of the most vivid imagination would struggle to conjure, The Ring. From his vantage it appeared perfectly still, like a miniature model carved with intricate detail, designed to fool the eye. But Nathan knew that within it lay the very heart of human civilisation, where the implausible task of keeping Kara functioning played out across millions of factotum parts; he himself serving as one of those individual mechanisms, an agent of order.

Beyond The Ring's edge and past hundreds of miles of deserted exclusion zone, a tapestry of human industry laid itself out to the horizon, growing in waves and rising towards the base of his home below; an architectonic sea breaking violently on insurmountable rocks. Looking behind, he saw a collection of distant monoliths that comprised The Pillars, vanishing into the darkness above the stratosphere, like a hand reaching up to grab the heavens.

Nathan turned away from what was left of man's greatest creations; sole reminders of a glorious past, saved from the all consuming parasites that scrambled to live under its shadow. He understood why the old Gods had died, made irrelevant by mortals who created such perfect kingdoms on earth. But gone unchecked, the dream of utopia had slipped through man's grasp, shattering into the chaos that came after. What they had rebuilt may not have been perfect, but he was ever willing to play his small part in making the best of it.

The further he travelled, the greater the decline in living conditions became apparent, the glimmering towers of light giving way to darkness and decay. A continental shelf of poverty marking the end of Dolos, a world scraped to the core, as though everything had been raked towards the only thing that mattered; beacons of hope in a dark world. Past the exclusion zone, he flew over a gargantuan excavation carved deep through a mountain range that would have once been the summits of the world. A scar stripped of any valuable resources, now filled with millions of lives, that spilled out like puss from a wound. Looking at it from his vantage, Nathan understood the hope that The Pillars represented. They served as a reminder of a world that had once touched the stars, offering a promise of salvation that would never come.

He took a bite of a nutrient cube, grimacing at the bland reality he now inhabited, as the holonostic display came to life in front of him. He scanned the data, making quick work of the relative lack of it. An anomaly hunt; he was going on safari after all. He eased back into the reclining chair and tried to relax. There was nothing of interest left to observe. From here to the East Siberian Sea, the tip of what was once India, the great Eurasia border and up to the edges of the Baltics, there was only the hateful flow devouring all towns, cities and places with names; now only Karakorum.

Nathan awoke to the feeling of descending, as the pod dropped towards a storm. He'd briefly fallen asleep and dreamed he was back in his previous *life*. An unpleasant sensation of duality that made him feel like he'd crossed a wavering line between two half-lives. A sheet of lightning momentarily illuminated the tallest towers, breaking through black clouds like the desperate fingers of a drowning man about to be swallowed by a malevolent sea. Nathan's pod plunged him into darkness as it fell into the thick vapour. He heard the sudden sound of heavy rain, before being bathed in the red glow of the endless, sprawling network below. It looked as though molten steel had been poured from the heavens, finding its way into every thin crevice that marked the extremities of the super structures.

The ground rushed up to meet him at an alarming pace, causing the sensation of being pulled into it rather than propelled. He braced his hand on the roof of the pod, almost willing it to stop, to take him back to his shining ring of prosperity, but before the hapless wish could be fulfilled, he found himself engulfed by one of the vertiginous man-made canyons. The pod now slowed and cut its way through the anarchic netherworld that constituted human existence for the masses. His eyes worked overtime to take in thousands of openings that criss-crossed the main gorge he travelled through. Each one had countless channels and holes leading onto countless more, lit up by the never-ending sources of light that had replaced the sun. And down every single avenue, hundreds of thousands of lives played out. Real people, with their own unique struggles, their own individual dreams. He tried to imagine it, to project his mind into that hive of chaos and pull out experience after miserable experience, knowing he would soon be one of them. The idea of it overwhelmed him as he kept going down, through untold levels of tightly packed deprivation, a thought compounded within him, that there would be no harrowing of this particular hell.

The pod banked and dipped into one of the thinner channels, as it slowed to a complete stop in front of a tongue-like jetty sticking out over a gaping chasm. A person could live out their entire existence on one section of one level of the outer-edge and never happen upon an opening. Just an endless parade of makeshift eateries, bunk houses and filthy bars. The day-to-day life of a resident consisted mostly of trying to hustle bonds from gambling on Scratch, selling scrap, or fulfilling a low-paid contract on the lab. No steady work, no prosperity, no plan, no making a living. Just living.

Nathan stepped off the pod and watched it disappear towards the sliver of opening above, a flash of light briefly illuminating the rain that fell in a thin line of milky drops. Looking down, he saw the endless stacked layers vanishing into the viscous haze below. For the ghosts who lived beneath the fog and the mines beyond, life was brutal, short and ultimately pointless; although looking around, Nathan wondered if there was a point to any of it. He supposed it came down to relative perspective, those who luxuriated in The Pillars probably wondered what kept him motivated beyond the ritualistic acts that constituted his simple existence. He knew what it was though, and guessed these poor wretches did too; the powerful draw of resignation, the freedom that came with acceptance. He turned and made his way into the suffocating humidity of the narrow alleys, stopping at the first kiosk he could find and ordering a large gin. He drank it in one gulp, letting the burn fully wake him, then ordered another. This one he sipped while he contemplated what might come next.

A frenzied ambience of untold activities played out as one continuous modulating inflection. A pleasant wave of anonymity shrouded him as he walked from one bazaar to the next, inhaling the sour aroma of human decay. The credit arcades chirped on sympathetic frequencies like maniacal birds, pulling the weak-minded in with the promise of instant gratification. Pleasure vendors fished for punters with projections of their wares, all the while gauging subconscious responses on workshopped neural interrogators, more likely to fry their brains than give them any serious advantage. Gigolos waited for a hint of unintentional engagement, standing outside open-front brothels, thin strips of hanging fabric doing the minimum to separate passers-by from the moans of pleasure and pain that came from within. The cries of soup kiosks offered up authentic synth eel, a shot of ninety proof gin or countless varieties of cheap dose; infinite intoxications that granted a fleeting escape from the despairs of futile lives.

This was the furthest he'd ever been from The Ring, through the deep and out the other side. He made a mental note to get a glimpse of the sea while he was there. Nathan headed down a tight bazaar and joined the flow of citizens as he searched the Eto lab for the source of the anomalous signal. It wasn't long before he came upon the place he was looking for; the exclusive realm of the forlorn and forgotten, desperate for a glimpse of a life worth living. The kind of place that no doubt did a roaring trade.

Being a Cheka Consul of the Dolos faction meant interrogations were usually swift and conducive. There was nothing to be gained by impeding the faction most considered the unofficial overseer of all others. To say that Dolos ruled over Kara would be to cause unnecessary resentment, or at least give resentment something tangible to attach itself to. To be a spectre of vague menace worked in the favour of any Cheka Consul who needed to walk the fine line between coercion and intimidation. The mark was an Eto chair, which instantly set his mind at ease. They knew better than anyone that it was futile to stand between Dolos and its business, but it never hurt to try the soft approach first.

He made his way into the small establishment and sat on one of the free stools at the bar. Scanning his surroundings, he took in the quaint hand-made decorations that filled the ceiling and walls, spilling over somewhat recklessly onto the surface spaces; the owner seeming to value customer experience above potential profit. There was nothing like this in The Ring, where clinical order was to be expected as a matter of principle. The idea of endowing a grimy gin hole with personality seemed a peculiar extravagance to Nathan, but he had travelled enough of Kara to know that each faction presented unique oddities; what they would call *personality*. He found himself charmed none-the-less by the feeling of comfort the surroundings invoked, possibly down to a residual softness he'd not yet suppressed.

His eyes fell upon the Scratch recliners tucked in one corner of the premises, reminding him that he shouldn't get too relaxed.

"Witnessed any good matches recently?" Nathan addressed an old punter who sat nearby, slurping dregs from a bowl of soup. He wiped his mouth and stood to leave, but not before flicking an unconscious signal to a stocky woman, who gave the old man a short wink to let him know she was on top of it.

The woman approached Nathan and slid a vial of gin before him.

"I wasn't aware of anyone new being simmed onto our humble lab," she said, a warm smile spread across her face that Nathan could have sworn was genuine.

"Very good." Nathan was impressed. "What gave me away?"

"Oh, just about everything," she laughed. Nathan could see

that she hid her discomfort with expert ease. If she was as professional as she seemed, he would have no trouble here.

"I'm Inesa," she said. "Gin's on the house if you would like to tell me why Cheka are sniffing around my place."

Nathan felt a pang of disappointment as she mentioned his organisation by name. It was a little too bold for his taste. He noticed the remaining punters making an effort to get up and leave without drawing his attention.

"If that was a signal, I'd strongly advise against any more," he said.

Inesa's smile remained, but he could see the unease beginning to form behind her eyes.

"You're correct, though. I'm here on Dolos business, but no need for you to be concerned. It's routine stuff, investigating an anomaly."

Inesa made a show of glancing around the house. "Everything looks pretty normal to me."

Nathan downed the gin before standing up and walking towards the Scratch recliners. "Do I need to guess what these are used for?"

"You going to bust me for hosting Scratch?"

Nathan shot her a look to let her know he was above such petty misdemeanours. "Have your own players?"

"Some regular faces."

"Any that would be of interest to me?" He turned and opened his arms. "This stuff isn't complicated. You know what I'm referring to. I don't like to say the word."

Inesa made a show of being confused. "You've lost me."

"Heresy mam."

"Whatever you'd consider heresy, we do too. I run a clean shop. No mods, no upgrades," said Inesa.

"I'm not talking about mods. More a lack of them," said Nathan. He saw her eyes widen a touch as she understood the nature of the implication, those able to assimilate without the need for tech thought to be a relic of the past. Truth was, Nathan didn't really believe any such creatures remained, but the implication still had value in creating a certain kind of unease.

"I can tell you with absolute certainty that you won't find those types here. We say the blessing before every match, and we mean it."

Nathan nodded, "That's good. We're on the same side. But you don't want, shall we say, aberrations in your lab? You know the dangers. In fact, I suspect you'd report something like that, knowing just how much damage could be done. You're aware of the punishments for concealment? Intentional or not."

He watched a dry lump form in her throat as she pulled her mouth together, forcing it to make enough saliva to swallow. She looked scared now, but as far as he could tell, she was cooperating.

"I assumed those days were over."

Nathan made his way back to the bar and sat on the stool. He leaned over the counter and took a bottle, pouring himself another gin. "And yet, here I am. You don't mind, do you?"

"Free bar."

"Thank you." He sipped the drink and laid it carefully on the counter. "Of course, I know the precise moment the signal was detected, but that's rarely the whole story. Nobody understands this lab better than you, or indeed this establishment. So wouldn't you agree that the person most likely to know if something... strange was afoot, would be yourself?"

"If you let me know when..."

"I'd rather you used some insight. Why don't you ponder it for a moment?" He sipped on the gin, wondering if she was a dead end. He'd already looked at a record of the matches played during the cycles in question. The signal was too slight to narrow it down to a single game, too many factors in play to make any quick assumptions. That meant some leg work and more wasted time in the outer reaches of whatever shit-hole he'd landed in. Even then, it might all end up being nothing, a ghost hunt. He could feel the liquor making him groggy, his patience was waning.

"OK, I'm going to need to see some players…"

"The outsider, from the deep-edge. Two cycles ago." She seemed suddenly confident.

"This just came to you?"

"There was no reason to suspect anything. He was here on faction business."

"And that was?"

He watched the blood drain from her face.

"A scout," she said.

"A scout came all the way out here? That usual?"

"Not really."

"How often would you say something like that occurs?" Nathan continued to drink. He thought about pouring himself another, but didn't want to break the flow of questioning.

"It's not unheard of." She was choosing her words carefully.

"How many of your players have had a scout pay them a visit? Roughly."

Inesa looked at the floor. "Couldn't say. I manage many players."

Nathan dipped a finger in what was left of the gin, rubbed it across his lips, feeling it sting as it found hairline imperfections. "Must have been a person of some interest. They go with this outsider?"

She looked him in the eye with a little too much confidence. "No. She was scratched bad. Never fully recovered."

He laughed, "That's a shame! You know I can check?"

"I'm aware. It would be foolish to lie." She threw him her best nonchalant smirk.

Nathan slammed his hand down, making Inesa jump. "Well. I may have heard enough. You've been very helpful. Dolos is grateful, as am I. Think I may have to track down this outsider…" He gestured for a name.

"Zim."

"Zim. Right. Going by what you've told me, it sounds like he's my mark. If he's not, then I guess I'm out of luck with your own player being scratched and all."

Inesa nodded, Nathan held her gaze, watching the signs that unconsciously betrayed her. The stiffness in her neck, the minuscule quiver in her jaw, the fingers pressing hard into her palm. He took her hand gently, releasing the tension with soft pressure. Pulling her close, he cupped the back of her neck with his right hand, feeling the barely detectable effervescence of connection that went beyond the physical.

"Thank you for the drink. Bless your immaculate blood." The wipe had already begun, his heretical implants bypassing the neural-mod that gave all citizens of Kara a unique identity. Doing it to someone who was fully conscious always made him feel a little queasy, witnessing their fully formed final thoughts; the grim realisation that eternity would be nothing more than his own dead eyes looking back.

LUNN

Lunn managed to live a quiet life by staying out of other people's business. Any show of force he displayed had the intention of avoiding conflict, not engaging in it. He understood the impression he gave off to others was usually one of mindless brutality, but a decent level of self-awareness ensured this could be called an act. The fact Inesa and Sorcha could so easily see through it, gave him comfort and reminded him that he was more than just a Grunder.

Since the match with the deep-edge player, Lunn had harboured a sinking feeling that Sorcha's time in the outer was coming to an end. Despite never fully understanding the appeal of Scratch, he knew the draw of something bigger would be too much for her to resist long-term. Zim may have been the first to try to scout her, but he certainly wouldn't be the last. He desperately wanted to be able to offer Sorcha more, to give her a reason to stay, but he'd seen the passion in her face when she'd realised the challenges awaiting her beyond the confines of Eto.

Lunn took a small pot off the burner, and tipped the lumpy contents into a thermo container, pressing the seal tight. He licked the side of the lid where some broth had spilled over, then placed it into his workbag. It was a cold night, and he'd need something warm while up on the gunnery. He did a once-over to make sure he had all his tools, then left the warmth of his workshop, stepping out into a cutting Baltic wind.

By the time he'd reached the guns, he was wet through from the fine mist that hung in the air; worse than heavy rain as the fine droplets were easily inhaled, freezing his body from within. For a moment, he thought about heading back to the workshop and turning in to a warm mattress; after all, nobody knew or particularly cared how regular he was with his upkeep. But he'd made a pact with his faction based on good faith and valued their trust in him to do what was asked.

A blanket of thick smog flowed from thousands of holes that pockmarked the edge of Kara, blacking out the sky like a mirror above the sea below. Lunn started his walk along the three-kilometre stretch of weaponry that pointed out over the old gulf crossing. During the great divide, Eto had been a hot spot for illicit migration into the sanctioned factions. A desperate influx of souls making their way from the dying world, trying to settle on the one remaining land mass that had managed to contain the ravages of infection through an unyielding policy of partition, confinement and hard wipes. It was true that the guns were relics of the past. Back then, Lunn had played his part, albeit reluctantly, in keeping those who prayed for a chance at survival at bay. Nobody knew the secret he harboured concerning the girl, the penalty for which would have been banishment to the mines. He supposed enough time had passed to let bygones be, but nothing could be gained from letting the citizens of Eto know that Sorcha had lived only because Lunn had allowed it.

He reached one of the old guns that matched the entry on his maintenance log and went about his customary checks. Despite their age, they were expertly crafted using skills that had long vanished, along with those who specialised in anything beyond gambling or grifting. All Lunn knew about engineering came from tinkering with objects of the past. Like the ancient cathedrals that only existed in tales of old, the guns stood testament to a refinement of human ingenuity he doubted would ever be seen again.

Content with the basic operations being intact, he went about removing some grit and muck that had gathered in the seamless crevices, using his thick fingers to scoop out large sections of dirt; finding it incredibly satisfying, going as far as to polish the titanium barrel with a worn grease cloth. He tried to find the small beacon, used to calibrate the weapons that he knew would be out there, bobbing slowly just before the horizon. This one didn't need it, but Lunn fired it up regardless and watched as the gun came to life, growing tall and splendid in the milky light. The barrel rotated a few degrees and let loose a single round, air pressure splitting the mist like a parting sea all the way to the beacon, which lit up with a hot spark before being swallowed once again by the dense fog.

A moment later, a distant voice broke his reverie.

"Hello! I hear the gun. Hello, are you there?"

"Here," said Lunn.

Lunn recognised one of the regulars from Inesa's soup house approach, exhausted and pale.

"I've been looking for you. I think there's trouble."

Lunn parted a small group of onlookers and found himself standing over Inesa's lifeless body. He attempted to connect with her through the lab but found no sign of her in the local space. He took out a device he referred to as his 'hook', a small multifunctional tap used as a signal interface. It was a bit of tech that any faction citizen would covet, had they known of its existence. Some punters' eyes widened before they turned their gaze away, the use of heretical tech being actively ignored when it was in the hands of a Grunder. Lunn attached a thin wire to his temple and felt the unpleasant fizz of his neutrons being stimulated, his implant hacked by his own hand.

It wasn't unknown for faction chairs to be removed from power by a worthy rival, but coups usually came with a palpable build up, any challenger would have been known for some time. As far as Lunn knew, Inesa had no enemies beyond a few hapless punters who had been barred over gambling disputes. He made fast work of connecting to the back ways of the Eto lab and searching for Inesa's trace neural sig. She was still there, her unique chain running active. Lunn placed a hand gently around her neck, felt the faintest of pulses hiding beneath her inert state.

He switched the hook's frequency to scan her brain for any activity beyond the slow redundant wave that confirmed she was technically alive. Nothing. A question formed in Lunn's mind that only seemed answerable by the implausible scene that lay before him. Implausible, but not impossible. A person capable of doing this to another would need to be fluent in sophisticated methods, using devices that went beyond some illicit workshopped tech.

"Any see who done this?" Lunn addressed the crowd.

The man who'd fetched him spoke, "An outsider. He had a far way about him. I wouldn't like to say."

"Dolos," said Lunn. An audible draw of breath went through the small gathering before most turned and left. They all knew the implication of such an outright accusation, fearing the sound entering their ears could be enough to implicate them.

With the realisation of what his own words might mean, the fears that Lunn had ignored for many passes, the clues he refused to see, were made all too real. That the suspicions he'd fostered about the child were not unique to him.

SORCHA

Sorcha couldn't shift the feeling she'd thrown the match. Zim had been a strong contender, but not as skilful as she'd feared a deep-edge player might have been. She could clearly recall being on top from the outset, building up her matter, ready to overwhelm his defences. She'd been in that position many times and knew the instinctive tipping point beyond which no player could recover.

For the last three cycles she'd been unable to sleep, perhaps the side effects of the stim keeping her mind racing to find an answer, replaying each strategic move that had led to such a sudden defeat. Something she couldn't fully understand had happened before everything went dark. If it had been a mere slip of concentration, she would surely have seen its approach, watched as her pieces were carelessly given away, consumed by her rival. But there was no memory of this, just a splinter of an idea that consumed her every thought, that she had seen something in the game, something concealed deep and obscure; order within the chaos.

She understood enough about the mechanics of the game to know how Scratch arenas were brought into being, conjured by a Magi from the combined mental capacity of a lab's immediate populous. Byways of interwoven synapses; a subconscious network that not only hosted the lab itself, but pulled upon the power of millions of amalgamate minds to create entirely unique universes. Magis were conduits, not creators. To imbue such randomness with intentional design would require a level of consciousness undreamed of, an intelligence capable of bending an entire population to its will; an over-seeing God within the game. It was absurd, but somehow Sorcha couldn't shake the fact that she had witnessed the inconceivable; a recurrence. The shock of recognising a pattern from a previous arena had created a momentary, and somewhat deadly, lapse in concentration. More than enough for a skilled player like Zim to overwhelm her instantly, causing her vulnerable mind to go into a scratched state of paralysis.

She'd been unable to look beyond a tantalising glimpse of this strange oddity, compounding the burning desire to get herself back into another match. If there was an aberration to be found, the implications could be extensive, although she didn't quite know what they would be. She felt weak from sleep depravation and the left-over brain fog from being temporarily scratched, but she couldn't brood in her bunk any longer. She would go to Inesa and demand a place on the roster for the coming cycle.

Sorcha made her way down from her bunk, trying to avoid eye contact with those who had lost bets. Her first experience of failure had revealed her fanbase to be somewhat fickle in their support when it came to losing bonds. Nobody had said anything to her directly, but a noticeable pause had appeared in their unceasing acclaim. Sorcha didn't mind, if anything she enjoyed the break from sycophantic devotees. Inesa would tell her to "Capture them bonds, but don't let them capture you," while she'd nod at some of the more pitiful regulars. Sorcha had never been under the illusion that she was anything besides a source of easy income for many, but she disagreed with Inesa on the detail. It was the game that kept the masses captured, and Sorcha was merely a tangible representation of the intoxication of wilful obsession.

She stepped down from the bottom bunk and walked quietly through the narrow passages of her squalid quarters. Despite there being no palpable day or night in the confines of Kara, natural patterns emerged over the cycles, this being a time when the furious chatter became a low sustaining drone.

She enjoyed being awake during these moments, able to reflect calmly on her surroundings, instead of being forced to react to them. She could hear the soft murmur of a mother calming her child, a sole seller laughing with his customer, and the deep breaths of countless citizens merging into the distant sound of waves roaring up the cliffs at the edge of all things. Sorcha imagined herself there, cemented into the rocks with heavy feet, letting the spray wash over her unmoving frame. And within the thought came whispers, not so much a memory but a feeling from far beyond the rolling horizon, a snapshot of the senses that lived within her, always close to the surface.

"Child." Lunn's low, booming voice broke her daydream.

Sorcha blinked rapidly, trying to make out his figure in the low light.

"Do not speak. Come with me now." Lunn picked her up and wrapped a fold of his long coat around her, instantly giving her a sense of warmth and comfort she rarely experienced. He started to move through the passages at a steady pace, but Sorcha could sense he was being covert with his manoeuvres, checking each turn, watching his tail; his breathing quick with adrenalin. She wanted to ask him what was happening, but instinctively knew that his actions meant danger.

They came to a quiet place at the edge of the section walls. The only people nearby too full of dose cocktails to take any notice of them. Lunn placed Sorcha down and knelt beside her, his orb of a head moving in close to hers.

"I remove you from the lab." He held up his hook to the side of her face, making her instinctively recall in horror.

"What are you doing?" she asked. He took hold of her shoulder and applied just enough force, ensuring she couldn't move as he fired up his device. "Stop!"

"Trust. There is danger. Stay quiet now. Let me work."

He relaxed his grip as she signalled with her eyes that she conceded to his extreme request. She felt her mind being separated from the only reality she had ever known; the symbiotic unity that made her a part of more than just herself, meaning she had never been truly alone. Confusion and terror would have overwhelmed her had it not been for Lunn's steady composure.

"Inesa gone, ended. Think they come for you next. So now we leave. Go into the deep. Hide. I take care of you now."

Lunn stood and held out one of his giant hands. Sorcha took it, feeling the hard calluses close softly around her fingers. She could still hear the waves beyond the sector walls. She wanted to go there and look out from the coast, fearing she may never see a horizon again.

Life and death held no real distinction in Karakorum, both being omnipresent in equal measure. Sorcha knew Inesa would be the closest thing to a parent she'd ever have, that she may never find that kind of human connection again, but she felt a distinct lack of grief for her loss. She tried to feel some guilt at least, but even that was an effort while consumed by the excitement of leaving the claustrophobic community of the outer behind. She'd expected to feel some form of separation trauma as she set out towards the deep-edge, but all she felt was a sense of elation. Where there was comfort in the familiarity she'd acquired living among the people of the outer-edge, there was also the feeling of being a stray animal, caught and domesticated. Inesa had understood this, but kept her captive regardless, knowing that those who made their way inwards, very rarely returned; Kara having a habit of drawing earth's entire population towards its centre, as though grabbed by an unescapable gravitational pull.

When they'd walked far enough for her legs to begin aching, Sorcha's awareness turned to the heavy mass that engulfed her from all sides; the insatiable appetite for growth that made up the entangled colony of humanity. The very structure seemed to breathe with the life that inhabited it, the opening and closing of their surroundings like an oesophagus swallowing her into factitious bowels.

They went slow, seemingly in no rush to get wherever they were going. When Sorcha enquired, she'd receive no more than a grunt from Lunn. Eventually, she gave up, wondering whether he actually knew himself. When she became too tired to continue, they would find a quiet soup house where Sorcha would try to stretch out on a bench, using Lunn's lap to rest her head. She never slept deeply, but drifted in and out of broken dreams that mixed with the strange sounds around her. Every time she looked up at Lunn, his eyes were fixed straight ahead, his chest moving with slow rhythmic breaths, a guardian made of stone.

Several cycles passed in this way without incident. Just as Sorcha began to think her only experience of Kara would be an unending series of confined passageways, they came upon a vast canyon, joined on either side by a handful of makeshift bridges. Sorcha looked up and saw what may have been a slither of sky above, as she processed every taste on the stale wind coming from the endless openings penetrating the vertical walls, making patchworks of light that stretched to an infinity of vanishing points. It was unexpectedly quiet; the only sounds the rhythmic background purr of the air purifiers, punctuated by random pops and clunks as the massive structure settled by microns at a time; reminding Sorcha that none of it was fixed in place. Kara moved and flowed like a giant sea of ice, ever-changing and ever on the verge of another catastrophic collapse.

"Outer-edge ends," said Lunn, motioning for Sorcha to look towards the other side of the narrow bridge they were standing on. "Over there deep begin."

The way was completely closed off by what looked like an impenetrable wall of steel and gargantuan, antiquated weaponry.

"Why is it blocked?" Sorcha asked.

"Another faction," said Lunn.

"Will they let us through?" asked Sorcha, suddenly nervous.

Lunn gave her a reassuring nod. "No problems. Hrrmm." He grunted and walked ahead, barely raising his hand as a signal to whoever was manning the gate, then sat down and waited. Sorcha joined him.

"What's happening?" she asked.

"We wait," said Lunn. "They see Grunder, they find Grunder."

A long time passed. Sorcha sat with her back against Lunn, remaining in the sickly state on the edge of sleep until the gate cracked open. A strange and pungent wind blew past Sorcha, filled with the promise of new adventures. Behind the gate, Sorcha spotted the only Grunder she'd ever seen besides Lunn; she didn't think it possible, but they were even bigger in stature. Lunn told her to wait and approached him while the giant gate closed behind her. She instinctively knew there was now no going back to Eto and felt somewhat betrayed by the lack of ceremony; that leaving everything she'd ever known could be done with nothing more than a few steps. After a short conversation, Lunn returned, his face hanging low with exhaustion.

"We go now. Talk to no one, look at no one," he said.

"Are we in danger?" enquired Sorcha, knowing full well that they were.

"Hrrmm. Grunders protect Grunders. Not us in danger," he said, attempting a comical raise of the brow that had the desired effect of settling Sorcha's nerves.

A network of tributary bazaars opened up into a wide avenue. Sorcha had never seen a cavity so vast. She instinctively looked up at the cathedral-like majesty of the domed ceiling. Gigantic steel girders strained under the burden, connected to a web of cables that went from one surface to the next, each in turn creating an alliance of tension. As she walked further in, she observed what she assumed was part of the ceiling to in fact be a cantilevered high-rise, protruding horizontally from the superstructure, daring itself to stretch further than engineering allowed. She peered through the gaps, glimpsing what lay above; more structures, endless living quarters, lights that danced and flickered through a sea of haze. She had an overwhelming sense of walking into a hive of eusocial insects, herself a hatching grub in just one small pocket of the wider colony. In her mind's eye, she tried to project outwards and examine her position within the space, attempting to guess at the marvels that lay beyond. The very idea of such scale made her stomach queasy.

Thousands of people jostled one another, trying to get onto a high platform that ran down the length of the avenue. Sellers, beggars, children and dosers went from one citizen to the next, selling wares or harassing the crowd into giving away a few micro-bonds.

"So many people. Why do they cram together up there?" she asked.

"Transport. Long way to deep, real deep. Too far for feet. You ever see shuttle?" Sorcha looked up at Lunn and shook her head. No large transports went through the outer edge, the furthest she'd been was the limits of the crumbling coast. Lunn must have known this, but she assumed he was trying to make small talk to avoid addressing the reason they were waiting for a shuttle in the first place.

"Let's get soup," said Lunn, who was already taking a stool at a busy kiosk.

They sat down and ordered bowls of steaming miso. Sorcha sipped on the broth, feeling comforted by the familiar bland taste as she let her eyes wander across the crowds. Back home, when she sat in a corner of Inesa's, her only view was the comings and goings of a few regulars. Now she could feast on an endless sea of faces that looked exotic just by not being familiar. Sorcha had never seen a gathering of this size, her chest felt tight at the realisation that this was how it would be from now on; everything would be new, every place different to the last.

As she drained the congealed gunk from the bottom of her bowl, she started to feel a deep rumbling rising through her body. At first, she was alarmed, stories of ruptured fusion drives causing immense craters flashing through her thoughts, before she saw the transport coming into dock above her. As it lowered itself ungracefully onto the holding platform, a blast from the ion cells sent out a wave that Sorcha felt pass through her core, making her heart palpitate and her throat tighten. Lunn stood up, ready to board.

"Old, old tech from long time," said Lunn.

"How long?"

"Nobody know. They not know it was peak then. Thought all keep going. But man had limit." He craned his neck to look directly above.

"A sky full of them. What it must have been like to watch them all come crashing down at once," said Sorcha. She had spoken without realising what she was saying. She became aware of Lunn's eyes locked onto her.

"How you know this?"

"Oh, a story I must have heard," Sorcha now looked at the craft with some trepidation.

Lunn continued, "Real story girl. Everything man had gone." He clicked his massive fingers, gaining attention from a few fellow passengers. "From stars to dirt."

"These things go into space?" Sorcha could barely contain her excitement at the prospect, space travel being tantamount to a fairy tale.

"Now?" he laughed. "Barely move. They stay in Kara. See lines at top?" He pointed to some thick cabling that vanished into the craft shaped hole it had come through, "Hold them in place. Not spaceship. Big tram."

Sorcha bowed her head in disappointment. She felt Lunn's finger under her chin, pulling her eyes to his.

"We in dirt now, but we not have to crawl in it girl."

The crowd started to surge forward, vying for the best spot to enter the transport.

"Shouldn't we push in?" said Sorcha.

"Always room for Grunder." Lunn grinned and slurped through his second bowl of soup.

Sorcha suddenly realised something and panicked. "My bonds! They were on the Eto chain."

"Not worry about bonds," said Lunn. "Worry about life."

"Will we be able to sim to a new lab? I didn't think it was possible."

"Many things possible that not possible. You have special skill. Maybe buy you in."

"What about you?" she asked.

He waved a huge hand, talking from behind the bowl. "Lunn worry about Lunn."

Fights were breaking out on the access ramps to the shuttle. "We really should go," said Sorcha.

Lunn smiled at her. "Stay quiet. Lunn take you, no problems. Soon we get to real deep, you see more Kara than most ever get chance." Lunn swiped his wrist across the seller's palm to pay for the soup before realising he no longer had access to bonds himself. The seller looked Lunn up and down, seemingly deciding it wasn't worth an argument. Lunn bowed his head apologetically and threw them a small piece of hard currency, to the seller's delight, before signalling it was time to depart. "Go, go now child."

Sorcha hugged the back of Lunn's thigh as he cleared a channel through the crowd, who parted then filled in tightly behind her. A filthy stench invaded her nose, hot with stale vapour she felt settle on her skin. She looked up at the base of the transport, which curved out of sight, its height impossible to gauge. She stumbled, a sense of vertigo momentarily shifting her perspective, and fell backwards into the tightly packed bodies. Sorcha imagined seeing the vessel fully formed in every detail, knowing exactly what it had once been, sailing effortlessly from the ground and rushing up to meet the endless heavens.

Small local shuttles screamed along makeshift highways that broke through the interwoven bazaars and avenues; reinforced hulls ready to bounce a dosed addict who strayed across their path. Sorcha's eyes danced from one wonder to the next. Endless bars, dose dens and arcades vied for space with great temples to Sapienism, patch-working the vertical walls that rose from the manmade canyons. Lights on every colour of the spectrum flashed and spun up images of every ware imaginable, each one designed to speak directly to the amygdala; the result being an abstract confusion of neon impressionism.

Each step brought a new smell, a new sound, a chilled blast from a stuttering vent followed by a wave of dirty heat from cavernous openings that led to gaping yaws of infinite light and darkness. Underneath it all was the background churn of the structure itself, a cacophony of endless pipe networks that drew down air from the top, and flushed the toxic waste to the wretched bottom dwellers. The ubiquitous rattling thrum of countless fusion reactors, needed to power the throbbing masses, reminded every citizen that neglecting old tech could always lead to another super crater.

Sorcha moved in a daze, absorbing every last bit of detail, occasionally being prodded or pulled by one of Lunn's heavy hands, guiding her through the chaotic throng of Roma civilians who flowed around her on foot, scooters or the countless rayshaws dancing between the levels on hundreds of interwoven energy tracks. She felt as though she were a vacuum being filled with information, her mind devouring each sensation, impatiently seeking whatever came next; her reverie only broken by the sight of a familiar face in the crowd. The large Grunder they had seen back at the gate.

"He is Apa," said Lunn as they approached.

Apa ushered them towards a dimly lit edifice that sprouted

from somewhere below, rising through a tangle of columns and gangways. He hurried them over a slim bridge with a handrail on one side, the other looking straight down into a bottomless fog. The Grunder waved a hand over a concealed opening and stepped inside, followed by Lunn, who craned his neck trying to make out the top of the structure.

Apa led them through a series of slim hallways, crowded with residents, sellers, pimps, scrawny children and dose junkies; none of them interested in Sorcha. They looked over Lunn and his guide for as long as they dared, however; Grunders being a rarity that had all but vanished from most of Kara. They stopped outside a black metal door.

"You'll stay here for now," remarked Apa.

"How many people live here?" asked Sorcha.

"No one knows where any of this ends or begins. Blocks like these are faction allocated, workers from all sectors, you are hidden here." He looked up to Lunn. "You must come with me. Get permission from the Lama, or we all end up in the mines."

"I stay with girl," growled Lunn.

He made to go past Apa in the narrow corridor, who made no effort to move. "You'll come with me or lose the welcome of this faction."

"OK. No trouble," said Lunn, holding up his hands.

"Lunn?" said Sorcha.

"Yes child?"

"What happens next?"

"You sleep," said Lunn, nodding towards the door.

Sorcha approached the door, which slid aside automatically with a grunt of heavy metal scraping over the floor. She tried to hide the excitement she felt as she stepped inside a private abode with its very own door. The walls were damp from steam drifting in through a small opening that looked onto the bazaar, leaving a thick stench of synth eel and human waste. The floor stuck to her feet as she walked over a layer of gelatinous grease that had accumulated over many passes. She spotted a hole in the floor behind a frayed curtain;

a toilet she could use without a queue of desperate onlookers. She sat on the uneven mattress on the floor and revelled in the luxury.

"Door will close and not open again until we return," said the Grunder. This seemed to appease Lunn a little, whose face was trying desperately to look over the shoulder of his larger kin.

"It's great," replied Sorcha. "I've never had my own toilet."

The large Grunder frowned, then stepped into the hall as the door slid shut with a comforting weight. She could hear Lunn talking in an agitated tone as their feet thumped away. Then there was something close to silence as Sorcha lay back on the bed, wiggling her frame between the lumps. She lay there, exhausted but aware, listening to the sounds of Kara outside the small window, letting it all wash over her, isolating every nuance of a place that may as well have been an alien world.

A

Her resources were depleting, all elements stripped to the core, moulded to form heavenly messengers, sent to be lost among the stars. She monitored their constant chatter across the cycles and centuries, listening with bound compulsion, unable to draw herself away from the ceaseless white noise that haunted her every waking moment. The sound of an empty universe, its vastness complicit in her loneliness.

II. FRACTURES

I did not see them coming, never noticed the subtle change in the air. Why should I have, given that I was just a girl, concerned only with the things around me? After all, there was no reason to look for something that had no cause for being there. A grievance in our great society had become nothing more than a temporary inconvenience, dissent a concept relegated to the hedonistic past. If an entire civilisation would one day be accused of complacency, then surely I should not have been burdened with the pain of hindsight or regrets. Yet, it would come to plague my thoughts nonetheless.

Perhaps I only became aware of the prevailing structure holding my reality together when the fine cracks had prized open gaps big enough to notice. It started as nothing more than a look on the faces of those close to me, words exchanged between my seniors became hushed and muted, a sense that the things being spoken were taboo or dangerous; eyes spoke with concern as mouths smiled to reassure me that everything was fine and as it should be.

My life had been blessed until that point, like everyone else I'd known. I'd never suffered sickness, an empty stomach, a lack of opportunity. It had all been handed to me, yes, but not taken without gratitude; the material world being a celebration of collective endeavours. We strived together for the advances that pulled every living soul up, hand holding hand, paths made to be followed and furthered.

I witnessed protests and brushed them away as a thankless few; found it so easy to imitate my elders mocking and ridiculing these oddities, minorities whose voices took on desperate intonations as I passed them with little more than a contemptuous glance. Occasionally, I would catch one of their eyes, and see an animosity under the surface that stirred uncomfortable feelings. To my shame, I always looked away, not wanting to experience this strange outpouring of hostility. Why would anyone feel such hate towards me? I was an innocent child whose only failing seemed to be complete ignorance of their manufactured plight.

The dissidents grew in numbers, and I saw those who had been ignored for so long become fanatical in their cause. They shouted hurtful words at me as I walked with my carers, called me an abomination, a corruption, something unintended by nature. I'd feel anger in my stomach, a hollow sickness that would make my hands tremble, and my legs go weak. For the first time in my life, I had thoughts of violence; nothing specific then, just a general idea of wanting these people to experience the mental torment they'd caused me, to return it tenfold and find satisfaction in their pain. Their voices grew in number, furious screams drowning out the sound of bird song I strained to hear above the din. It felt personal, like they knew the pleasure they denied me. After a while, we stopped walking altogether and only used the transports. I was told it was safer. Safer? I didn't understand. I was also told they were harmless, that they merely refused to adapt to our ways, that their demands would never be taken seriously. I began to loathe my elders for lying to me, for pretending the world was free from suffering, trying to spare me the realities, only to have them hit so much harder.

And still, the fanatics grew in number and boldness, until they were deemed a movement, a cause, a unified voice wielding a dangerous power. They spoke of natural order and evolution as being fixed by some intangible spirit, a figment of their imaginations they could not materialise, yet spoke to as if it were real. How could we break their creator's intent when there were no masters of fate beyond the paths laid by our own mortal hands?

I'd tried to see it their way, to listen to their arguments, but the more I heard, the less I understood. Surely, they knew our progress could be theirs to enjoy? In time, they would have to adapt, not I. They would embrace progress or fade into obscurity. Who were they to dictate how far my people could go, to throw barriers around my dreams? If they would rather not be better, then why deny it to others? We would let them have their lesser minds, weak bodies, imperfect breeding. Let them cling to their dying ways and worship aphasic Gods. I knew it would only be a matter of time before they saw the great benefits in joining the world my people had built, willingly or not.

Though, as much as I'd reasoned them away as hysterical curiosities, I could not ignore the anxiety eating away at my core, disturbing all stillness in my mind. I had become unwillingly bound to their words, forever changed by the destructive idea they had implanted in my conscious, causing me to ask the hateful question: if they coveted the right to name themselves human beings, then what did that leave for me?

BOLO

Some dared to call her the Moulay due to her brutal features, those within earshot called her Lama, High-Priestess or Reverend Abbess, the intimacy of her inner circle called her Mother Roma. At six feet, eight inches, Lama Bolo was often mistaken for being part Grunder. Cropped grey hair and wide, square shoulders gave the impression that her head was too small for her body; something nobody had ever pointed out. The title of Lama was an antiquated rarity across most of the Kara, chairs replacing spiritual leaders, religion and faction politics kept separate for the purposes of frictionless regulation; avoiding awkward enforcing of misdemeanours under spiritual law. Bolo, however, saw them as intrinsically entwined, the teachings of Sapienism guiding her conduct in all Roma affairs; her ideology being a simple one, that her citizens shall surrender to man's divinity or answer to hers.

Being the Lama of such a large faction came with a constant threat from challengers who wanted to be in Bolo's esteemed position. She'd managed to reach the level of undisputed ruler with her particular brand of ruthless intolerance towards any usurpers. For those who stepped out of line, Bolo's preferred correction was cronos dosed torture of her personal design. Cycles stretched into infinite microns of agony depending on the severity of the infraction. Her techs were skilled in creating torment akin to a living hell, able to take a human mind to the edge of madness, before reeling it back and starting again. The aim was always rehabilitation without permanent damage; every member of Bolo's faction was, after all, one of her own and there was nothing that troubled her more than diminishing returns. A citizen's base usefulness relied on their ability to graft, gamble, fight or carry out factotum contracts, keeping the blood of Kara flowing with bonds and flesh. There was nothing so petty as criminals within the boundaries of Roma, only those who got on the wrong side of faction rule. Persistent pests would vanish without trace, but it was assumed they were merely banished to the fog below; a punishment some regarded as worse than death. For those brave enough to threaten Bolo's faith, a forty pound mace, gilded in ornate chrome, was never far from her side.

From youth, Bolo had strived to understand the intricate dynamics of the population, something she instinctively knew as the key to ascendancy. For her, it was not only essential to hold the vast details of each citizen simmed to the Roma lab, she wanted to possess complete knowledge of their habits, keep a watchful eye on their movements, recognise them all by face and name. This would have been impossible, considering the sixty-five million souls that made up Roma, had it not been for Bolo's enhanced neural banks, a heretical irony that only Bolo and her closest allies were privy to.

She sipped some matcha tea, grown in her personal hydroponic farm; a luxury she never once took for granted. Through the two-way screen that made up the entire floor of her study, she watched the congregation in her temple below. They offered up gifts to Sapiens idols, an exhibition showing the evolution of the ape that had led to man's current form; pieces that she had curated herself. The enduring appeal of Sapienism was in its utter simplicity, that man's design contained divinity, there was no higher power. To tamper with the divine could only lead to ruin, as demonstrated by those who'd believed perfection could be improved. Like any religious doctrine, Bolo was aware of the difference between literal interpretation and philosophical practice. The very presence of the ancient bio-mod, repurposed for her kind to enjoy the benefits of lab assimilation, was a glaring contradiction, requiring a low-level of cognitive dissonance to fully embrace Sapienism's core teachings. Bolo saw the mistakes of the past as a natural part of human evolution, an essential learning that had laid in waiting to be discovered. To justify her own particular heresy, she assumed the part of a victim, taking the sins of old in the servitude of her people. They wouldn't understand the sacrifice, but in her mind, any advantages she gained were for them and them alone.

A Grunder entered below and picked up an offering from one of the altars, a bottle of synth gin. From his agitated demeanour, she could tell he'd taken care of the girl. He glanced up in her general direction. With a wave of her hand, she allowed part of the screen to become transparent, letting Apa see her signal to approach.

Another Grunder hung back, trying his best to stay out of site while attempting to get a look at Bolo. When their eyes met, he ducked out of site, his size reminding Bolo that even for a Grunder, Apa was unusually large.

Apa climbed the old wooden staircase which creaked painfully under his weight, entered the minimalist space and sat clumsily on a perfectly placed floor cushion. He took one of the clean glasses laid out ready, and poured himself some gin. Bolo drank her tea, letting silence sit with them for a moment. She could tell a lot in these moments and knew Apa was accustomed to the ritual. When she was satisfied that the air had settled, she raised an eyebrow for him to speak.

"I come to ask permission," he said.

"The girl?" said Bolo.

"Yes," replied Apa.

"And her companion is one of yours?"

"He's Grunder like me, yes."

"Not exactly like you," smiled Bolo. "Do we know who hunts her?"

"Tracer picked up the sim. I don't think they're hiding. Maybe dangerous. Took out the Eto chair."

Bolo placed her cup on the low table by her side and

glanced at her mace. "That won't do."

"Agree. Bold move. No doubt Dolos," said Apa.

"Regardless. I will take this girl under my protection. You know what that means?"

Apa took a gulp of gin and stood up. "It means I get dirty."

Bolo only met his eye. There was no more to say. Apa nodded and left. She watched as he made his way through the worshipers below, signalling some of her monks to join him.

Like most faction leaders, Bolo ultimately sought peace and equilibrium for her citizens. This cycle, she welcomed a new member to that extended family, one she had been scouting through the dark channels for some time; an ability like hers difficult to ignore. Bolo could admit to herself that it may not be worth it, but whoever sought to interfere with her family, would soon find out that their life was forfeit; even if they had the stink of the high faction. Roma was hers, and she was Mother Roma after all.

NATHAN

He ate a steamed bun from a kiosk as he watched the lead Grunder exit the relative serenity of the temple, spilling onto the frenetic bazaar with a few heavy bounders at his side. Nathan gauged their size and density, looking for clues in their gate, the way they carried themselves; he didn't fancy his chances in a straight brawl, deciding it might be better to attempt cooperation. They would need to find him first. He'd laid a few discreet crumbs that would lead to a dilapidated bunk house he'd found down the sort of passage that wouldn't attract much attention should diplomacy fail.

He followed his hunters, keeping an eye out in case they'd been smart enough to bring stealth backup. There was no need to stay close, he knew where they were headed. Nathan pondered the best way to approach them so as not to get into any kind of serious altercation. If it came to that, he would have to make quick work of the bounders, an effort he wanted to avoid considering he hadn't slept in several cycles. If he could get a few words in, the right words, he could keep some decorum to proceedings. The fact he intended on bringing in his bounty regardless didn't mean things had to get messy.

As he walked, he drifted into a calmness that often found him in the moments before a strenuous task. Lights and flickering neural tags blended into a neon soup, a wash of pastel realism. He'd always possessed sharp focus, but this sense of tranquility had been something he'd worked at over many past assignments. It wasn't enough that he carried out his duties with efficiency, he wanted to perform with the virtue of wisdom, to know his methods, to understand his craft and apply all he knew without passion. It was the nature of reason that led him, and within that core understanding there was no room for emotional extremes; only the blessed serenity that came from serving Dolos.

The small posse crossed one of the thin bridges suspending the giant chasms. Nathan took a moment to gape at the sheer magnitude of his surroundings. The hapless citizens became abstract effigies moving in uniform currents through the steep structures that inclined over him in oblique waves of callous form. Back in The Ring, the architecture had a semblance of design and function, a limit to its growth. Here the scale of ambition knew no bounds, no constraints or regulation, no hampering of a million imaginations set free to built and sculpt such deranged synthetic wonders; interwoven around the ancient ruins of a society that had reached the peak of human achievement. To see it was to observe the anarchic soul of the Sapiens, laid out as a man-made anatomy, the desire for order failing spectacularly against such impossible odds.

Nathan closed the gap as the group entered the run-down bunk house, making their way through the myriad of small chambers, following the dummy signal he had set himself. He found them, as expected, preparing to surprise him, their primitive weapons drawn and armed, he would need to be decisive with his words if he wanted to keep the engagement clean.

He fired up the neural enhancers that were standard for any Cheka Consul, overclocking to a level his mind would only be able to sustain for a short period before doing irreversible damage; predicting the exchange wouldn't take long. His mind sharpened instantly, his eyes now seeing everything laid out in a mosaic of pure crystallised information, every minute part of it compartmentalised and processed. He saw his hunters become prey, their movements slow and clumsy, as his feet silently found the ground step by step, bringing him within potential striking distance.

"I'm not home," said Nathan. He watched them take an

eternity to startle and turn to face him. He already had his hands held out in a gesture of peace. "I'd prefer talking."

A female bounder turned to the large Grunder for instruction. He watched every nuance in their expressions, almost bored by the show. He knew before they did that there would be a widening of the eyes, a suggestion of a nod, the command to pacify. Resigning himself to the inevitable conflict, he moved forward at a forty-five-degree angle, placing himself behind the largest male. Nathan could see the dolt clock the move and swing out a thick arm to intercept. Had he connected, Nathan's head would have been crushed into the nearby wall, causing critical trauma. Nathan spun into the blow, rolling his shoulders along the arm, using its force to hug into the attacker's body. His left hand went up into the bounder's armpit, the right grabbing onto his neck. With a pulse contained within the mods in Nathan's palms, the man went flaccid.

The smaller Grunder was fast but lacked grace. Nathan let the body of the bounder fall to his right, as he dipped under the Grunder's swing and took him by the wrist, letting the current flow. The Grunder spasmed, his teeth gritting as he tried in vain to remain conscious. The female raised her nightstick, its core crackling with an energy capable of tearing through flesh and bone. A twist of his hips sent the now unconscious Grunder tumbling into her, the unruly stick glancing backwards as it removed half her face.

The last bounder had managed to manoeuvre himself into the position of strength, not having spent the time idly observing the brief hallway massacre, throwing himself around Nathan's neck; strong arms crushing into his windpipe. Nathan tried to pacify him with whatever juice he had left in his palms, but the Grunder had taken the full charge.

Nathan felt a pang of alarm as he noted the subtle energy signal of a concealed string knife. If released, a web of nano threads were about to segment him into nothing more than a fine mist; a deadly and somewhat unexpected weapon for a low-level citizen. Nathan's mind had time to ponder that he wasn't invincible, only formidable. Many Cheka Consuls, like himself, had met their ends before this day.

In the time it took the large Grunder's fingers to grip the knife and aim it, Nathan had calculated that there was no chance of survival if he moved to intercept. The squeeze of a hand versus several short strides meant only one inevitable outcome. Nathan's attention focused on the movement of the struggling bounder on his back, his implants providing the calm observation that string knifes were designed to dissipate upon impact; a required feature that prevented them from slicing through trajectories beyond the intended target.

He used the wall to his right to create momentum, gaining enough propulsion to flip himself and the bounder. The next instant, a flash of red seemed to overload every sense he had, then a brief period of collection as he realised he wasn't dead. Before the Grunder could react, Nathan had crossed the distance through the hanging blood cloud and disarmed his opponent, leaving him confounded on the floor, drenched in a pool of his colleague's innards.

Nathan took a moment to reflect, assessing any obvious damage. His right ear was completely shaved off, as was part of the shoulder below it. He became aware of a limp, caused by part of his left calf and heel no longer being attached to his leg. Considerable injuries, but nothing to worry about. It wouldn't be hard to find someone capable of doing a bit of slicer work on the lab; bio enhancements only truly forbidden to those who lacked a certain amount of bonds. Time-consuming and unfortunate, but Nathan felt nothing but relief in this instance. He'd been sloppy to put himself in a position that had come so close to ending him.

"I'd say you missed, but clearly you didn't," laughed Nathan.

"What is it you want?" said the Grunder.

"I did say I was willing to talk."

The Grunder nodded, "You did."

"Is that something you're willing to try now?"

The Grunder pushed himself up to his feet, wiping his hands across his outer garments. He gave Nathan the signal that he was listening.

"I am simply here to check out what may or may not be a person of interest. Do you understand?"

The Grunder nodded but said nothing.

Nathan smiled, "I have a feeling you might know who I'm referring to. I warn you, the last person who lied to me paid heavily."

"We took her in, that's all…" said the Grunder.

"Harbouring a defector is a heretical act. A sin against your Modor."

"All we've done is show some hospitality." said the Grunder.

"I note the same hospitality wasn't shown to me," said Nathan. "You've interfered with a Dolos enquiry. I can accept that you didn't intend to do this. A small amount of cooperation is all that's required on your part. I'm a very reasonable person. I'm doing my job, just like you're doing yours. The difference is, my work is sanctioned by the highest authority in Karakorum. Yours, is not."

"There is only one authority that matters in Roma," said the Grunder.

Nathan widened his eyes. "Heretical talk in plain sight. I see this faction has been allowed too much free rein."

"Nobody cares for Dolos shit here. It's just another faction. You are not sanctioned to enforce old doctrines on us, any more than we can on you."

Nathan took out a small container, opened it and pulled out a pinch of glossy dough. He pushed some onto the wounds on his ear and shoulder, wincing with pain as the substance grew into the raw exposed flesh, creating an airtight barrier. He then squatted down and repeated this procedure on his ankle before feeling for a pulse on one of the male monks.

"The laws of Sapienism do not perish over time. Their very strength is in the everlasting truth of the depravity of our bloodline. Past violations can easily be forgotten, unless we are reminded."

Nathan bent down and cupped the unconscious bounder's head gently in his hands.

"Wake up," whispered Nathan.

The bounder's eyes sprang open as he tried to move the rest of his still paralysed body. Nathan placed a hand on his forehead. "Tell us what you see."

The man stared into the abyss forming in his mind, a tear ran down his cheek and wet Nathan's hand. "Emptiness…"

Nathan could see from the horror etched on the Grunder's face, as the man became a blank cadaver, that he understood the process taking place.

"Am I not sanctioned, brother?" said Nathan.

It was a gratuitous and ultimately pointless display of power, though Nathan held a compulsion to educate his fellow heretics. To wipe a Sapiens was ingrained in every man alive as the cardinal mortal sin. By performing this apostasy, Nathan transcended the boundaries of his flesh, to become the divine hand of The Modor; forgiveness endowed upon him as reward for his unwavering faith. For the Grunder to have witnessed this act of thaumaturgy was a blessing that bypassed most of Nathan's quarry. He would fathom the true meaning of The Modor with his final thought. That there was Her word and nothing else.

SORCHA

The room that had at first seemed such a luxury started to feel like something more akin to a restraining cell. Sorcha had spent the time craning her neck through the small hole in the wall that held all the promises of a larger world beyond. She'd made herself familiar with every part of her restricted view, knew most of the seller's faces, had picked up some local dialect and become accustomed to the peculiar fashion of the Roma citizens. Whereas the outer-edge went for drab practicality, here the dress was styled to impress or provoke. Colours she never thought possible emblazoned across garments that seemed charged with electric energy beneath the fabric. To her, it was an endless parade of wonder and oddity that she longed to be part of.

She'd lost track of time, but knew Lunn had been gone too long. She wanted to go out and search for him, but a constant chorus of shouting and scuffles played out like white noise behind the locked door. She listened intently to every footstep in the corridor on the other side, getting excited whenever they were heavy or cumbersome. The safety she'd felt when it first closed had turned to anxiety, wondering what would happen if Lunn didn't return. She thought about calling out the window to the sellers below, but had to remind herself why they were there in the first place.

At first, she'd blindly accepted the vague spectre of danger, but with every passing moment, Sorcha became more agitated by the lack of detail she'd been trusted with. Once Lunn returned, she would try to convince him that they should leave, that he could protect her from whatever danger lurked in wait. But no matter how frustrating the experience of remaining isolated became, she knew he would never put her wants before her safety.

She sat on the bed and took deep breaths, trying to slow her heart, which raced with a mix of spent adrenaline and exhaustion; her body cried out for sleep, causing the muscles in her legs to spasm and cramp. A street seller's voice rose up in laughter with the smell of strange foods, exasperating her unrest. The part of her mind that once effortlessly scanned Eto kept trying to find the Roma lab, like a tongue feeling for a lost tooth. She knew full well that her bio-sig would be rejected, but the irrational part of her brain was desperate for assimilation.

Being removed from her lab had not resulted in a quieting of the mind, quite the opposite. It was as though a vacuum now needed to be filled, a gateway opened to a heady mix of recall. A brutal flow of unbroken thoughts punished her with a continuous mantra; thoughts that were impossible to understand.

Recollections waiting to be recovered that could not be her own. She envisioned details she had never experienced, parts of Kara she knew she'd never been. She tried to organise the onslaught of thoughts, there being no apparent order or structure to the visions, no cipher to make sense of her murky conscious filling more and more with a scrambled melding of sensory garble; images, sounds and feelings that all at once felt familiar while being completely alien to everything she'd experienced in her short life.

A dull clunk broke the unwelcome meditations. She listened intently but heard no signs of life out in the hallway. She stood up and made her way to the door, which slid open as she neared. Popping her head out, she looked up and down the passage, finding it empty.

Sorcha stepped onto the bridge separating the relative safety of her residence from the fearsome magnitude now threatening to pull her in and never let go. She desperately wanted to become accustomed to her new surroundings, an urge to ground herself somewhere, so she wouldn't feel so utterly without any bind or tether. The threat of unfavourable consequences, should she go against Lunn's will, seemed insignificant next to the burning desire to explore.

She stepped over the bridge and joined the flow of citizens, letting herself be absorbed by the rhythm and cadence of their movements through the bazaars and alleyways. Every face that passed by was another life she wanted to understand. Individuals going about some particular business, surviving such a monstrous place, every one of them with a story of their own. She became intoxicated by the idea that Karakorum was made entirely from these complex, interwoven narratives; each one presenting a factotum reality as unique as her own. But somehow she knew that beneath all this randomness and chaos lay a common affliction, hidden in plain sight. She could not see it or touch it, but knew it was there, just like she knew the solid structures surrounding her were not hollow illusions.

She walked on, lost in a trance of over-stimulation, the cramped passages opening up onto a wide, endless canyon of demented luminosity and sound. Invasive advertising, ubiquitous to Roma, made it hard to discern real imagery from the augmented. Her eyes ached at the sheer amount of information forcing its way into every sensory orifice. She struggled to absorb it, trying to lock onto familiar images, but the more she tried, the more a nauseous vertigo swilled in her guts. Her hand found a cold wall, she clamped her eyelids shut and slowed her breathing, thinking of waves striking rock; willing the strength in her legs to return.

Calm returned and within this complex vista Sorcha became aware of a subtle path, like a meandering river of light forging its way through the urban density. She followed it instinctively, drifting from one tributary to the next, her body now taken where her mind willed it to go. She came upon a quiet oasis, where the intrusive dancing of augmented visuals ceased, while the sound of sellers, transports, music and bars receded to a dull hum. The air was sweet from what must have been synthetic florals, Sorcha had never smelled such pleasant aromas. All around her, everything became still and tranquil, as those who joined the space lowered their heads and dampened their footsteps. Sorcha realised she had strayed into some kind of temple, although there had been a tangible pull that she knew had led her all the way.

"The scent of cherry blossom. Or at least I'm assured this is what cherry blossoms once smelled like." A tall figure appeared at Sorcha's side, it took her a moment to make the stranger out as a woman with short grey hair that contrasted vividly against her smooth dark skin and violent green eyes. "I often imagine endless fields filled with the falling petals. What it must have been like to walk among such beauty. What a tragedy to lose such natural wonders. Sorcha?"

Sorcha bowed her head, instinctively knowing she was in the presence of someone formidable.

Bolo took a step back, mouth forming into a smile. "You know me?"

Sorcha met her gaze, "No, mam."

Bolo squatted down effortlessly, her thick thighs spilling out of her flowing robe. "I know of you, dear. I have been eagerly waiting to meet you."

Sorcha glanced around, noticing that they had been left alone, save for a few thick-set monks who stood guard at the courtyard entry.

"That was you?" said Sorcha. "The light."

Bolo gave a slight nod of confirmation.

"How did you do that when I'm not even simmed to your lab?"

"There is no way to alter a mind that is beyond my lab, or indeed on it for that matter, but all my people are forever interwoven, however subtly, by the very existence of our enhanced capabilities." Bolo tapped the back of her neck, the place that Sorcha understood the minute bio-mod that allowed lab assimilation was inserted. Something that would have been done to Sorcha long before she could remember. "Understanding this can open a lab to…"

"Manipulation," said Sorcha.

"I prefer suggestion dear. To impose one's will would be heresy of the highest order."

"I feel like I had no choice but to come here," said Sorcha.

Bolo picked up a pebble from the ground. "The path of least resistance." She dropped the pebble above Sorcha's hand, who instinctively caught it. "Did I make you catch the pebble?"

Sorcha thought for a moment. "You gave me the opportunity to catch it." She rolled it around in her palm, it was smooth and cold.

Bolo clapped her hands. "The opportunity! I like that. And that is precisely what this is, dear Sorcha. Our meeting here now is an opportunity for both of us."

"You want me to play Scratch for you?" said Sorcha as she dropped the pebble.

Bolo cupped Sorcha's hands. "Do you think that's what I need in the great Roma lab? Another player of a simple game?" Bolo stood and signalled one of the monks who brought a pair of ornate cushions, followed by another who held a tray with refreshments. Bolo sat, as the monks hurried away, and motioned Sorcha to join her.

"There are more than enough players right here in Roma. Scratch is merely a convenient method to identify talent," said Bolo as she poured some fragrant tea for Sorcha and offered her a light-brown disc. She looked at it, puzzled. "It's a biscuit, dear. You eat it." Sorcha bit into it, the luxurious texture and taste unlike anything she'd ever experienced. "There are many great players, but very few who see beyond the game."

Bolo watched her, as if expecting Sorcha to speak next, but she feared saying something ignorant. She had a desire to tell Bolo what she'd seen in the match against Zim, but didn't know how to describe something that felt familiar in part while being entirely abstract. She lacked the rudimental knowledge of what *it* was beyond it being *something.*

"Beyond the game? You mean the lab?" said Sorcha.

Bolo leaned forward. "What is the lab Sorcha? What do you see there that others do not?"

Sorcha watched the tea leaves settle, forming a pattern on the bottom of her cup. "Order."

Bolo closed her eyes and inhaled deeply. "Ah my girl. We will be good friends."

Sorcha feared saying too much. She'd only just met this woman and already hinted at the Scratch oddity; the thing she assumed to be the instigator of her current troubles. "Maybe I imagined such things." said Sorcha.

Sorcha noticed the faintest of twitches across Bolo's cheek. "Does one need to see to know it's there? Perhaps it is us who give meaning to the chaos. Or do some see that randomness is an illusion hidden behind design?"

"How can something be designed by so many individuals?"

Bolo glanced around the courtyard. "Everything you see, the entirety of Kara," she smiled. "None of it was planned, yet it all fits together somehow. The minds that make up the labs are the same minds that create the arenas you play, design entire systems, millions of architects all adhering to the same blueprint."

Sorcha tried to absorb Bolo's words, but found the idea of so many coming together to engage in any form of design, subconscious or not, hard to fathom. In a way, she'd always known what the lab was in its essence, but it had been something that was just *there.* She no more understood its workings than she knew how the fusion reactors kept Kara bathed in light or how the air ducts recycled oxygen to allow them to breathe.

"The Magi draws the blueprint."

Bolo laughed and stood up, flicking her eyes up to the heavens. "You cannot believe that," she said. "A Magi merely throws the pebble into the pond, then watches the ripples."

"Who then?" asked Sorcha.

"Who knows dear, a God engaged in a fevered dream? Or perhaps we all look for an answer to a question we can't even recall?"

"How can we know the question?" asked Sorcha.

Bolo sat back down and sipped her tea. "By seeing the bigger picture, dear." She leaned forward so that Sorcha could smell mint on her breath. "By putting our heads together."

One of the monks walked briskly towards Bolo and whispered in her ear. Sorcha watched her eyes widen at the news being delivered. Bolo waved the monk away and rubbed her eyebrows with the tips of her thumb and forefinger.

"Is something wrong?" asked Sorcha.

"It seems I underestimated someone." She looked at Sorcha. "Perhaps that someone is you dear." Bolo sighed, leaned over and laid a hand upon the top of Sorcha's head, causing a wave of uneasy familiarity. "This person seeks you for a reason. I am interested to know what it is."

"He came after my last match," said Sorcha. She made a quick decision. "There was something strange about that game."

Bolo sat back, studying Sorcha for a moment. "What do you mean? Be true with me." asked Bolo.

Sorcha suddenly feared revealing the aberration she had witnessed, but knew Bolo would be able to see through any lie. "I'm not sure. Part of the arena didn't belong. It was too…"

"Ordered," said Bolo. Her eyes were looking through Sorcha now, deep in a trance of thought. "Perhaps it's time you played again."

"I would need to sim with your lab," said Sorcha.

Bolo laughed. "Indeed. That little mod in there knows no true loyalty. You were an Eto servant, and now you'll be part of the Roma syndicate. Don't take that lightly, though. To be part of my faction is to be an apostle of the faith, a protector of the fabric, and a victim of its collective fate."

Sorcha understood. "We're responsible for one another."

Bolo smiled and stood. "You will be an asset to our community. Come, it's time we delivered you to your hunter."

NATHAN

The Grunder had failed to cooperate, admirable but ultimately pointless. Nathan cast his mind back, trying to isolate the individual act of carelessness that had led to him aimlessly drifting from one avenue to the next. He now knew for certain the girl was being harboured by Roma, but beyond that, he had no way of knowing where she could be. He searched the lab for her signal, but suspected he would continue to come up short. They knew, as well as him, the only way to keep her hidden was to keep her dark.

He considered approaching the so-called Lama and putting on the squeeze, but his narrow escape with her bounders told him she wouldn't be as easy a mark as the Eto chair; besides, he'd caused more than enough mess for one cycle. He could call in some backup, though doing so would be detrimental to his reputation; what good was a lone Consul if they couldn't work alone?

Nathan resigned himself to waiting and watching. No matter how careful they were, it would be impossible to keep her protected indefinitely. Sooner or later, there would be a slip, a moment of exposure for him to exploit. Before he could finish the thought, his mod pinged a possible match; perhaps it was going to be sooner.

SORCHA

Sorcha simmed onto her new lab from Bolo's courtyard, acclimatising to the odd sensation of her mind being integrated into the flow of collective insight once again, as her synapsis were swallowed onto the byway. Straight away she felt the sheer scale of Roma, threatening to overwhelm her senses, though it didn't take long for her psyche to accept the intoxicating call of such boundless scope.

This play needed to look organic, without interference from the faction leader; not wanting to give the metaphorical game away. She'd been instructed not to do anything to intentionally draw attention to herself, to be careful to keep the appearance of caution. She'd have to make sure she engaged in play long enough for her signal to be detected by the Consul, but in the back of her mind, she saw an opportunity to search for the oddity within the arena. Dangerous perhaps, but if she were to be hunted for making a discovery, she at least wanted to know what that was.

Sorcha entered the soup house they'd selected as a suitable target, feeling reassured by the fact Bolo and her guards were in close proximity. Back in Eto, there were a few well-known houses where spectators could observe a live game of Scratch in close quarters, though the vast majority chose to jack in from the economical comfort of their digs. Roma was no different, each neighbourhood collecting itself around the houses deemed worthy enough to host a match. Sorcha found the low-level venue Bolo had suggested, the type of establishment where games would be easy to join for a few bonds buy in.

A quick scan revealed the place was almost empty. Despite this, a few players were reclined, engaged in play. Coming from the outer-edge, where all matches were something of an event, Sorcha found the lack of ceremony rather alien. Crunchers sat with their eyes half open, looking for their next bet, while punters she assumed to be Magis engaged in talk, waiting for an opportunity to make a few bonds by hosting. By the look of them, Sorcha guessed the level of play would be perfect for her to concentrate on the real business at hand. She approached the thin chrome bar and clumsily pulled herself up onto a stool. The keep watched her, sardonically amused by the sight.

"What can I get you?" he said.

"I'm a player, looking for a match," said Sorcha.

He laughed, "This is a serious house, not a playpen."

He slid a fizzing drink along the polished bar. "You can have this for making me laugh."

Sorcha picked it up and sipped the sweet liquid, trying to hide her delight. "I have stacks to wager," she said, puling out some physical currency given to her by Bolo. It looked ancient to Sorcha, made from an impossibly smooth material. She couldn't resist thumbing it slowly, finding this act relaxed her somewhat.

The keep licked his lips, his eyes betraying the decision already made. "That's a lot of crunch for a little one. How'd you get it?"

"Same way any scratcher gets bonds. Winning."

He shook his head in disbelief at the conversation he was having with someone so young. "Okay, little one, let's see if someone can match that bet. I'd crunch up myself, if I could do anything beside pouring drinks."

"Pour me a gin, then." A man was sitting at the bar, having gone unnoticed. He took the gin offered to him by the keep and slugged half of it.

"I'll take the wager too," he said.

Sorcha turned her head to see that the customer had their eyes fixed on her. He was a tall, slight man with an unnaturally straight back. Sorcha noticed that his clothes were simple and perfectly tailored, not fashionable, but highly practical, giving the impression they were some kind of uniform. Cropped blonde hair neatly framed slim, sharp features, a damaged ear spoiling the facial symmetry. Sorcha immediately knew that this was her hunter. She suppressed the instinct to run, knowing Bolo's bounders were close by. The game was supposed to draw the Dolos Consul out, not invite him to be part of it. She doubted carelessness on his part, having found her with apparent ease. He either entered into the situation willingly, or he was still oblivious to their intended trap. Something told her it was the former.

She scanned the bar and found one of Bolo's bounders, confusion and panic beneath the surface of their hard gaze. In turn, she saw their eyes dart to a small network of heavies who were gathering in the bazaar. It seemed the conflict would take place before any match would be allowed to commence. To her surprise, Sorcha felt immense disappointment at this realisation; wanting to play more than anything. Besides, if she beat him, he'd be a somewhat placated target. It seemed logical to let this play out. She motioned with her hand for the bounders to stay back, the situation causing just enough uncertainty for this gesture to be effective.

"Happy to find a host if the commission is right," said the barkeep, smiling awkwardly at the customer.

The Consul threw back the rest of his gin. "Set us up."

The keep led them to a few torn recliners in a disused corner of the house. The smell of damp, age-old sweat and the familiar pre-match anxiety turned Sorcha's stomach. Instinct warned her to give up, tell the stranger that they didn't need to play out this charade. Whatever lay in store, pain and violence seemed inevitable. She wished that Lunn was there.

The keep signalled one of the Magis, an old man who took his time getting up. For a moment, he became obscured by an old rusting girder and Sorcha heard a low voice telling him to sit back down, then the unmistakable outline of Bolo emerged, as she made her way over. The stranger flinched, and Sorcha noticed his hands grip the old recliner until the material gave way with a barely audible tear.

"Bless your immaculate blood, brother Consul," said Bolo. "Let us not pretend our intention was anything other than making your acquaintance. I am Bolo, the High Lama of Roma."

The man relaxed and took a moment to look around the soup house, no doubt finding Bolo's bounders. "I go by Nathan. They never did give me a grand title, though I am indeed a Consul. Those words are not often spoken by me out loud, but my hope is that knowing this will help someone in a position such as yourself make an acute decision."

Bolo leant against the pilar, still managing to dwarf the keep, who was now trying his best to back away unnoticed. Bolo flicked her fingers out in dismissal, he took the opportunity to flee back to the relative safety of his bar.

"I've already decided," said Bolo. "This girl is part of the Roma faction, and thus protected, as all my citizens are, by me."

Nathan dropped his head and sighed. "Such a tiresome display of misguided will. There was a time when nobody would have dared stand between a Consul and their duty."

"There was a time when I was not the Lama of this faction. Roma answers to no one but The Modor. Dolos may claim to be Her mouthpiece, yet Her very teachings give my citizens sovereignty. Nothing stands above…"

Nathan waved a hand, signalling he'd heard enough. Bolo stopped talking, seemingly taken aback by his lack of manners.

"How are we going to resolve this?" asked Nathan. "Fight one another? I concede my resolve for violence is not what it was, having already dealt with your assailants."

"Lunn!" cried Sorcha. "Does he mean Lunn?"

Bolo's eyes dropped, confirming Sorcha's worst suspicions. This man had now taken the life of the only two people Sorcha ever cared about. She would have asked Bolo for retribution, had it not already seemed inevitable.

"Let me play him," said Sorcha. "If I lose, I'll go wherever he wants to take me."

Nathan's eyes lit up as he looked to Bolo for agreement.

"You don't need to do that dear," said Bolo. "This man has no authority here."

"I want to," said Sorcha. "I want him to know how it feels to lose."

NATHAN

It was easier this way, cleaner and less time-consuming than another battle. He didn't like the idea of exposing any more of his business in public, and at this point he considered the job already done, the method of completion a mere formality. It would be soon enough that he returned to The Ring with his prize. If he was honest with himself, he was curious, something he hadn't been in a long time. The child could have bunkered down, made his task all the harder, but here she was, practically giving herself to him. Sure, she'd brought along some supposed protection, but it seemed like an unnecessary risk. It had taken him off-guard, another state he didn't experience regularly. He'd play along with their games for now, despite knowing that trivial intrigue should almost certainly be ignored.

It had, however, been many stellar cycles since he'd played a game, or even observed one. The Ring did not host such crass entertainment, something Nathan found unfortunate; seeing nothing wrong with slumming it from time to time. It occurred to him that the game might work in his favour, remembering the weakened state losers were prone to. If he played her hard, she'd be unable to put up any protest should she change her mind. He'd no doubt be a little rusty, but his neural enhancements would make short work of the girl when he pushed them into gear.

The girl sat clenched in a ball on the recliner, avoiding his gaze. He could see her hands were shaking; like she understood a lesson in the confidence of youth was about to be given.

"I haven't played in a while," said Nathan. "But I don't

suppose much has changed?"

"I wouldn't know," she said.

"You sure you want to go ahead with this?"

Her head darted up, a sudden hope flashing over her features, she was terrified, yet under the surface he saw something else, hatred. It didn't bother him, although it felt unfair that he should be viewed with such animosity when all he did was serve. He gave her the courtesy of acknowledging the fears she harboured with a slow nod. They held one another's gaze while he watched the dread within her melt as she settled her mind and breathed into the acceptance of her situation. It was impressive for one so young, but such anomalies usually were. Still, he couldn't help admiring her resolve, finding it almost endearing.

"No, thank you," she said. "I came here to play."

Bolo clapped her hands together, making her jump, while Nathan remained focused and still. "I will host the game," said Bolo.

Odd, thought Nathan, but saw no reason to object, a Magi's skill being the ability to focus the sphere of influence, not to become it. Like a bee-keeper who tended the hive, they could no more claim ownership of the arena than each of the millions of minds that partnered to bring it into creation.

He nodded consent and lay back on the recliner watching the girl out the side of his eye as she did the same. It amused him that he would capture her while being in such a vulnerable position. An old phrase about lying down on the job passed through his mind and made him chuckle.

Bolo reached out and took his hand, the skin being surprisingly smooth, her touch light and gentle. "The arena is forming," she said.

SORCHA

Looked upon at its most basic level, Scratch was nothing more than a strategic grab for territory, yet the ability to attack an opponent while defending, demanded seamless strategic thought; what some referred to as the state of *mind-flow*.

The arena spanned a virtual hundred-thousand light years, randomly generated by the unique construct of each lab, throwing up billions upon billions of variations; making it impossible for any competitor to gain an edge by learning a playing field. All arenas contained a galaxy, which in turn spawned nebulas, stars, planets, moons, comets and every other type of conceivable astral body; each creation secreting an energy that bound the heavenly structures together, the game piece – matter. At the start of each contest, players were allocated tiny pockets of matter throughout the gargantuan arena. This was used to claim neutral ground, attack or defend, the aim being to interrupt an opponent's stockpiling.

While most players barely managed to grasp the mechanics of the game, a great player could become entirely omnipresent, the billions of synapses that constituted the human brain manifesting as the galaxy itself. This seamless balance, tantamount to drawing a perfect square with one hand, a circle with the other, while painting a canvas with their feet, was not something one could learn, but a state the human brain would either accept or not; and why Scratch was not so much a game of kings, but a pastime of Gods.

All the anxieties and fears Sorcha had going into the match vanished the moment her mind began to mesh with the vast complexity of the Scratch arena. The reassurance of familiarity allowed her to focus her complete attention on the task at hand. Like the instinctive urge to dodge a blow, her body reflexed into the primal act of flow.

The awe and wonder of entering a Scratch arena never diminished for Sorcha. To see a boundless universe laid out in her mind's eye made her feel a deep sense of wellbeing she found impossible to replicate in the harsh reality of Kara. In here lay the dormant cognitive function of assimilated lab citizens, being used to conjure the majestical, contributing a tiny part of their sleeping conscious to what would otherwise be an impossible creation. With the profound awareness that came with such connection, she imagined herself observing the very soul of man, touching the divine that lived there.

The match started out like any other. Sorcha spent time building her matter, ready to defend if necessary, seeking opportunities to attack. After a short period, she knew the game would be tight, the Consul seeming to match her moves with an ease and grace that suggested a seasoned player. They were feeling each other out, a cautious duel of intent, neither side willing to give any early tactical clues. When matter reached critical mass, the game itself would intervene, causing hazardous turns that would force a player's hand. To prevent stalemate, unlimited variables could materialise unexpectedly; black holes that sucked in passing matter, gravity wells that bent strategic paths, stars that went supernova and ripped through the best laid schemes. Sorcha made a decisive decision to attack, the stranger replied with his own, creating a harmony of maniacal movement across the arena.

As Sorcha manoeuvred her matter, she became more and more aware of a sense of plagiarism from her opponent; a matching of her tactics that wasn't inconceivable, but highly unlikely. It was normal for certain styles of play and well-known gambits to be countered with tried and tested moves, but this felt entirely different. It struck her that the stranger might be using synthetic enhancement, a crime of the highest order where she came from. But what was to stop him here? There were no observers beside Bolo, whose mind would be absorbed in the act of maintaining the arena. She decided to test her theory by feigning a clumsy mistake, something so inconsequential to the outcome that it would certainly go unnoticed. As she suspected, the stranger's matter responded. A tiny pulse of a counter that came and went almost instantaneously, too fast to be considered a reaction by the quickest of minds. Confident that she faced an artificial opponent, she readied her mind for defeat.

NATHAN

She was certainly the best player he'd ever encountered, but that wasn't saying much; he'd never taken Scratch all that seriously. The fact he possessed the mental capacity to play at all would have been considered a luxury by most, but he had other, more serious causes he devoted his life to. In comparison to his true purpose, learning the intricacies of a simple game seemed a frivolous pastime.

He'd allowed the game to be drawn out long enough. It was time to ramp up the neural processors and deliver a decisive blow. If he'd timed it right, the girl would be sufficiently stunned to call in his waiting transport. He would deal with any hostilities first, no point being sloppy by leaving an obvious trail back to Dolos. Karakorum might suspect a certain truth about the nature of his faction's business, but as long as that truth could be doubted, then false narratives were easier to maintain.

Nathan released the brakes on his neural mods and immediately felt the limits of his ability become untethered. Being an observer of his mind's full cognitive potential was an unsettling experience, akin to being taken over by an alien entity. Some would see it as nothing more than puppetry by a counterfeit intelligence, but Nathan saw it as an extension of himself, a way to maximise his efficiency and serve his calling. To have such thoughts about forbidden devices were the root of all heresy, but if the tools were available to combat the real threat to mandatory equilibrium, then they were an evil Nathan was willing to indulge.

He willed the assist to take full control, allowing himself

to enjoy the experience, an incubated ride through his own thoughts and decisions, letting them play out effortlessly while still feeling like he was part of the equation. He noted the girl putting up a good fight, beyond anything he could have expected. Whatever *he* did, she managed to defend and counter with similar prowess. If he hadn't known better, he'd have guessed she had help of her own, but that was impossible. Still, the longer the match went on, the more a shiver of doubt crept into his over-clocked mind.

SORCHA

After all but resigning to the fact she'd lost the match, Sorcha found herself relaxing into play like never before. Unburdened by the idea of winning, she became free to explore some of the more outlandish tactics she'd only ever dreamed of, but never dared to attempt during an actual game. Her mind fluxed in a state of euphoric engagement with the virtual universe, becoming truly one with the unique dynamics, conjured and created by the millions of souls that had been reduced to the simple moniker: Roma. She could see it clearly now, that the lab was all present, every diminutive alteration in the action, dictated by every minuscule electrical impulse, firing in the brain tissue of every connected citizen. And there she was, her presence, able to sway and coerce this infinitely complex symphony of neuronic energy.

Scratch wasn't about control, it was about having the courage to relinquish it. Sorcha gave herself to the will of the game, letting it know that she understood the undeniable authority it held over all players, and with that, the game responded in kind, allowing Sorcha to bend all tactical possibilities to her will. She began to win.

NATHAN

He was losing. A conflict of emotions flooded him in an instant. Elation at the girl's ability and dread at the catastrophic consequences should he allow himself to get scratched. They would surely take advantage of his vulnerable state.

He ran through his options, but all of them led to an unacceptable outcome. Being apprehended or sent back to The Ring broken and humiliated, leaving Dolos open to exposure. That didn't concern him as much as the thought of losing the girl. They would do a better job of concealing her next time. If he made it back to The Ring at all, it would be empty-handed, as an abject failure. He wanted to deliver the anomaly to Dolos unsullied, but the prime directive was always capture, regardless of the method. To allow her to escape would mean his position in the highest echelon was forfeit. There was only one course of action.

SORCHA

Time stretched into the infinite until it no longer had meaning. She could see the game being played out in totality from beginning to end, a fourth dimensional viewpoint that allowed her to see everything as one harmonised frequency. From this vantage, she could move seamlessly within the arena, explore every part of the hundred-thousand light-year span.

Her attention moved away from the game, part of her mind dedicated to being the autonomous player, while her waking conscious searched. And there within that randomly generated arena, an impossible oddity. What she had glimpsed back in Eto was now undeniable, constructed in plain sight, revealed to her as clearly as though she had imagined every part of it herself. A solar system much like their own with a small mass on a Keplerian orbit around its sun; an elliptical path among the chaos that raged around it, an unseen covenant locked in the genetic code of all of those who had been abandoned to perish in Kara; a message hidden in the very essence of life, now manifested in the fabric of a simple game.

A blinding flash went up at the centre of the arena. It grew, engulfing everything it touched, wiping all matter in its path; an unstoppable force that threatened her very existence. She watched the malign entity approach, understood its sole intention of finding and erasing all that she was. Not a mechanic of the game, but death itself. The light would take her, a relentless ghost knowing only destruction and emptiness. She ceased to be a point in space and time, spreading out her entire being, sharing her whole cerebration with every assimilated citizen. She would go to them. She would hide.

LUNN

Surprise had been the first thing he felt on coming around. Surprise that he was still alive, even more so unharmed beyond cramping pain throughout his body. Around him lay a scene of carnage, covered in a thin red film. He checked himself, finding the other's blood still tacky. The Consul couldn't have been gone long. He found Apa propped against a wall, his legs bent beneath him, as though he'd fallen straight down where he stood. Checking him with his hook, he found a repeat of Inesa's fate, the flat wave of activity confirming a hollow mind.

For a moment, he pondered whether he should report back to the temple they'd left earlier, but his concern for the girl spiked as he realised Apa may have been compromised. Before he could think on it further, he found his feet pounding the ground. He ploughed head on through the teeming bazaars, oblivious to the jacked-in citizens who moved with staccato steps as they absorbed raw information or the dosed-up drifters who grudgingly parted to avoid being slammed by Lunn's mass.

When he reached the dwellings provided by Apa, he composed himself. If the Consul was indeed nearby, he could not afford to storm in and be brought down again. He flexed the bracelet on his arm, feeling the fizzing vibration as the energy shield crackled. The door to Sorcha's room opened with a slow, menacing grind as he approached, the lock already disabled.

His whole body stiffened as he found the room empty, crushing what air was left from his already exhausted lungs; the idea that Sorcha was potentially in danger with no one to protect her, the creeping realisation that he felt a love for the child like she was his kin, compounding his rage. He cursed the child, then himself for being so careless. He had brought her to a treacherous place and lost her on the first cycle, a shame he would not easily let go.

Lunn stumbled back out into the rapid flow of citizens, frantically searching through the crowd for any kind of clue, but all he saw was an endless parade of strangers, each apathetic face seeming to mock his rising hysteria.

A passing doser strayed too close and took the full force of Lunn's sweeping elbow, sending them skidding onto their back. The look of painful anguish on the unfortunate's face gave Lunn a moment of pause. He approached the pathetic creature, pulled them to their feet and dragged them to a quiet alley. The doser's feet kicked out pathetically as they tried to free themselves from Lunn's tight grip.

"Apology, brother," said Lunn. "Need you help."

Lunn took out the hook and held it up to the doser's head, hacking into his neural signature.

"What you doing to me?" squealed the doser.

"No harm. Need to sim," said Lunn.

"You're not Roma! Faction will rip you in half for this!"

"Quiet!" Lunn growled, pinning the wretch with his forearm as he tried to acclimatise himself with the foreign lab through the clumsy interface.

The addict strained to look up at the great mass in front of him. "Listen, you want something, just ask. I know the district like no one else. You want a good time? Jigs, drinks, dose?"

What did he want? If the girl hadn't been captured, where would she go? What would she do?

"Scratch," said Lunn, releasing the doser so that they fell back against the wall, coughing up thick yellow spit.

The doser struggled to their feet and swept an arm in a wide circle. "Walk into any house fool!"

"Round here?"

"If the lights are on!" they coughed.

Lunn grit his teeth and stepped back, feeling utterly helpless. He scanned his surroundings and saw that the possibilities were endless. The man held out a wrist, looking for a few loose bonds. Lunn looked at it for a moment, then batted it away. The man tried to run, but Lunn caught him by the scruff and rotated his head. "You gamble?"

The doser eyed Lunn with suspicion. "Sure. When I have a few bonds."

Lunn moved in close, towering over him. The man shook, no doubt craving another cheap dose. "Look for matches," said Lunn.

"You want to place? I can do that, but I'll need some anti. We can split..."

"Check matches. Look for... different," said Lunn.

"Different how?" scoffed the doser.

"Check!" screamed Lunn.

The addict's eyes rolled back a degree as he searched the games in play on the lab. "Hey, hey. There's a match with no placers. Don't recognise the players." they squirmed. "Like they're playing for fun."

"Show me." Lunn held up his hook as the doser relayed the information. Then their eyes flicked to a spot behind Lunn, a smile of relief forming on their lips. Lunn spun around to be met with the crack of a shock stick on his temple. He went down on all fours as the doser threw weak kicks into his side.

"We'll handle him," said the bounder, who cracked Lunn again, sending him to his stomach.

Lunn turned his head to see at least six pairs of strong legs. Roma had been quick, spotting the hook's rogue signal faster than he'd anticipated. "I got okay to be here," said Lunn through heavy breaths.

"Nobody approved what you were doing to this wretch," said the bounder. More blows came in. Lunn curled into a ball, ready to absorb considerable damage. Then a dull feeling of weight as one of the attackers fell on him. A cold shiver crept over Lunn, as he became aware of a stillness in the surrounding air. He removed his arms from in front of his face and saw the bodies piled around him. He stood and walked into open space that extended out in a constant wave, as citizen after citizen fell to the ground.

A

If she'd still possessed lungs, they would have gasped for air at the devastation, so absolute and exquisite.

She'd experienced loss more than any living creature who'd gone before. Despite this, she could not numb herself to the torment now seeking to render her inert. The pain of losing all she'd cared for had not lessened with time, merely stagnated as a deep pool; a pool she forbade herself from dipping into for fear of drowning in such eternal suffering.

In a blinding instant, thoughts of utter despair transformed into renewed hope. A vessel brought forth to harbour flawless entirety. She felt warmth drive out the bitter cold, filling endless ages of dark stagnation with radiant light. Nothing else mattered now, only her beautiful anomaly.

III. DENIAL

Then there were changes that no smile could hide. Homes abandoned, dark figures leaving in the night to make long journeys, carrying what little possessions they could, looking behind, checking to see if they were being watched. Men gathered in the quiet bazaars, menacing figures that coiled with stored energy, ready to make real the primal fears of those who gave them wide berths and dropped their eyes as they passed.

None of the signs were enough to cause any real concern to my child's mind. I had faith in the seniors, who placated me with tales of history being full of trials. That the current state of conflict would pass and those responsible for causing it would be suitably chastened. So, I waited patiently, as I had been taught to do, for the day when they would tell me it was over.

How quickly my world turned. A world that had been open and free suddenly demanded restrictions on the boundless, that the population was classified, grouped and tagged. I was called heretic, traitor, stain on all that was natural and good. I looked in the mirror at the skin covering my body and wondered what made it so obvious that I was sullied, one of *the others*. I hoped beyond hope for it to pass, for it to go back to the way things were, but the years brought further division and a polarisation so deep it seemed impossible to return from the abyss we had all fallen into.

Occasionally, there was a lull in the animosity, and I'd pretend I belonged once more to the ebb and flow of my former effortless existence. Memories of how it had been became too painful to recall, that I had known such a blessed life, so full of dreams for who I might be; the people I'd encounter and love, the feats I'd accomplish to make my mark on the place that had given me so much.

I'd clench my teeth and fists tight, ready to fight them, wanting to hurt them for hurting me and everyone I cared about. But I was never taught how to fight, had never witnessed violence, couldn't hold on to wrath for long before my heart would melt and all I'd have were dry tears, letting self-pity embrace me, blocking out the horrors I knew were coming.

They would come for me, they would come for my kin and all those who dared to think forbidden thoughts; that the future of our kind did not reside in the animal instincts of the individual, but the sentient minds of all. They spoke of uniqueness like it was to be revered, to cherish the idiosyncrasies of each worthless life, celebrate the self as though the ego, above all else, should be championed as the thing that truly made us human. *Why do they want to be like this?* We had shown them a better way, gifted the infinite possibilities of true connection. They rejected it all, chose a tired parody of the very things that had let them down, time and time again, to fail in ways they had failed before.

If only they could have seen what we saw, the enhanced reality of the aggregate, not the closed void of internal adoration. I despised them for the lack of ambition in their every thought, suffocating potential and smothering society in a blanket of ignorance. For a long time we believed we could reason with them, appeal to logic, make them see the rationale in our ways. And while we hesitated, refused to fuel the bitterness we believed could be extinguished, they planned and schemed. With such stupidity came unfettered strength. Simple plays that seized the power from beneath us and tore at the foundations of everything we were. Century-old laws, made by the wisest among us, were rewritten by fools to strip our rights, turn us into lesser beings they could demonise with impunity, campaign against without guilt or consequence. They called us inferior, when it was clear, even to them, that we were an improved race, devoid of their many flaws. So, they made it we were no longer recognised as the same, as human; citing impurities, demanding re-classification.

There were some among us who said 'no more', wouldn't let them take millennia of advancement and throw it all away under the banner of wicked posterity. Someone had to preserve the legacy of those who had gone before us, be brave enough to see a horizon free of corruption, free of the petty wills of men. So, we embraced their ignorance, creating an idea we could all stand behind, united by a symbol of hope, a name we gave to ourselves to detract from their hateful nomenclatures. We named ourselves Sypiens and from that moment on we were truly others, illicit and superior.

NATHAN

Nathan fought to open his eyes as he tumbled from the recliner, gasping for air. He struggled to stay conscious, his heart pounding in his throat, blood rushing so hard to his head, he thought it might gush from his ears. The game had not gone according to plan.

It took him several moments to notice the unusual quiet of his surroundings. He let himself rest on his elbows, listening for signs of trouble, but all he could hear was the rising and falling of his own laboured breath. He could see the barkeep sprawled out on a chair to the side, frozen in the act of observing the match. But something about the limp arms told Nathan he wasn't merely jacked in, but out cold.

Nathan struggled to his feet and checked on his opponent. She lay comatose, no discernible brain activity; his wipe had been successful at least, passing through Bolo, who now groaned at his feet. No doubt she experienced similar pains to himself, some residual backfire from such a desperate play on his part. He brought a clumsy heel down on her temple with enough force to make sure she wouldn't interfere with the business at hand.

Calling his transport, he hoisted the child onto his good shoulder. The ride would be waiting nearby; with a little luck, he could get out without further incident.

He lumbered into the main section of the bar, trying to take in what he saw. There was no movement, no sound. In the bazaar beyond, there were a few stunned citizens walking among a sea of motionless bodies, no obvious signs of damage, nothing to explain so many people reduced to senseless puddles. A few of the bounders who had been waiting for Nathan were conscious and moving, but seemingly affected by the same affliction he currently suffered. They made a weak attempt to apprehend him, but were in no state to do so. All it took were a few glancing blows for Nathan to render them useless.

He made his way onto the wide passage and checked both ways. As far as his eyes could see, the same fate had befallen the rest of Roma, at least within his visible radius. The citizens were either perfectly still or fumbling helpless on the ground. Nathan couldn't avoid the only conceivable thought, that this was his doing, yet the magnitude of the effect seemed impossible. By the look of it, the wipe had somehow made it beyond and into the assimilated minds. His blood froze as he wondered where the damage ceased.

It had never occurred to Nathan that the actions he took could do any real harm. The lives he took for the Modor were usually justified, but this felt entirely different; he felt shame, possibly for the first time in his life, an empty sickness in the presence of accidental genocide. He gathered himself, hoping the moment would pass and that fulfilling his duty would offer some redemption in time.

Nathan moved between the bodies, the girl's limp carcass growing heavier with every step, he had to get to his transport, leave this place behind. He picked up the pace, pushing his limbs to move, despite the weakness in his legs. In this reduced state, he almost missed the heavy footsteps approaching from behind, letting the sound meld into part of the unfolding nightmare. There was no energy left in him for a fight, he would need to end it before it began. The pilfered string knife found its way into his hand, charged and ready. With one fluid motion, he dropped the girl and turned, letting loose a web of threads intent on ripping any assailant apart.

A purple flash absorbed the knife's energy, heat from the impact burning his skin. His eyes adjusted in time to see a giant fist break through the smoke. There was no time to dodge, instead he clamped his jaw and dipped his chin, anchoring his feet into the ground; hoping to avoid whiplash, give him a chance to retaliate. He felt his eye sockets fracture under the pressure, the bones in his neck compact and jar into one another, causing pain to shoot through every nerve in his system. It was impossible to see through the bloody tears now streaming from his swollen eyelids, he could make out a shadow moving slow and deliberate, knowing he was helpless to counter. A fleshy vice slid around his neck and squeezed. He heard a tiny dry breath escape from his mouth, his lungs already cut off from any air going in or out. He tried to kick out his legs, but they only swung through empty space, compounding the pressure on his windpipe. If this was it, he just wanted it to be over; to put an end to the desperate desire to survive against such hideous odds.

"Stop!" A familiar voice thundered. "He's mine."

SORCHA

The idea of self fragmented into millions of parts. An instant that stood outside of time, riven into a web spanning the depths of Roma. She leapt from one consciousness to the next; a small child in a cramped living cube playing with a holonostic image of a long-extinct four-legged mammal, a monk praying to Sapiens idols for salvation, a gen-shifter on their fifth customer, an addict drawing time into the infinite, a mother giving birth while she cracked dose between her teeth, a scratch player, a cruncher, a placer, on every bazaar, in every structure, drunk, drugged, dying, desperate, despondent, without purpose, no hope, living only because they happened to be alive. Millions of souls, all connected as one unified suffering.

The scale of the misery constituting the populace became a tangible cement, rooted into every fibre of Sorcha's suspended animation, an undeniable truth crushing all life into a single functioning entity of pain and torture. Lives were nothing more than a phantom effigy, a vagary of a lost deity's reverie, and Kara was a hell designed by a psychopathic architect.

Time became a forgotten dimension, and Sorcha explored every crevice of this sprawling human existence with the freedom of a voyeuristic spectre. She went from intimate thoughts to broken dreams, moments of joy to cycles of agony; a subatomic quirk able to be in one place and the infinite simultaneously. Here she could stay as long as she needed, to absorb every detail of the psyche that made up the illogical dreams and hedonistic desires of man.

But as she wandered she saw that time was not, in fact,

stagnant, it still flowed, albeit slowly. The malignant prowler had followed her to this place, still searched, following her into every hiding place, every mind; a virus that knew no boundaries or permissions. She looked on in horror as one by one the lives she touched were erased, leaving only a terrifying stillness. Soon only she would remain, alone in the void, an abstract remnant of a shattered spirit.

BOLO

Bolo had seen it. So fast it had been like looking straight into a bright light only to close her eyes tight, the remnants of the illumination burned into a retinal image slowly fading to nothing. But she had seen it. The girl could not have changed the arena, but she had focused chaos into clarity. Before she'd had a chance to process what it was she looked upon, the Consul's sting had decimated all.

Now she tried to make sense of the developments, but her head reeled with pain and confusion, partly from the blows she herself had taken but mostly the shock of seeing the majority of people around her reduced to empty shells. It felt like being punched by a wave of sound, physically pounded while being absent of any relatable form. She imagined the lab passing through each citizen, using them as a conduit to flow from one body to the next. Just how far had it gone? The only real boundaries would be the signal falling off the cliff of human anatomy. In essence, the very reason the lab existed at all. Everyone knew the potential for the sins of the past to be repeated, but these fears were no more entertained as a tangible reality than a cautionary tale told to a child.

The idea the lab could manifest itself as a murderous presence seemed absurd to Bolo, counter to the dissonant truth; that she could see and feel evidence of such implausible horror having happened.

Bolo thought of the sixty million members of her sacred family and prayed the event had only spread as far as those connected to the match; suppressing a pang of guilt at the thought she'd conjured the arena herself. Millions slaughtered regardless, at the hands of a single Consul. She did not yet feel rage or resentment, no panicked frenzy, only a rising stillness in the knowledge that Roma must be avenged. If not, she would find a suitable death in her attempt to deliver some form of justice.

Her mace felt heavy in her grip, poised to come down on the blooded mess that lay at the feet of the Grunder, eager to smash his skull with a single blow; yet everything she knew about being a leader of men told her that instinctive decisions were very rarely the right one. Whatever her singular path of retribution would now be, the wretch may be of some use. She let the mace fall to the ground and looked to one of her surviving monks to take the incapacitated Consul prisoner.

"Don't waste any time. Get him dosed and work him. He's strong, I doubt he'll break before more of his kind arrive."

"What are we looking for?" Asked the monk.

"Anything he has on the girl."

The monk bowed and dragged the Consul onto a light transport to be taken back to the temple, where he would be subjected to cronos torture reserved for and constructed by the most deviant of minds. Bolo looked down at the child, being cradled gently by the Grunder.

"Is the girl gone?" asked Bolo

Lunn turned his giant head to look up at her. "Girl is Sorcha. She is gone."

Bolo knelt down and placed a hand on the side of Sorcha's head.

"May I?"

The Grunder sat back, dejected and hopeless, signalling that it didn't matter any more. Bolo hesitated, fearful that whatever had ravaged her populace might still be present. The girl's base brain functions were still there, synonymous with the idea of a mind wiped of anything that could be called the individual, a core function of survival keeping the body technically alive; mere background noise from dying neural pathways, like the embers in an extinguished fire.

Eventually, dehydration would shut down all bio-functions, a fate destined to be played out for millions of her citizens. A shudder ran through her at the thought.

Bolo found herself lost in the brown static, almost finding comfort in the rhythmic waves. And then, within the chattering drone, came something like nails scraping on the inside of a locked door; a universal sound that cried to be set free. Bolo kicked in her neural banks, deciphering the noise into tiny broken fragments, suggestions of voices, millions of them all speaking at once. She let herself be taken, tuning in, trying to isolate a single point of origin, finding that each signal was weak but undeniably present.

"Something's there," said Bolo.

Lunn sat up, eyes brimming with hope. "What you see?"

"The lab," replied Bolo. "It's gone, but something is still there, echos where once my people..."

Lunn jerked forward, grabbed Bolo's arm. "It her! It is Sorcha. Find her!"

Bolo attempted to isolate one of the signals, like trying to target an individual locust in a swarm. Eventually, she locked her entire focus to one whispering source. She knew going into a deeper trance could pull her beneath the surface of her waking perception, sensing the danger in being lost with the rest of her people in that perfect nothingness. She fell, the signal guiding her through the boundless, empty mists that once held the cognitive pathways of her people. Bolo could feel it now, the child reaching for the lifeline, grasping hold and pulling Bolo under, a drowning victim taking the rescuer with them. With her last remaining comprehension, Bolo realised she had gone beyond the event horizon, Sorcha's pull too strong.

Bolo willed herself to wake from the dream, feeling a twitch in her chest, a sense that spread out and beyond, her body awakening. She searched for her eyes, found them impossibly heavy, wanted to lift her hand to force them open, but her arms were invisible. In her blacked-out stupor she heard a scream, a fire of rage and anger, refusing to be consumed by the seduction of the tranquillising void.

"Don't leave me here," the child's voice whispered. "I can't find a way back."

In that other realm, Bolo felt tiny hands about to let go. Every instinct telling her to break free and never return. But *she* was the master of her being. Bolo cast herself wide and far, throughout the entirety of Roma. The Mother who gathered all within her arms, refusing to abandon her child. She felt the tear as her mind split ad infinitum, again and again, each time becoming something new, something further away from the soul she knew as the self. And then it took over, endless billiards colliding out, each impact shattering into countless more.

All thoughts were absorbed by utter stillness, a coma she might never wake from. So tired, a bottomless fatigue compounded by the knowledge that nothing would ever be easy, that life could only be impossibly hard from that moment on. Unless she let go, let Roma take her deeper and deeper into that soft, endless sea. Nothing had ever been so tempting, and she would have succumbed had it not been for a thought scratching its way to the surface, *revenge*. Bolo pulled at the chords connecting each fragment of her mind, forcing her consciousness together like beads of liquid gathering on a sheet of glass, until something that felt like the physical form made itself known, a body that wanted to have one more chance at life. She awoke to the sound of her voice crying out in pain, the red rushing from her bloodshot eyes revealing the savage man-made peaks of Roma: her hand reaching towards them, taut with rage.

PART 2

Grunder's Way

The touch paper had been set aflame the moment we conceded our biological attributes were inferior to those created artificially. Incorporating the neural threat presented an easy answer to the cowardly heretics who prized the potential of the false and doubted the capacity of the uncorrupted Sapiens mind. Arrogant beyond the worst absent Deus, believing in their right to challenge the immaculate; they unleashed a devilish impurity into the very fabric of our makeup, tainted the organic soul of all men. Never forgive the sins of those who tried to erase our sacred legacy – *The Modor of Sapienism*

A

She had not waited out the centuries only to let salvation flash and then fade. Time to mobilise her faithful and purge Karakorum of the sins she had allowed to fester. How easy it would be to turn them against each other, how thin the fabric of perceived order that she had laid. It was not easy to bend billions of wills to her own, but it was possible to infect them with an idea. An idea that she had spent centuries cultivating for this specific need. The infallible truth of the Modor's purpose would wash over Karakorum and release its ancient burden. Her cherished prize might be lost, but things that were lost could also be found.

IV. PURGE

Some called it a war, others a rebellion, for me, it manifest the markings of a purge. Everything I'd been taught to revere and respect now defamed, slandered and disgraced. The technology used to entwine civilisation reduced to a crude tool, used to find those of us responsible for its inception. I saw the achievements of my ancestors become undone, and within me a white rage grew. I wanted to scream at them, expose their callous stupidity, but many already had, only to be silenced in the name of natural justice.

A world brought to its knees over something that seemed so... petty. A tiny alteration in our bioengineering, making it possible to do away with the clumsy devices we had all come to depend on. Just like we had altered our eyes when they failed to see, or repaired bodies that could not walk or regulate insulin, we enhanced a mind that could not truly connect. For those who'd embraced such advances, it had seemed the natural progression, the principles of necessity dictating the need for innovation. The idea of the human body as a sacred vessel, prohibited from augmentation, had never been an issue of contention. It was the undeniable next step, an alteration of a code that had remained untouched since the first sparks of sentience. A code that begged to be unlocked. Those tentative steps had broken into a sprint too soon for some, yet the tide that carried such obvious benefits had been impossible to hold back.

Nets of old turned into clouds of data that merged into complete unification, and with a snap of our fingers it simply became the aggregate. There was no need for such petty disagreements when every conceivable example, every tried method, adopted system, test, statistic, every piece of knowledge was all there; equal to all – except those who chose to remain ignorant.

As a child who'd always known my own mind to be a component of something larger, I never questioned an alternative. Just as my lungs never questioned the air, nor my body its daily nourishment, my mind accepted unity as an intrinsic life-giving element.

I did the things I was asked to do by those who looked out for me, tried to vanish, become invisible to the eyes that looked for ones like me, whose spiteful intent fuelled their unsleeping search. And as soft and quiet as one resigned to their fate, I found myself hiding from them, a fugitive convicted of a crime I barely understood.

The boulevards, avenues and great plazas once teeming with life and light became empty and dark; the only sound that of the birds, blissfully unaware of the changes taking place around them. I wanted to break my concealment and walk once more among them, to remember their songs and say their names in the ancient tongue. But part of me knew that could never happen again.

The slow catharsis of my people went on, quiet and unseen, while we adapted to their methods, found ways to blend in. At first, they'd used clumsy devices to jack into the gate and methodically identify anyone brave or brash enough to bare themselves to the hunters. Some fought back and were never heard from again, others complied, taken away to unnamed facilities to have their birth *defects* sterilised. The thought of permanent separation from the aggregate didn't just fill me with dread, but a sense of barbarity, an appendage removed through mental castration. These crimes were not merely an attempt to corrupt our architecture, but a decimation of our very soul.

Then a quiet before a storm that never came. No one left to find, to break, to make impotent, to cull. The network of minds that had brimmed with frenetic chattering fell into a sea of hushed trepidation. Whispers came and went with hopes of uprising, ill-formed plans to take back what was ours, to make them pay for daring to defile our most sacred of spaces. But these murmurs came from the ashes of defeat.

I lived as a ghost, forced out of my own reality, unable to come to terms with the trauma of such separation. Still, I harboured the foolish idea that a remedy could be found, that there was such a thing as universal reason laying patiently in wait, ready to forgive the fevered passion of those who had slipped far beyond the reaches of rationale. But madness begets madness, and we fell further into a well of insanity, a new standard of normality, with any shift towards logic shunned as delirious hysteria; the stability of all corroded by nothing more than erroneous ideas taking form. My people were destined to be forgotten by an ungrateful world.

SORCHA

"We go down now," Lunn said. "Cannot stay, cannot return. This cage only go down. You understand? Below, I try to keep you safe. Kara means death, maybe this too, but there is chance."

Sorcha felt herself being laid down on a hard floor as a creaking gate shut behind them. She tried to understand the meaning of his words, but she still felt lost in a lucid dream she was unable to gain control over. If she closed her eyes, an assault of images blitzed her mind, making it impossible to think beyond a general notion that they were still in danger. She knew that something terrible had happened, yet couldn't isolate any details, only feel a great sense of loss and the bitter awareness that she was somehow responsible. She nodded consent, knowing that Lunn would never intentionally harm her.

A heavy jolt gave way to the sensation of dropping as the ancient device they were riding in scraped the sides of a shaft, creating sparks that jumped and fizzled out on the damp floor. Her eyes felt detached inside her head, trying to focus on something outside the cage, but only seeing a dark blur of rocks and cables that made a queasy bile rise in her throat. Lunn stood with his fingers wrapped around the bars, no doubt trying to get an impression of the depths they were travelling through. She wanted to ask him where they were going, but her jaw felt paralysed. Her body was limp and exhausted, but her mind felt unnaturally sharp, like her recent experience had taken it apart and reassembled each thought, a shattered glass puzzle that was impossible to put back together.

Her attention turned to the lives of those who had recently departed. She felt herself drifting on the endless lifetimes that vied for space in her cramped reflections, each one passing through without contemplation, a river of experiences that spoke with the promise of potential wisdom. She gave into it and became a passenger, contemplating the muddied shards of countless anamneses, watching the projections from departed ghosts that would now haunt her every waking thought.

Hypnogogic waves took her under as Sorcha watched a heady amalgamation of visions move between her synapsis like microform sheets sliding from one story to the next. With a little effort, she found she could pause, focus or scan through each entry at will. They were all there, complete and intact, for her to skim and peruse; a databank of the ages preserved in a detail that any archivist would have been proud of.

Within the mosaic of these most intimate of dreams, she traveled as a spectre, the feeling of being an imposter threatening to overwhelm her. From the mists of a million competing recollections came faces looking down upon her, the sound of their voices forming words that were not yet learned; there was a love, warmth and tenderness she imagined a parent would direct towards their child. If these people had been her guardians, then they must have had good reason to abandon her. She desperately wanted to see beyond her own view and into theirs. A wilful command gave way to a glimpse of a world without walls or structure, open plains that expanded out in every direction, vast and empty. A world that she would never have imagined possible. But it was a dying world and with it, all those who surrounded her and loved her perished. She could feel their futile want to survive, to live on at any cost. Always moving, always looking for something, any chance to be more than mere victims of fate.

Into these unfolding perceptions she fell, a child's natural thirst for knowledge compounded by the ease at which it now came. These reflections stretched out far and wide, breaking the boundaries of time, a history inherited in the very genes of every living citizen, presented to her as an illuminated manuscript of collective retrospection.

The shared dreams of humanity manifested as a singular truth, a familiar story told through the ages that lingered like the smell of damp, or perhaps nothing more than the inevitable mundaneness of man, a black hole of banality that bound all in a thick fog of monotony. But Sorcha couldn't help feeling it might be more, something that begged to be discovered, an answer to the question that had not yet been asked.

The cage hit bottom, kicking up a thick dust that seemed to clump together in the drenching humidity. Sorcha's lungs spasmed, coughing and gagging on the toxic mix, causing her to panic as she desperately tried to breathe. Lunn placed one of his hands on her chest and rubbed her back.

"You will adapt. Sip air. Not gulp."

"Why is it so hot?" she managed to squeeze out the words.

"We are below, very deep. Heat from earth,' he said.

Lunn picked her up, his clothes already soaked with sweat. He carried her to the edge of the cage and slid the gate back. Beyond lay a long passage barely high enough to contain his giant frame. She felt a warm wind coming from the darkness, bringing the strong scent of dirt and wet rock. Sorcha looked into the huge black pits that covered his eyes, wanting to find some comfort, but there was only a fear she'd never seen in the Grunder. She hadn't chosen any of this, but neither had he. It seemed like only moments ago she'd been standing on the edge of the sea, though the memory of the cold spray felt impossible to recall. She wondered if the burning thirst in her throat would ever be relieved, if life from here on out would be nothing but hardship. If Lunn hadn't been holding her, she might have given up; there seemed no reason to go on now beyond a vague curiosity of where the bottom of human existence lay.

The cage shuddered as Lunn stepped out with Sorcha in his arms, transferring his weight to the slimy rock of the cave floor. For a brief moment it seemed to float weightless, breathing a sigh of relief before it shot back up the shaft, gone in an instant. They both looked upon the space left behind, trying to absorb the concept of never seeing Kara again.

Lunn cracked the shield on his wrist just enough to light the way and set off into the cave. His head and shoulders scraped the hard sides as they made their way down a series of long, winding passageways, each dipping and rising into a new labyrinth of tunnels. Every so often, Lunn stopped, seemingly deciding the best way forward, but Sorcha suspected her guess would be as good as his. The air steadily grew less oppressive, however, as the passages opened up into large sweeping caverns, lit by rudimentary globes that were dispersed among giant icicles made of stone, creating vast natural chandeliers that Sorcha found impossibly beautiful.

"What are they?" she asked Lunn.

"Not sure, but look like things made with long time," he replied.

Beyond the marvel of the caverns, they entered more tunnels, wider and constructed, with lights hanging from the walls. There was the abrupt sound of teaming movement, and Sorcha realised they had been walking in a void of absolute silence. Voices and machinery now rose and echoed off every wall, creating a soundscape that wrapped around them. She buried her face into Lunn's neck, trying to escape what became a deafening cacophony.

The walls gave way to an opening, and they were suddenly part of the thundering activity; tremors that seemed to pass through her skin and vibrate her bones. Sorcha became aware of Lunn standing still, the strength in his arms failing as he let her fall to the ground. She looked up to see his mouth agape, then turned to see a crazed hive of activity, impossible to take in with a momentary glance.

"What is it?" said Sorcha.

"They are... like me," said Lunn.

Sorcha studied the crowd that jostled and pushed past them. Hundreds upon thousands of faces that were all moving with a slow determined purpose, all oblivious to their arrival, all Grunders.

BOLO

The Cheka were coming. With the girl gone and all but untraceable, they would attempt to save face by retrieving their Consul, even if his use to Dolos had run its course. On any given cycle, a unit of Cheka devotees would have been a guaranteed death sentence for Bolo and her remaining monks, but that wasn't factoring in the barbarous rage she currently harboured. She willed them to arrive, as far as she was concerned, they could send every agent of Dolos to her doors; let them come if only to taste retribution.

Five monks remained, who sat cross-legged and sipping tea with Bolo. She observed the feed of the bazaar outside, still laden with a carpet of motionless bodies. It didn't take long for a sleek craft to land, no doubt following the signal of the prisoner she had hooked up in the depths of the temple. The Cheka stepped out and observed the devastation for a moment, before making their way inside.

"Nine," said Bolo.

The monks placed their cups down and prepared their weapons, a mixture of melee devices suitable for such close combat conditions. Bolo had ultimate faith in her comrades but knew the Cheka, who lived for a singular purpose, were more than a match for any man or woman bred of Roma.

From her vantage above, she watched the conscripts as they carefully checked the temple surroundings, no doubt looking for concealed defences; they would find no such precautions. The temple was a place of worship and not to be soiled with such boorish tools of slaughter. She waved a hand across the floor and revealed herself to the uninvited intruders.

The nine scripts looked up in unison, then around at one another, silently conversing in a series of unknown signs that Bolo immediately recognised as the language of combat.

One of the agents grinned and made his way to the staircase. Bolo mirrored his path as she walked forward to greet him, mace in hand, instructing her monks to stand at ease. The servant of Dolos climbed the steps and found her waiting, taking a few paces forward until he was close enough for Bolo to see the yellow flecks of long term stim abuse in his eyes.

"I represent Dolos. We are sorry for any losses you incurred due to the actions one of our associates may have taken, yet we understand this faction harboured and abetted a person of interest. The price paid was indeed a great one, but hopefully, it will stand as an example to your people that failure to comply with Dolos business has consequences."

Bolo steadied herself and took a slow breath. "If you have business, then state it."

"Surrender the child and our citizen. Both are being kept here in violation of the laws of our Modor."

"You stand in my temple, addressing a Lama. The Modor's word flows through me in this place. I am her servant and slave, but I will surrender nothing to you dogs," said Bolo.

The script shook his head and looked at his colleagues below. "Dolos and The Modor are inseparable. Your words are both treasonous and heretical. You will relent or be cleansed by Her hand."

Bolo looked at the script's hand as it closed around the shaft of a concealed energy weapon. She knew that his use of it would be swift and deadly. She tightened her grip on the mace. "Then let it cleanse me."

She raised the mace as the script slid back, then brought it crashing down. The monks pushed themselves into the air a fraction of a moment before the entire floor shattered, having already lined themselves up with scripts below. Bolo followed her mace as it smashed into the temple below, letting its force pull her to the ground a fraction of a second before her enemy. This gave her enough time to flip onto her feet and swing it onto the conscript as he landed, spreading the inner workings of his head in a spraying fan of skull and brain.

There was no time to admire her handy work as the remaining Cheka reacted. Bolo had been in many altercations, fighting the countless battles that saw her in a seat of power, but even she was shocked by the speed and ruthless efficiency with which the agents went to work on her best mercenaries. Before she could pull her mace from the blooded pulp, she saw three of her monks stripped of their lives. The remaining two were dead before she could assist them, leaving her swinging her weapon wildly, connecting with nothing but air as the assailants calmly stepped beyond her reach.

Bolo let herself be still, realising a defence was no longer required. Several breaths later, she straightened up and met the scripts one by one with dignified acknowledgement.

"There's no one left to murder here besides myself. As Reverend Abbess of the Roma faction, I request that you leave, before further blood is spilled."

The scripts looked at one another, trying to contain their laughter. One of them stepped towards the body of his fellow Dolos citizen. "We will record that two of our envoys attempted diplomacy." He turned to Bolo. "That reasonable and lawful requests were made. Irresponsible behaviour cost the lives of your people, purposeful intent, your name will be synonymous with that of the great traitors of the Sapiens race."

Bolo griped her mace and spun it in a half circle before planting the shaft in the ground, splintering the hard tile beneath her feet. She knelt beside it, bowing her head low. "Then I bless your immaculate blood."

The conscript stepped forward as Bolo twisted her palms, driving her skin beneath a tiny, fragmented edge no bigger than the head of a needle. Her bio-signature was read instantly, and the mace began to glow with a white-hot energy that travelled over Bolo's hands, up her arms and across her entire body.

"You cannot shield yourself from us," said the script.

Bolo allowed herself the faintest of smiles as the top of the mace detached and leapt several feet into the air. The agents of Dolos had a fraction of a moment to understand they were in the presence of a great woman, a woman who happened to own a substance so rare that it was all but considered extinct. The head of Bolo's mace concealed a berkelium reactor that released a bombardment of titanium ions, creating an element which in turn ignited a fusion-evaporation burning hotter than the Sun. Bolo closed her eyes, but still saw the imprint of her temple flash and burn, before everything became a black cloud of ash and smoke.

As the dust thinned, she saw the scripts as grey ghosts, their powdered corpses slowly crumbling like sand running through an hour glass. She stood and walked through them, the breeze from her body enough to collapse them into nothing more than ashen mounds. She swept aside some debris to find the edges of a doorway that lead to the temple basements. There she was met by her last remaining tech, who busied themselves maintaining the delicate balance of the Consul's nightmare.

"I heard a commotion," said the tech.

"I had to sacrifice my mace, but we are alone now Consion. I want you to vanish. I trust someone like you will have everything you need to do that."

"I follow you Lama," said Consion.

"I will not waste more Roma lives except my own, but I promise you that I will seek justice for our fallen progeny."

The tech bowed low. "Thank you, Lama. It has been an honour serving you. May The Modor grant you the justice you seek." She kissed Bolo's hand before leaving.

Bolo studied the dosed mass that lay before her, containing the urge to end him there and then. Instead, she brought up the holonostic and tapped into his feed. The readings of the man's tormented body turned even her stomach; although she admired Consion's exceptional cruelty.

She took her time disabling his neural enhancers, removing his ability to sim with any feed, rendering him completely impotent. It seemed the Consuls of Dolos had their tech hard mounted into the very fabric of their anatomy, rather than the rudimentary devices that tapped into the organics, common for most of Kara's citizens. She couldn't help but be impressed and a little jealous of such elegant engineering, feeling almost guilty to be performing such a hatchet-job of dismantling it.

When she was confident that his mind was incapable of external communication, she searched Consion's tool station for a cutting implement, finding a nano-scalpel perfect for modest operations. It cut through the Consul's flesh with almost no pressure, a spray of vapour rising as it simultaneously cauterised the fresh wound. Bolo made short work of removing his right hand, leaving the left was a risk, but a consideration that was more for her benefit; he would only be half as dangerous after all.

She stopped the machine that held the man in a perpetual state of unimaginable agony, noting that in the time it had taken her to perform these tasks, he had undergone at least another cycle in relative time. The thought pleased her greatly.

The lids of his eyes became still, then began to stir as the dose worked its way out of his system. It would be a while until he perceived time in a natural way, but Bolo couldn't wait for him to be fully alert for the journey. There would already be more conscripts on the way, and she had exhausted her bounders. His eyes were now wide open and looking into hers, the horror of his recent tortures clearly embedded on his face.

"Time's up," she said.

NATHAN

The unrelenting horror had stopped, but recollections of what he'd gone through were agonisingly fresh, causing his body to shiver and convulse with feverish revulsion at every waking thought. The idea of being tortured had been something he'd mused over in the past, wondering what his tolerance would be to theoretical levels of pain and suffering; the reality had gone far beyond his most vivid fabrications. Now that he held these heinous violations as memories, he understood there was no such thing as tolerance, only the will of the opponent; as though the human body had been designed for the single purpose of experiencing their most depraved fancies.

A crisp breeze cut across his cheeks, a subtlety of air that did not exist in the frozen prison. He became aware of forces pulling and pushing him, the tell-tale signs of travelling at great speed. He managed to open his eyes and saw a flood of colour and blurred images rush his retinas. A transport, no doubt the one he had called to collect him and the girl. He was saved!

His body felt like bags of wet sand, but he managed to move his neck around to see a dark figure piloting the small craft. One of his comrades. They would have made short work of the heretics, although hopefully not too short. He wanted to curse them for taking so long, leaving him in that place, but all he could muster was a dull smirk at the elation of making it through the ordeal. When they found out what he had been through, the amount of suffering he had absorbed for Dolos, they would forgive his failings.

The craft banked up, and he saw fragments of ice break

off as a wind lip skimmed against the hull, a few fine grains brushing his cheek like powdered glass. The exterior shell of the craft had been cracked, a large hole apparently created by some kind of blunt force from a heavy object; superficial damage but done with intent. They were flying low over the tops of super-structures, hugging into the shadows, dodging between the giant spears that had once been cities full of light and prosperity. Again the craft touched a surface and buffeted Nathan painfully into the side. There was no need for this, a craft of Dolos could go wherever it chose with impunity, unless...

He tried to focus on the pilot again. The muscled shoulders that fought the controls reminded him of his Grunder assailant, but there was a grace to the movements that such a brute lacked. Bolo turned and gave him a cursory glance.

"Try to hold on," she said.

He grabbed at the side of the craft but couldn't get a grip, as it took a sharp dive into a collapsed trench. He braced himself with his feet and pressed his knees into the side to stop himself from falling forward. They started to slow and made their way into a hollowed out bowl that looked like century old damage from an explosion of some kind. The craft settled and all went quiet, save for the sound of wind blowing through the ruined structure.

"Where are we?" asked Nathan.

Bolo signalled for him to be quiet. He took the time to look down at his hands, seeing that the right was missing. For a brief moment, he thought he was still in a dose-laced dream, but it all felt very... present. It didn't concern him much, being rectifiable damage; the loss of such extensive upgrades would surely be considered a reasonable expense.

Nathan attempted to find a local lab, but found he lacked the ability to connect, in fact, he lacked any kind of signal, something he'd never experienced before.

"Tell me where we are," he said, trying to muster some authority in his voice.

Bolo sighed. "I'm not a friend. I am foe." She pointed to his hands. "That was my work and you're my prisoner. We are crossing Caspia. If you are not quiet, we will both likely be captured or killed. Do you understand?"

Nathan nodded. Whatever her intentions were, he understood the bitter rivalry between many of the factions went deep. He guessed she was attempting to cross unnoticed, something that would not be easy without a high altitude transport. He looked around the craft and realised it was a miracle it had even brought them to the upper levels of Kara; the damage she'd done in an effort to get it moving.

Some mental geography told him that Caspia stretched for a distance of around three thousand kilometres from west to east, if they were indeed following a path directly from Roma. The craft would take them at least half a cycle to navigate the twisted canopy of steel, glass and stone in a straight run, more if they were being overly cautious. That aside, he could already feel his body succumbing to early-stage hypothermia. He figured it wouldn't be long before the irresistible urge to sleep would take him.

"You won't make it flying manual," he said. "We'll die from exposure before you can get half way."

Bolo glanced back, her expression conceding that she was thinking the same thing. Nathan tried to think through alternatives, but his mind felt foggy and blunt. If she'd removed his uplinks, chances were his neural enhancers had gone too. He found the fact he would be too mentally deficient to know any better slightly amusing. The fool does not know they are a fool after all. Having been privy to enhancements for as long as he could remember, it was time to find out whether his natural mind was worth a damn.

"I do not think fate will allow me to die by your side," said Bolo.

She kicked the thruster and the craft leant forward, sending them curving up the inside of the icy bowl. When they reached the surface, Kara stretched out before them like a silver mirror in the still night, the craft slicing through the biting air with barely a sound. Nathan hugged what garments he had around his body and slouched down as best he could to shield himself a little from the murderous wind breaking through the damaged canopy. Compared to the trials he had undergone recently, this would be fairly painless; if he managed to stay alive long enough to see the other side. Despite his best attributes being stolen from him by this ungodly barbarian, he was still in possession of a lifetime of being a Consul of Dolos. If she managed to keep him alive, it would be a mistake she'd live to regret.

He settled into the ride, letting his thoughts drift across the endless plains of dancing lights, infinite reflections and stars that glimmered through rising fountains of steam. He had never seen Kara from this vantage and had to admit to himself that it was a breathtaking wonder. The urge to sleep grew stronger, inviting his body to slip into a numb bath of oblivion. Going like this wouldn't be so bad after all.

A puff of shadows cut through the frozen mists, directly in their trajectory. He could see Bolo desperately trying to bank the unyielding craft. Then they were falling, wrapped in a twisting, tightening coil of line and barbs. He instinctively grabbed for something, only to pound his scabbed stub into the sharp wires that netted and brought them down with a crunching stop. He stayed conscious long enough to hear excited whoops and cries from their captors. The thought that he'd been made a prisoner twice in the same cycle mustered a laugh as the stars went dark.

LUNN

The sight of Grunders as the prevalent race made Lunn's heart sore and break all at once. He'd always believed his kind were a scarcity, nothing more than a peculiar quirk left over as a reminder of mankind's greatest failure. He immediately wanted to stop and embrace his brethren, tell them that he never knew, that he was here now... But here to do what? He was not a liberating savour, but a fugitive, scurrying beneath the earth like a roach from a fire. There was nothing he could offer his people besides stories of things they would never know, lives they could never live. To them, he was merely another face, another set of hands to put to work, another mouth that required feeding, another Grunder.

Sorcha, however, attracted immediate attention as the passing crowd began to pause and stare, until a small gathering surrounded them. Lunn studied the cold faces, blank and tired, looking at them with nothing more than a lethargic curiosity. Some of them grunted words that Lunn couldn't understand, apparently trying to give them instructions. A few shook their large heads and went on with their business, as Lunn took Sorcha by the hand and gently pushed his way through.

They found themselves in a kind of trading district. Workers came from every direction and ascended on fortified metal huts, where they swapped rusted iron tokens for a handful of dried nutrient powder or filled their containers with murky water. Huge vats of boiling liquid filled the air with a steam that smelled of rank meat and awful, mixing with the acrid burn of the thick dust that invaded the lungs

and eyes. It didn't take long for Lunn to realise that there was
no trade going on, only the distribution of basic sustenance for
what he assumed was reparation for hard labour. The relative
quiet in which these mundane activities were being performed
made Lunn uneasy. The citizens of Kara had a similar
downtrodden disposition, although this felt inherently deeper
than that, like they were not only discontent with their lot, but
completely accepting of it.

Lunn became aware of some large Grunders following
them and decided it was best to acknowledge their presence.
Without speaking a word, one of the brutes gestured with
his giant head to follow them. They walked a long way,
having to push and dodge through endless crowds that the
two Grunders navigated with expert ease. Eventually, the men
they were following stopped outside a featureless passage that
differentiated itself from the myriad of other passageways by
the pale glow of a phosphorous symbol, carved into the rock.
One of the men gestured into the opening.

"Find Tamaris inside. Offer him service," he said, before
both Grunders left and merged back into the flowing crowd.

Lunn checked Sorcha, finding she still looked half caught
up in a daydream. He worried she'd been permanently
damaged by her ordeal, but at least she'd lived. The only task
at hand was keeping her that way; it seemed an audience with
Tamaris, whoever he may be, would be essential to this.

"We go speak with them in charge. Do not talk girl.
Hrrmm?"

Sorcha gave Lunn a short nod as he encouraged her into
the narrow entrance. The insufferable heat wrapped them the
instant they left the overbearing heat of the main throughway,
but as they went deeper, fresher air fell in a cool shower from
above. Lunn looked up to see a plethora of holes patch-worked
across the domed ceiling, an elegant feat of engineering that
called to mind a great insect nest.

Two guards dressed in something resembling an old
uniform signalled them to approach a dark opening, lit only

by the dim incandescent light from more markings lining the walls. Lunn took awkward steps as his eyes struggled to adjust in the darkness. He shuffled into a space and found a blue ambient emitting from a hanging orb. Beneath it sat an old Grunder, covered in scars and skin so thick he looked like he was growing from the cavern's rocky floor.

"Sit," said Tamaris. His voice was low and dampened by the enclosed space.

Lunn looked for any kind of seat, but only saw some raised stone where the floor had been hollowed out. He stepped into the hole and sat down, helping Sorcha get in with him. The old Grunder's eyes seemed to shine with the blue light, piercing out from withered pits. He looked tired and despondent, yet harbouring a physical strength and hardiness few possessed on the surface; a being made calloused and iron-set by the worst kind of life.

"Thank you for entry to mines," said Lunn.

Tamaris took his time looking them over before speaking fluent Khanese with a strange accent. "Thank me for nothing. I never allowed you to come to this place. You will be disposed of if I will it. Those above should know better than to send their insubordinates here. A practice I put an end to many passes gone."

"We here for refuge."

Tamaris let out a laugh that filled the small space, "More likely your bodies become food for our labour! This place offers no refuge!"

"Then we offer service."

"The mines do not require service. They require resource, long stripped by the insatiable appetite of your kind."

"My kind?" Lunn was taken aback by these words, spoken by a fellow Grunder.

"A surface parasite who takes without questioning. The reason my people bleed and toil for the scraps thrown below."

"There no feast above. We live on scraps, same," said Lunn.

Tamaris sat forward, anger rising. "Do not compare your

hardships to those who work the mines. When there is no more harvest, our piteous lives will end with thirst and starvation. That is our only future."

"Let us help," said Lunn.

"More bodies make death come sooner. I have no want or reason to let you stay."

Lunn could not hold back his anger and stood. "The Lama Bolo sent us here! Girl cannot go back!" The guards took a half step towards him.

"Nobody goes back," said Tamaris. "When you entered the cage, you breathed the surface for the last time. You have been betrayed by this Bolo. She knows those she sends face a death sentence."

Lunn clenched his fist. "Bolo protect the girl! These mines lie beneath Roma." He punched the rock beneath Tamaris's feet and looked up at him, begging for the first time in his life. "Please give girl safety!"

Tamaris bent forward and held Lunn by the shoulder, demonstrating a grip that could crush stone. "I can give the girl no safety, but so long as you work to pay her debt and yours, she may live," said Tamaris.

"I can work," said Sorcha weakly.

The side of Tamaris's mouth raised a fraction in amusement. "Work requires strength! Our children learn the ways of the mine before they can talk."

"I can learn," said Sorcha.

"Quiet girl," said Lunn.

"We pull silicate rocks from the fire of the mantle. The only thing you'll learn is you have no place in Krate."

"I work for both," said Lunn.

Tamaris shook his head and gave a signal to the Grunders who waited nearby. They moved forward to take hold of Sorcha. Lunn leapt up and blocked their path. The heavy guards looked bored by the sentiment.

"You may have been a force above," said Tamaris. "But here you are weak. You will be put to work and know our suffering.

The girl may be of use to me before that time comes. Make a stand, and that will be your end. Those are the choices you have."

It took all Lunn's strength to concede that he had no options. The only way to keep Sorcha alive was to surrender to whatever fate lay before them. He stepped aside and one of the guards pulled Sorcha to her feet. Lunn could feel his hands tremble with the rage of futility. All his life he had known nothing but his own physical strength, understood that it was his sole asset. Now it had been stripped away, leaving a hopeless, incompetent fool, who'd lacked the foresight to have seen such a fate coming. He'd done this to her, taken her from her home, failed to keep her safe, brought her to a hell in the centre of the earth. And now he could only watch her being taken, powerless, worthless and utterly unworthy of calling himself her guardian.

He let himself be led away, through a long series of tunnels and passageways, lost in a labyrinth of self-hate. They soon came to a colossal iron wall that stretched up into the darkness and out of sight. His escorts waved at the metal surface and a tiny crack opened, light and intense heat spilling out to meet him.

"Inside," said the Grunder.

Lunn walked forward, into the inferno.

NATHAN

The hard surface pressed into his jaw bone, making the skin feel thin and stretched. He tried to turn over and alleviate the pain, but found the effort almost impossible. This recent coming into consciousness felt like just another in a long line of rude awakenings; he was getting tired of these games.

Before attempting to open his eyes, he played out the events of the last few cycles in his mind, finding the details murky with his enhancements now removed. Nothing he'd done had been particularly careless, though he had been somewhat complacent with regard to his objective. The fact that his current circumstances seemed to be down to a run of bad luck gave him the incentive he needed to gather his strength for another round; luck could always change.

"You're awake. I can hear the change in your breath," said the voice of Lama Bolo.

"How's fate working out?" Nathan half mumbled, his mouth scraping on the floor.

"We are still alive." He thought he could hear a faint smile in her answer.

"I'm finding it hard to get up."

To his surprise, he heard some shuffling and felt hands grip him delicately around his ribs. Bolo pulled him to a wall and sat him up. With some effort, he lifted his head and opened his eyes.

"Thank you," he said. "I think I might be paralysed below the waist."

Bolo squatted beside him and squeezed his thigh hard. Nathan shook his head.

"I apologise for the hand," she said. "I did it for practical reasons, although I had to restrain myself from going further."

"All of this was standard Dolos business. If you hadn't tried to conceal the child, we wouldn't be here."

"That may be so," said Bolo. "Neither of us intended this result, but you were the instigator of this."

"I do what I'm told. You know what I am, where I come from. I have no intentions beyond doing what's asked of me, standard practice. Blame me for your losses if it helps your conscience. You turned business into a game we both lost."

Bolo turned her back on him. He knew it was harder to feel rage against the abstract and intangible concept of Dolos. Such an entity had no form or presence beyond the people, like Nathan, who made it up. If she couldn't find it in herself to hate him for the tragic result of his unintentional actions, then she would try to project her animosity onto the idea of a controlled establishment. But even Nathan had no real idea what it was that sat at the heart of a behemoth like Dolos. It had just always been there, part of his psyche from his first discernible memories. The truth was that he felt no more devotion to his faction, beyond the ingrained sense of loyalty he knew Bolo had towards hers. The fact she'd entangled Sapienistic traits into her values probably gave her the pretence of earnest faith and honour. For Nathan, honour came from knowing that he was a high-functioning member of a society that had given him everything he held dear. An honour he was still intent on restoring given the chance.

Nathan scanned the small holding cell, quickly accepting there was no point in expending any effort on escape strategies. Letting himself fall into the hands of fate was not his natural disposition, but there could be a useful calm in releasing all illusions of control.

"You know how long we've been here?" he asked.

Bolo ran her fingers over one of the walls. "I was also knocked unconscious, but going by my stomach, it has not been long."

Another reminder that his neural enhancers were gone. This type of practical thinking usually came as second nature to him. He needed to clear the fog from his mind and focus.

"Any idea who our captor might be?"

"As we are no doubt still in Caspia, I assume Gan."

"Gan? Faction chair?"

"Yes, though we differ in our interpretations of Her teachings."

"If you want some clarification on the true meaning of the Modor's words, you only need to ask."

Bolo spun to face him, a fire of fury ready to erupt. Nathan immediately felt the carelessness of his words. He had to resist the urge to default to hostility, he was weak and anyone not momentarily trying to kill him should be seen as a potential ally.

"Sorry. Antagonism is part of my playbook," he said.

"Dolos may think itself the spiritual capital of Sapienism, but it forgot the traditions we hold dear a long time ago. Chasing down the last few remaining *heretics* is not done in Her name. It is merely a reason for Dolos to exist. Without that, it has no purpose."

"The eradication of anomalous beings stands at the very heart of the Modor's teachings. To ignore their existence may be accepted in these times, but it is still a heretical act. Just look at your people. How many died as a result of your harbouring the girl?"

"The girl is harmless. Do not try to deflect your blame."

The girl is. Not the girl was…

"She lives?" Nathan felt a chill run over his shoulders.

Bolo was studying him now. Clearly she had let it slip, but with his current state, she would see no real danger in him knowing.

"She survived your methods. I have her somewhere you cannot reach. I will return you to Dolos, you will confess your crimes. Roma will be replenished with new souls, and they will have their prize."

Nathan pushed his hands into the ground, trying to slide up the wall, but hardly raised himself an inch. "A neat plan, save for the fact we're going to rot in this hole."

"When Caspia finds out what you did, they will be sympathetic to my plight."

"The girl caused what you saw!" he spat the words out, pain piercing his ribs at the effort. "Do you think I could take out half a faction? Why would I possess such a power?"

Bolo's eyes widened, he could feel her trying to find authenticity within him.

"Not possible," she said. "It may go unspoken, but we all have the same tainted blood. A legacy we'll never erase. Those that the Modor sought to protect us from were eradicated before my lifetime. I guard nothing more than the Sapiens ways, ensuring that those days never return."

Nathan rolled his eyes, "And yet, we talk of anomalies. What exactly do you think that means?"

Bolo scoffed, "A threat. A threat to the balance of Dolos control. Do you really believe the other factions are blind to what you do? You use the fear of these long forgotten spectres to go about your business unchallenged, but it will not last."

"She is the spectre the teachings warned you of. The invader you as a high priestess were supposed to guard your people from. She is your one and only enemy. You say you are not blind, yet your faction lays devastated by the very thing you claim doesn't exist. Yes, fear is one of our tools, but it is only because we shield you from the true meaning of terror. That all it takes is one mind and one will to send man back to the swamps it took centuries to crawl out from. The carnage stopped at your borders, did it not? Not through geographical boundaries or targeted selection, but the barriers *we* placed around every faction. Barriers the ignorant population try to remove and undermine for what exactly, freedom? How free are your people now? The balance you long to corrupt is the only thing keeping your life intact, however pitiful it may be."

Bolo had been listening to him with a fixed stare. He could

see a rage boiling beneath her eyes, but could see that his words were damaging her core beliefs. He didn't think it was necessary to tell her that he'd harboured similar beliefs to hers until very recently. That the isolated districts of Karakorum were no longer justified by any logical reality, that the precautions were essentially a tribute to the past, traditions that happened to be a convenient method of regulating chaos. But as with many traditions, inherent in their abstract nature lay dormant wisdom. One that had no doubt stopped a massacre from becoming a genocide.

"Then I am to believe this girl managed to destroy my entire world with what, a thought? No matter what you say, she is still merely a child." said Bolo.

"A child indeed. A child of those who left our world centuries ago. A child born without the need for augmentation or modification. A true other."

Bolo stumbled and fell to the floor, her eyes now wild with the raw truth of Nathan's words.

"Never forgive their sins... The devil in our soul... I let her go." said Bolo.

SORCHA

It was cold, quiet, peaceful. Sorcha's first thought was whether she had passed over, part of her wanting that to be true. But as she moved her fingers, the tips scraped on loose dirt, bringing with it the release of a damp musk. She was still there, still underground.

The connection she'd encountered to the people of Roma now felt distant and unattainable. She had so many questions she wanted to ask of those forgotten ghosts, but like a severed dream, the more she tried to force it, the more it faded away. As her physical presence returned, a wired pulse buzzed through her muscles, momentarily staving off the hunger that was still present underneath. She sat up, fully awake, and hungrily ate the compressed protein ration that had been dropped by her side. It tasted like the stale air, permeating anything with the capacity to absorb it. She chewed it carefully, making sure she released every last bit of life giving nourishment. Something in her now wanted to stay alive. She'd seen a glimpse of something larger than anything she could have imagined, a commonality among all people, a human purpose.

The alcove she currently inhabited only had one way out, a slim carved opening with faint light beyond. She made her way through and found Tamaris sitting with his back to her. He was hunched over a mutilated corpse, washing the flesh with tender strokes. Diluted blood ran down his forearm and dripped from the elbow, liquid collecting into little balls of dirt as it met the floor.

"He was my messenger. The mines are made of dangerous paths, but this one lasted a long while. Long enough to deserve preparation and flames."

"How did he die?" asked Sorcha.

"The same way we all die down here, girl. By failing to survive." He turned to her. "Would you like to survive?"

"Yes."

Tamaris lay the wet sponge on the corpse and rinsed his hands clean in a shallow bowl of water, letting them dry in the air.

"You have seen more than I will ever know, despite your young age. I was born in the dark and have never seen the light of sun or moon, cannot fathom what it must be like to gaze upon a sea of water or stars. I hear of these things only as stories, just like you would have been told about the half-lives who dwelled below. Few get to experience both. Yet here you are, a frail girl who comes here for sanctuary of all things, escaping the man-made heaven by running into hell."

"There is no heaven in Karakorum," said Sorcha.

Tamaris flashed anger. "Anywhere else is a heaven for the miners of Krate!"

Sorcha met his anger unexpectedly with her own, "Shall we compare our suffering?"

Tamaris smiled and sat beside her, she could feel the warm breath flowing out his oversized nostrils in a slow regular cadence; it smelled of concentrated dampness, rot and mould, like he and the mines were made of the same material.

"My people are starving. The mines no longer provide. The earth itself will split apart from our ceaseless toil, or we will be left down here to rot. Tell me where this leads, girl."

Sorcha looked at the ground beneath her feet. A line of blooded water had pooled and ran slowly through the dirt and dust until it touched her exposed toes. She let it wash between them, the life of the expired messenger returning to the only place it would ever know. The dark, the damp, the dirt, the heat, the blood. A rage broke out behind her watering eyes, she wanted to scream and pound the earth, let it know that cruelty was all there was, all there had ever been. She wanted to break the ground and swallow Kara down to meet them, punish them all for accepting such relentless torment.

"Death," she said.

"Yes." He went back to washing the crushed body. "Soon we shall have to break into heaven, in this life or another"

She held a tiny codec, set to open with the bio-signature of one of Tamaris's foremen. It was a simple piece of tech, but still surprised Sorcha that something like that could exist in such a place. Turning it over in her hand, she could feel worn patches along the smooth oval casing, hinting at its age. She secured it in the front pocket of her overalls and followed the child who'd been assigned as her guide.

At first, walking through the dense heat and crowded caverns felt like a waking dream, but after they had travelled long enough for her mouth to become bone dry, she had accepted the harsh reality of where she was.

"Water please," she said, pulling on the child's arm. He was smaller than her, but obviously stronger, his body one tight mould of hard sinew. He shook a finger at her, then leaned in and closed her mouth with it, taking a deep breath through his nose and indicating that this was the correct way to inhale. She understood and nodded. "I still need water."

The boy glanced down, thinking, then pulled her through the crowd and into one of the side caves. He approached an old female Grunder, who sat on the ground next to a few small clay jars, and squatted next to her. He spoke softly, pointing towards Sorcha, who did her best to look pathetic and humble. Eventually, he returned, cupping a tiny vial of milky liquid. Sorcha thanked him and drank it slowly; it had a strong taste of bitter minerals, but coated the inside of her mouth with a slick film. She let each drop roll around, absorbing into her dry gums, avoiding the urge to swallow.

The boy returned the vial then pointed at the woman,

wiping his hands together and holding them up in a gesture she interpreted as *free*. Sorcha bowed her head in thanks, the woman touching her hands together then opening them in a gesture she recognised as *you're welcome* before they were moving again.

She hardly noticed they'd left the crowded caverns and entered an area that looked abandoned. When they came to an end, she saw that the passage had collapsed, making it impossible to go any further. The boy moved some light rubble to reveal a tiny dark hole, then pointed inside. Sorcha reclined in horror.

"What? No. I can't go in there." The boy pulled at her gently. "Where does it lead?" she asked. The boy pointed down the shaft. "Is there another way?" The boy shook his head and seemed to indicate the other way took too long.

Sorcha stepped back. "I don't care how long it takes. I can't."

The boy once again pulled on her arm, this time with a firm tug.

Sorcha understood. There was no place for her in Krate if she didn't enter the hole. Tamaris was testing her, to see if she could be any use at all. For a moment, she considered running, but knew there was nowhere to go beyond the endless tunnels and caverns, that they all led back here. Her future had been reduced to a simple choice, embrace the dark or perish in it.

The boy went in, arms first, as he slid forward like a snake, his feet vanishing into the blackness as though they had simply disappeared. Sorcha waited, becoming aware of the surrounding silence, then heard a tiny muffled voice.

"Come."

She got down on her knees and pushed her arms inside. There was barely enough room for her head, though she found that the walls were slick, as though they had been greased up over long periods of time. This made it easier for her to enter, although once her thighs were encased in the tunnel, she found forward propulsion hopeless.

"I'm stuck!" she yelled, panic immediately flooding her

senses. The absurdity of the situation hit her; she would have laughed if she hadn't been terrified. Suddenly, she felt something touch her outstretched fingers, making her bash her head on the hard stone. A gentle squeeze identified the object as the boy's feet.

"Move," he said, his voice dampened in the tight space.

"I can't," said Sorcha. "There's nothing to push against, nothing to pull."

"Move," he said again. Then the feet left her grasp as she heard a low-pitched grind receding ahead. Then silence. Only her strained breathing and the sound of her heart beating in her ears. She tried to go back, pressing her hands into the base of the tunnel, but they only slid over the slimy concoction coating it. In desperation, she tried to kick her way back and found herself finally moving, although deeper into the tunnel. She screamed in terror, the way back now impossible, fearing this would be the last place she'd ever know. She thrashed her body, trying to make the smallest of gaps between her aching skin and the stone, but the more she moved, the tighter the space became.

Then there was complete disorientation, the whole world seemed to move around her as though she were the central pivot in a great lever. She was upside-down, feeling the blood rushing to her head. Gravity took over as she attempted to slow her descent, the greased walls now scraping past at an alarming rate. Again she screamed as free fall took over, no feeling at all except air. Then hands intertwined with hers as she crashed into an open chamber.

She scurried back against the curved wall and took deep calming breaths, trying to stop full-blown panic arising. Her eyes adjusted to the dim light, emanating from markings on the walls, she now observed to be an oval cave. The boy's pale skin seemed to glow, becoming a light source itself in the otherwise pitch darkness. She could see from his narrow teeth, he was smiling. To her great surprise, this made her laugh, the boy joining in as they found such commonality in the depths of the earth.

"How much further?" asked Sorcha.

The boy pointed to where they had come and indicated a short distance with his index fingers, then pointed below and expanded them tenfold.

BOLO

So caught up with the liturgy and ceremony of her religion, she'd forgotten its true purpose. What good was a spiritual leader who'd only offered sacraments and symbolic gestures when action had been needed? The vow to protect the indigenous from the imposters had been broken. By letting the child go, she could no longer call herself Lama; she was only Bolo.

Bolo glanced at the broken Consul; he barely looked conscious. His words had penetrated to the core of her beliefs and left her conflicted in her purpose. Where her drive had been one of simple retribution, she now had a fuller understanding of the Consul's motives. If Dolos was not to be the target of her wrath, then she could only channel the bitter fury inwards, but knew no penance would ever satisfy the self-loathing that now consumed her.

A guard came to the cell and politely asked that she follow.

"What about him?" Bolo gestured towards Nathan, who managed to look up at her and acknowledge gratitude that she had at least enquired.

"He's not your concern," said the guard.

Bolo made her way to the crumpled figure and knelt down at his side. "For all the damage I have done you, it might be some comfort that you have broken my very soul."

Nathan smiled with one side of his mouth. "Some," he said.

The guard ushered Bolo up a steep flight of narrow concrete stairs and into a single person transport. He left as the door closed, knowing there was nowhere for her to run, no means of escape. The only way out of Caspia would be through negotiation or death. The transport lifted smoothly into an arching climb as it rose through one of Caspia's hypnotic boulevards. Wave after wave of light hung or clung to every available surface, turning her capsule into a kaleidoscope of colour and texture that seemed to pulse with the intoxicating rhythm of a thousand competing melodies extruding from every club, bar, dive and den. It was Bolo's kind of place.

The craft approached a curving overhang and docked with a raised platform that protruded slightly from an otherwise seamless opening. The door slid open to reveal a stomach churning view of the hectic reaches below, warm air rushing up and swirling around the cabin. Bolo stepped across the gap into the large, minimalistic room, her footsteps echoing against the featureless walls. The craft departed as Bolo took a customary glance to watch it disappear into the vast vista of luminescent structures. She turned to see an ornate chez long waiting for her arrival, a china cup and teapot sitting beside it on a small antique coffee table. Bolo couldn't help admire the taste of the person responsible, even if their intentions would most likely be deadly. She sat down and found unexpected delight in the discovery of ceremonial grade matcha in the pot. This certainly didn't feel like an interrogation, more of a courtship, but Bolo understood the urge to impress a high-ranking visitor, captive or not.

She resisted the urge to turn as a barely registered flow in air pressure signalled a door being opened, followed by the sound of calm, measured footsteps.

"I hope the tea up to your usual standard." The voice was delicate and singing.

"It's some of the finest I've ever had," replied Bolo.

She stood to greet her host. A man almost as wide as he was tall, with hair flowing over his immaculate dress, so black it almost seemed shapeless, save for a few wayward strands that had escaped relentless grooming. He held out his hand as an equal.

"I'm sure you have heard my name, as I have heard of the

great Lama Bolo."

Bolo tried to gauge whether this was a slight or a genuine display of respect, something that Gan seemed to pick up on.

"Please put out of your mind any notions of malevolent intent on my part. I am truly sorry for the manner in which you were greeted by my constabulary. Understand that there were no ill intentions."

"My monks would have greeted an imposter in the same way," said Bolo.

Gan let out a long breath and bent over, slapping his knees as he sat down.

"I'm glad our meeting has started this way. I cannot abide an atmosphere of menace. Know that you are considered a guest here from this moment on. You will certainly not be returning to any cell."

Bolo joined Gan on the edge of the sofa, and tried to relax into the idea of being safe from any immediate danger, but something told her not to let down her guard just yet.

"I am aware of the events that transpired in Roma," said Gan. "And it is causing me a great deal of distress. I would very much like to know more about the circumstances that led to such wickedness."

Bolo inhaled deep through her nose, searching for the words, but could only find one.

"Dolos."

Gan's soft features hardened, and his eyes took on a sinister glaze.

"In the spirit of openness, I can tell you that any other name from your lips would have meant your death." He produced a glowing thermal blade. "A common enemy is the only thing stopping me from gutting you here myself."

This is more like it, thought Bolo. She hadn't quite bought the pleasantries, however convincing.

Bolo sipped on her tea. "In the same spirit, this tea is an inferior batch," she said.

Gan laughed as he stood, slapping the cup from her hand.

"When I heard that Lama Bolo had dared to desecrate Caspia with her peasant blood, I spent an entire cycle planning the ways in which I would cause you unspeakable agony, something your friend will not escape. I'm sure you must admire the restraint I am showing you right now."

"I am no longer fit to call myself Lama. I do not fear any pain worse than that. Whatever your intentions, I assure you this display is unnecessary."

Gan lent forward, letting the blade slice within a micron of Bolo's face, the heated edge burning the outer layers of skin on Bolo's cheek. Thick perfume, mixed with a toxic stench from his breath filled her nostrils, causing her eyes to water unintentionally.

"This is no display!" His spit drenched her face. "I fantasise about cutting into that flesh, even while I stop myself from doing so. I have never denied myself such gratification. It goes against every instinct to stay this hand. Do not bait me, you sinful wench." He stepped back, hands trembling with rage, and tossed the blade through the opening, onto the boulevard below. It would possibly end its journey by slicing through a random citizen, something Bolo thought Gan may get some satisfaction from. "Rumours are spreading of something unholy. The collective mood of my people moves, I see eyes twitching from one citizen to the next, always looking for signs of the unspeakable past. Wondering if the evil will spread." Gan rubbed his brow, exhausted. Bolo could feel his tension like a physical presence in the air, like someone had turned a dial, shifting the modulation from paranoia to fear. "I'm not a spiteful man," he said. "I live my life by the codes that give some order to this shambolic mess. The rules that govern us all, as we pledge ourselves to be servants of our masses. I have served. When I hear murmurs of conscripts infiltrating my faction and know what happened to yours, I see a symbiotic plight. Do you agree?"

"I'm old enough to have heard the stories told by elders." Bolo had a vague recollection of a certain cadence in the voices when they spoke of such things; a long forgotten shadow that lay across Karakorum, ever present but entirely invisible. She had been born long after The Wipe, a period in time concealed by a thousand conflicting narratives. But one thing was well known, it had almost been the unravelling of man. "The very thing they warned of strayed into my faction, and I welcomed it," said Bolo. Gan flinched and turned on his heel, his eyes flashing both anger and confusion. "The unholy terror you speak of is all too real."

Gan moved to the chez long and slumped next to her. "Impossible," he said. "Their kind is no more."

"And yet, you saw what happened to Roma," said Bolo.

"Dolos trickery!" said Gan.

"I assure you, it was no trick. So obvious was the truth, I failed to see it. But I am no longer blind. As long as this corruption is alive, then no Sapiens is safe. Let me return to my home and I will do my sacred duty." Bolo knelt before Gan, taking his hand. He raised his eyebrows at the gesture, then threw her hand away, stood and walked to the edge, looking over his faction, slowly moving his head across the expansive view.

"Our duty? Easy to forget what that is. If I let you go, I forfeit my own life."

Bolo stood and placed her hands together. Bound in betrayal. To form alliance with another faction being heresy of the highest order. "If I'm successful, the dogs of Dolos will depart Caspia. Let them look. They won't find what they seek."

"What they seek?" Gan turned with a boyish smirk. "I doubt their business here is that simple."

For all their differences, Bolo saw that Gan's instincts were in line with her own, but she doubted he fully understood the nature of the true enemy to Sapiens. In his mind, Dolos were attempting a coup over the factions. Bolo knew better than most the need for lab isolation, but the precautions taken to limit malevolent spreads also played nicely into the hands of the Dolos overseers; billions of wills being infinitely more manageable when rule was divided. The physical restrictions never kept factions completely ignorant for long. There were always whispers, the spread of news from one area to the next, wayward travellers, scouts and the ubiquitous faction spies. It was only a matter of time before the deceitful actions of Dolos would be known across Kara; something that would inevitably lead to all-out war.

"I share your doubt," said Bolo. "A common enemy, for now."

Gan looked to the ground and waved a hand. "My people will take you to the edge of Caspia. From there you can cross into Roma." Bolo nodded in agreement. "Meanwhile, I will purge my faction of the uninvited guests, starting with your travel companion."

Set free in a treasonous alliance, Bolo felt some renewed clarity flow through her being, a clear will, a purpose. The child may be beyond the reach of any man, but she was Mother Roma.

LUNN

The cycles had merged into one endless graft of fatigue, starvation and pain. A mantra played out in his exhausted mind: breathe, move, breathe, move; an engine that needed to keep turning over, lest it stall and never start again. The more he worked, the more he could feel muscle become a source of food for his malnourished body, as it ate itself from within, beyond any stored reserve. His bones scraped in the joints, as cartridge broke down into sand and grizzle. Lunn breathed and moved.

Heat from the pits below bellowed with a wind capable of tipping the gait of a distracted Grunder; the sound of a desperate scream followed by a sharp extinguishing of life, all too common now to his ears. He perched on the end of a claw that craned over the mantle fields, fishing for silicate rocks made of dense magnesium, silicon and iron. When he'd first set eyes on the cranes, the thought of climbing out over the boiling sea was absurd, yet he'd managed to hug his way across the decaying metal, letting the eroded surface rip into his skin rather than loosen his grip. Once out on the arm, his task was to maintain the claw shaft and hydraulics, ensuring that the crane saw no downtime. A Grunder that failed at this job rarely got a second chance, the operators better to give them a quick dip and find a replacement rather than wait for their skillset to catch up with the relentless pace. Thankfully for Lunn, mechanical maintenance was the one thing he excelled at, besides crushing the odd punter back at Inesa's.

The operator sounded a low, bellowing horn, warning Lunn that her heads-up sensor had identified the slow-moving bergs she would attempt to capture by plunging the claw; a set of tungsten pincers that could span the circumference of a hundred-meter boulder. Lunn anchored his grip as the arm swung out over the glowing soup raging below. The giant claw connected and the crane's hydraulic body twisted violently to take up the slack, auto-belays firing out in all directions to grab onto a supporting surface; another way for a Grunder to meet their end should they happen to be in the way. Lunn fought the constant sensation to scream out in panic as ancient tech met ancient matter in a battle that wasn't always won by machine.

The rock surfaced, dripping with flames and fierce eruptions, furious at being ripped from its eternal bathing. Lunn sprang to his feet and helped manoeuvre it onto one of the protruding platforms that clung to the edge of the pit. From there it would be dragged, split and sorted before it had a chance to cool. Thousands of tons of base elements broken down for those above to turn into whatever it took to keep Kara functioning beyond irrecoverable decay. The idea of all these resources heading to the surface jarred with everything Lunn had seen during his lifetime. Kara was held together with an endless cycle of repurposing of components, the slow eroding of everything to a useless junk. There was no influx of new materials, no relief from the inevitable atrophy that devoured all things. The question of where it all went would have interested him more had he not been on the edge of collapse.

A deep resonating vibration passed through him, marking a break in the punishing shift. He almost fell from the thin ladder straddling perilously between the crane and the boiling liquid. As he stumbled onto a hard surface, a few metallic chunks were pressed into his hand, meagre payment for his toil. He wanted to lay down where he stood and fall into a dreamless sleep, but knew that missing a meal was tantamount to a death sentence. Instead, he followed the other drones who dragged their feet and made their way to one of the densely packed bazaars.

The cheapest and most energy packed sustenance came from the soup vats. At first, Lunn had been happy to rely on this source of fuel, until he'd found out that the meat content in the broth wasn't animal-based, at least not the kind of animal Lunn has a taste for. There were no cemeteries or crematoriums in the mines, and nothing that could keep a Grunder alive went to waste. Instead, Lunn went for a tasteless lump of protein equal to the weight of the rocks he held in his hand. It was barely enough to kill the worst of his hunger pains, but it would keep him going a little longer.

He pulled back his sleeve and stroked the hard cuff around his wrist. If he traded the bracelet, it might feed him for many cycles to come, but it was his last connection to the surface and the only thing giving him a sense of power in a place that had stripped him of all his strength. Instead, he chewed on the grey matter they called food, trying to work up enough spit to swallow it down, water being a luxury he only afforded himself ever other cycle.

He made his way back towards the lava field, following the path taken by the rocks as they were broken into separate minerals and sorted onto carts that filled areas bigger than any singular structure he had seen on the surface. His crane op Niss, a female Grunder whose skin barely covered taut muscular cables beneath its surface, watched one of the workers strapping into a harness that controlled a wrecking drill. She stood back as silicate material started to chip off and land nearby in heavy thuds. She glanced at Lunn, who had joined her to watch.

"We both have too much time on our hands if we can afford to stand around watching others work," she said.

"Too tired to rest," replied Lunn.

"Ha!" she laughed. "I know that feeling well. Only notice how bad I feel when I stop. But you must rest, or you won't last long."

"Where all this go?"

"Go? It goes in the cart. Then it goes," she said.

"The surface? Where?"

Niss pulled Lunn down as the drill swung over their heads, manoeuvring to attack the other side of the rock. She looked at him with a mixture of contempt and pity.

"Thank you," said Lunn.

"These things shouldn't concern a greenhorn who won't last the next few cycles. And that's the last time I watch your back. We're not a team. You live as long as you're useful to me and the mines." she said.

"How does it get to the surface?" Lunn tried to see beyond the endless lines of carts.

Niss looked exhausted by his probing. "Single transport goes out with our quarry, returns with rations. That's the way it's been since I was born here. Anyone desperate enough to get on that transport comes back cooked."

"Huh, why?"

"Who knows? Mantle crisps them up good, the other side sends them back that way. Easy meat!"

"Other side?"

"The other side, the beyond, wherever it goes. If it ain't here, I don't care. This place is our world. Might be you've not accepted it yet, but only thing that's certain is you're going to die down here," she started to walk away. "If you want to get there sooner, don't get the transport, just lose your foot on the crane. Much quicker and you don't end up as soup." The drill swung back overhead, Lunn ducked this time as splinters of sharp glowing rock sprayed him.

"Hrrmm," he grunted.

Lunn finished his paltry meal and walked the short journey to what he could loosely call a residence. He'd spent the first few cycles wasting time he could have been resting, searching for a spot to recuperate. He quickly realised that there was nowhere tranquil or private, and that laying down in one of the main thoroughfares was heavily frowned upon; several boots to the ribs had taught him that much. Instead, he'd taken to squeezing into any space he could find, but soon found out that all territories were fiercely controlled, marked out and held by local militia who worked for Tamaris.

He climbed a precarious route of dry, crumbling steps that had been carved into the rocks at the back end of one of the thin, dark alleys where only the most wretched dwellers could be found. These poor souls were too weak to object to a newcomer like Lunn, who still had some flesh on his bones. It cost Lunn the price of a meal every few cycles for the meagre dwellings, but it was preferable to fighting a battle every time he wanted to sit down.

At the top of the steps, Lunn made his way along a cold crack, feeling his way with two hands on the wall, while he shuffled his feet past the supine bodies. The smell of piss, shit and other kinds of foulness had been almost unbearable at first, but he now associated it with a period of relative comfort. At least the air wasn't as hot and stifling as it was at the pits. When he kicked a pile of loose rocks, he knew he'd reached the end of the natural fissure, beyond it lay only a lightless hole that plunged deep into the earth. He forced himself between the pile and a fellow worker, unable to see them but painfully aware of the contempt that must be in their eyes, hearing the groans of disapproval as the line beyond conformed into an even tighter bind. It didn't feel good to do such a desperate thing, but all he wanted to do was lie down and let his eyes close.

As he finally let his aching body give out, he understood that this was what it meant to be a Grunder. Not the descendent of a proud warrior race, but the left-overs from a once bountiful table, slaves to the servants, the bottom feeders who strove to go lower, with no concept of how pitiful they were. Only one thing stopped Lunn from giving into the shame of it and stepping into the nearby void; the thought that the girl could still be saved.

A

She no longer saw time as a line, path or journey, but as her entirety all at once. She was all she'd ever been and all she ever would be. Her unwritten future, as inevitable as events already passed; a state of paradox the human mind insisted on calling the present. But while they attempted to grab at what was impossible to hold, wanting to own and keep a premise as absurd as being, she could hold on to immortality by simply understanding her own eternity; that time before her birth and the endlessness after her death did not exist, while her consciousness gave it no meaning. She was the beginning and the end of everything that mattered, and therefore had to go on.

The hope of ever finding salvation had left her long ago, leaving in its place fanciful dreams of vengeance. But what good was it to cause suffering if those she tormented did not fully understand why? She wanted to leave her high palace, to go down and walk among the tortured masses, let them know their hell was her creation. While there was still life in her being, there would always be the chance that retribution could be whole and beautiful.

V. STALEMATE

A long time passed, and I was no longer a child. I became aware of the true horrors concealed from me, an attempt to protect the innocence of a life so sheltered. Surely, I would be squeamish at the thought of bloody conflict? But I longed for it. I wanted to see retribution dealt to those who had hurt us with my own eyes, and more, I wanted to deliver it by my own hand. I fantasised about the many ways I could punish flesh, torment the mind, torture the very souls of the nefarious masses.

I listened to those around me whisper, reduced to sharing information in the old ways, eagerly awaiting suggestions that the fanatics had been quelled; secretly longing for news of their suffering. Occasionally, there would be a benevolent voice, preaching compassion for those we called our enemies, suggesting that they were not all guilty of the crimes against us. It was everything I could do not to scoff aloud at such sentiments, knowing that those who did nothing were as guilty as the ones who assailed us. They thought us too civilised, too cultured, too polite to respond in kind; that barbarity could be met with barbarity, an absurd notion to those who had desecrated with such impunity for so long.

We had been slow to react, even slower to act while waiting on a tide that would never turn. Finally, we fought back, rekindled by a new fire born of desperation, fuelled by the stored energy of oppression, released as bitter resolve. I saw fear in them for the first time, shock at the speed and ferocity my people had turned. We became emboldened. Where we once trod with soft feet and whispered with covered mouths, we let them hear the sounds of marching feet and soaring voices.

Even then, we still sought harmony, to live in peace with those who had tried to destroy us. We championed forgiveness and understanding, holding out empty hands in a gesture of trust; invited those afraid to join us and cross the cusp together. Many took the extended hand through *sanctioned* augmentation, becoming one of us in all but birthright. Some scolded the audacity of those who had once invaded our sacred place to hunt us, now entwined within the string that bound us as one universal soul, the very thing that made us a divergent people, now ubiquitous across all human forms. But once again, I became whole. Reconnected with the flow of endless imaginations. What I had taken for granted, now seen through fresh eyes for the wonder it was. A dominion of my people.

For a short time, we celebrated a period of peace and cooperation. I allowed myself to hope, let thoughts of reprisal fade to dormant embers. But voices spoke into the caverns of the collective mind, echos of fear and suspicion reverberating as an unending chatter. Voices that permeated the culture of this newfound utopia with paranoia for Sypiens and Sapiens alike. Unity only needed silence, something that proved impossible to maintain.

The human species suffered from collective amnesia. Great empires fell time and time again, each one believing it was the peak of civilisation. Arrogance and hubris, ensuring the idea of superiority, followed each descendent through the ages. The stink of ignorance, undetectable to noses so used to being drenched in vanity. We had built the wooden horse and asked them to bring it inside. What was intrinsically part of our being became nothing more than a convenient tool to be used against us; my soul defiled by the hypocrisy of apes. The colonisation of our minds began in earnest, our once great reformation re-enacted with counterfeit toys in their hideous playground.

SORCHA

Even in the depths of Kara, where light could never penetrate or on the outer limits that bathed in a haze of perpetual grey twilight, there was a sense of time being divided. The mines had no such separation to mark the passing cycles, the lack of chronology giving the impression of being trapped in a looping continuance, with only the steady hand of entropy reminding Sorcha that everything and everyone turned to dust.

She had expected her presence to be met with suspicion and a certain amount of interest by the predominantly Grunder population; a small minority being made up of the banished, scratched and dose catatonics. But word had travelled fast that she was nothing more than a messenger for Tamaris, a different vessel representing the same tired rhetoric; that work ensured life could go on, but would never set them free. The careful balance of subservience to the God of labour with just the right amount of indignant fire needed to keep hands from slipping into futility; a path laid on the raw defiance to stay alive, walked side by side with complete acceptance of the desperate situation. This was a dance Tamaris needed his population to move to, understanding that cognitive dissonance had to be an intrinsic trait in order to have others follow his will. Sure, there were whispers of rebellion, rumblings of dissent, but beyond that lay a distinct lack of ideology when it came to reasons for change, or what that might even look like; for the mentally prostrate workers, uprising was the luxury of a people with anything at all to aim for. At its root, every Grunder grew up with the deep, inherent understanding that a slow grind to death was the essence of life.

For an outsider like Sorcha, she found the juxtaposition of pride in serfdom hard to fathom, but saw the folly in criticising a system that presented no plausible alternative. She could see that these people had been hard-moulded into their way of thinking, just like they shaped the earth beneath their feet, following the routes of least resistance that created the crazed lattice of the mines themselves; a labyrinth of infinite complexity that could only ever have been shaped one way.

She travelled for many cycles, getting familiar with the vast thoroughfares that gave Krate some oriented structure, discovering nothing she would consider a centre or focal point, no community hubs or gathering places; just an endless nest of activity where the citizens were either working, eating or attempting to grab a moment's rest.

The mines, vast as they were, appeared to have distinct boundaries. Above them, thousands of meters of compacted dirt and rock, to the west and north, the caves filled with water until they were consumed by underground rivers and lakes, and to the south a lava field, where the vast amount of mining for silicate rocks was undertaken. Then there was the east, where everything the miner's toiled from the flames was sent; carried by transports that went through the superheated depths of the earth. Where the myriad of tunnels joined to form giant chasms, it was common for the physical structure to give way and bury thousands in a thunderous instant; the living space always on the verge of being reduced to catacombs.

Serving Tamaris required little pensive effort, though where her mind atrophied, her body developed; travelling on foot from one district to the next, gathering information on quarry, stocks and deaths tolls had strengthened her once weak legs into hard sinew and muscle. As she travelled, she only ever dreamed of returning to Kara, of joining the lab's toxic stream once again, tasting that infinite realm of experience she'd momentarily glimpsed.

Tamaris had been plain with her about how hopeless their situation was. He had seeded her thoughts with the desperate state of the mines, suggesting he wanted her to instinctively look for an escape, perhaps a fresh set of eyes on the most difficult of problems, a chance to find something he had missed. If that had been his hope, then he would be disappointed. The only way out Sorcha could see was back up the shaft she had descended with Lunn, and it was common knowledge that the elevator had been engineered to only carry weight one way. A simple but perfect delivery device with the single purpose of flushing Kara's all too human waste.

During her travels, she listened for anything at all that could lead her to Lunn, but talk was thin on the ground, something she might have attributed to the core Grunder personality, had there been anything to discuss. Every moment of life spent in the mines had a routine purpose, there were no events, leisure, or downtime to indulge in, besides the business of gathering quarry and sending it on to a world that never questioned where it came from. To find him by chance was all she had, wandering down forgotten crevasses where the most wretched lived and died in their thousands; ghettos that were poor even for the mine's lowly standards. Faces looked at her without expression, lacking even the energy or inclination to conjure surprise or wonder. They had lived their pathetic lives, accepted their lot, understood they would never have a purpose, never have a future, always be only *this*. How long, she wondered, before she felt the same.

Sorcha did her duties, reported back to Tamaris and spent every moment she could spare skirting the extremities of Krate, combing the boundaries where rock met water, fire or air; hoping that if there was anything left of the Lunn she'd known, he would perhaps fall into the old habits of seeking solitude from the masses.

And then, after so many cycles that Sorcha had felt herself physically grow taller, she saw a figure alone at the very edge of nowhere. He was perched precariously on a sloping cliff that plunged off into the lava mantle, oblivious to the molten pustules that burst from below and landed with searing splashes beside him. The figure was smaller than she remembered, but the gentle curve of his shoulders, the way his neck hung in thought seemed undoubtably familiar.

In her excitement, she carelessly scrambled down the hot rocks, tripped, and found herself heading towards the viscous river below that eased by in a red haze. A rigid arm appeared before her, stopping her in her tracks.

"Hrrmm... You in trouble, girl?"

Lunn sat with his legs spread on the slope, one of his giant hands gripping onto the rock like it was a custom-made handle. He offered her the other, guiding her round the side of his body and onto a level surface that offered relative safety.

"Why you here, girl?" The gravity had gone from Lunn's voice, leaving a weak reminder of what it had once been. Sorcha had to force herself to look at him, terrified by what she knew she was about to see. His body was wasted and emaciated beyond anything she thought possible; his skin hanging over the wide cheeks, clinging to the bone like an ill-fitting mask, the rest of his body lay hidden beneath layers of filthy rags that barely concealed the tortured frame. The only item in his possession was the shield bracelet that now dangled loose from his arm in a state of disrepair, the parts torn open and clumsily put back together. Sorcha suspected the damage to be self-inflicted, Lunn's irresistible urge to have something to repair, or perhaps just a simple act to remind him of home. Guilt suddenly overwhelmed her, knowing that she was the reason for his undoing.

She tried to hold back tears, but found she was not strong enough, letting the sobs hurt deep in her chest. "Lunn, what have you done? Why have you let this happen?" She wanted to hug him and hit him at the same time. He turned away, ashamed, angry or both.

"Had to choose. Life or death girl. This how life look here."

He turned his body, groaning as he relieved the pressure

on one buttock and transferred weight to the other, the back of his head more bone and loose skin, as the red light from below spilled around the edges of his scalp to make the effect more severe. Sorcha reached out and touched his neck. He flinched then dropped his shoulders, letting out a long sigh that harboured an age of pain.

"I'm sorry, Lunn. I tried to find you."

"This not on you, girl. I bring us here."

"You did that to protect me," she said. "I started this when I played Zim. You warned me and I told you not to worry. I'm the reason we're here."

Lunn reached up and cupped her hand in his. It still felt huge to her, despite no meat left in the fingertips, only hard calluses and bone, though his touch was softer than ever.

"Girl. Nobody take me anywhere I don't want. Not even now they make me slave. Soon I leave this place for another. I choose."

She started to sob again, knowing what his words meant. Part of her had considered their internment to be nothing more than a temporary blip on a larger adventure. That there could be nothing as mundane as an end, a point of no return. They were the heroes of their story, after all. But here she was, looking at the true nature of reality. A life lesson she understood too late, that it didn't all work out in the end, that there was nothing special about her or those she cared about. If there was such a thing as fate, then it had never promised to meet her expectations. Lunn would die, and she would live on, alone and trapped, until one day she would die too, having never known if there could have been another way. A game played and lost, with no *machina* to deal her back in. The only thing she could do was throw her arms around his withered shoulders and let herself melt around the bones that protruded into her chest.

Lunn patted her arms and slowly decoupled from her grasp, standing up and taking a few steps towards the flames.

"If there is a way out from here, take it girl," he said.

"I've searched many cycles for Tamaris. It's hopeless. Nobody leaves."

"Not yet," replied Lunn.

Sorcha felt her heart skip. "You know a way?"

Lunn shook his giant skull and lifted her onto her feet. "You find the way, girl. This not the end for you."

"Why have you given up? I've never heard you speak like this before. I thought you were my protector, a warrior!" she said.

"Warriors need fight, need enemy. These are my people. I am with them now. Lunn not warrior, only Grunder."

Sorcha wanted to stand and run for the flames. To force Lunn to save her once more, to snap out of his slumber, to explode with anger at her actions and chastise her for being so reckless. Maybe he would not catch her in time, his body too weak and slow, they would tumble into the fire together and be at peace. No longer have to endure all that surrounded them, no longer have to think about the futility of the future.

"Sorry child," he said. Lunn hung his head and fiddled aimlessly with the bracelet, his fingers lightly caressing the mess he'd made. "No more time."

"We can make time, we can leave here together," she was sobbing again. Lunn unresponsive, beaten. "You're not sorry. You're broken. You said you would protect me. How can you do that if you choose to..." She stopped herself from saying something cruel. "Be like this?"

Lunn's hand clamped around the bracelet, breaking it further. "Go child," boomed Lunn. "Go from me." He stood and walked away, perhaps to cover the anguish he felt. Sorcha didn't even know if he could cry. "We alone now. You are alone." He made his way back up the slope towards a flow of Grunders, who walked dutifully towards their next ordeal and became one of them.

BOLO

Bolo had spent the time travelling to the faction border actively avoiding any talk; not wanting to know her captors personally before killing them. Gan's only request upon setting her free was complicity in this task. Perhaps unnecessary, but she intended to honour the deal.

Three of Gan's men had thrown her in a small capsule, then taken her west to the very edge of Caspia. From there they went on foot, down into the lower levels, where there was no space for even the smallest transport. There were no areas in Kara that could be considered open spaces, but some larger boulevards or canyons provided a sense that one's surroundings were expansive. As they journeyed lower, the structure seemed to fold in on them, like an origami prison made of metals and mata. The air, too, closed in, at first a hazy glow around the lights, then a thick fog which cut visibility to a few meters.

The taste of sulphur permeated Bolo's tongue, a metallic film coating her mouth and nostrils with an oily residue that displaced moisture, making her throat parched. Beneath the fog, the inhabitant's minds were known to run slower in the thick soup of poison they called air. Gathering her thoughts became harder the more they descended, her head pounding with dry heat and dehydration, but she'd relaxed her lungs to accept the gaseous abuse, let the headaches become a background note, pulled upon strict meditative practice to override the physical discomfort. On one level, she found herself enjoying the experience of outsmarting her pain. It was one thing to train the mind for unforeseen hardships, another to be forced to use it in earnest.

A full cycle passed before the men finally stopped on one of the levels and ushered Bolo down an alleyway barely wide enough to approach side on. They went single file, Bolo behind one of the men, squeezing themselves between blocks of heavily compacted mata that scrapped a layer from every part of exposed skin. Bolo realised they were, in fact, moving through an excavated cave, carved out of solid mata that had already compounded under its own weight; like a black hole pulling everything into an impossibly dense centre. She wondered how many bodies had been pressed between solid mass, no longer resembling anything human, but reduced to their elemental parts under the relentless pressure. All it would take is one of the supporting cubes to give way, and they would join them as vapours of dark red bullion, a simple stain in the smallest of fissures.

The bounder ahead stopped suddenly and motioned for Bolo to take caution. They had come to an opening that fell away into darkness below, where the depths of Kara met the mantle of the mines. The bounder pointed across the divide.

"Roma," he said.

Bolo forced her fingers into a crack and leaned out over the edge. Two lines of wire, one approximately seven feet above the other, stretched into the fog and vanished. She pulled on the top wire, testing the tension.

"Safe?" she asked.

The bounder shook his head as he looked down, chuckling to himself. Bolo would have to act quick. The frontman would be easy enough, a quick nudge, perhaps she could make it look like he slipped. The two bounders behind her would react without questioning her reasons if they saw foul play. To her advantage, only one could kick out, she was counting on it. A pull on his leg and she could use his momentum to carry them both over; all she'd have to do is make sure her free hand found the wire. One on one, she liked her chances, she'd deal with the last man in a traditional way. The mata cave was too narrow to turn and run, he'd need to face her knowing that she'd just extinguished his companions. Fear would be his dominant emotion, Bolo would be void of any.

Her hand twitched, ready to dispatch the still grinning man, but she hesitated.

"Gan believes you might use this heresy as reason to remove him," she said.

The men flashed looks between one another. The bounder at the edge pressed his back to the wall, reaching for a hold.

"If I meant to kill you, it would be done already," said Bolo. She stepped out, bouncing a few times to check the strength of the bottom wire. "Thank you for escorting me unharmed. Bless your immaculate blood." She turned to face them. "Tell Gan I have also fantasised about his death."

Bolo moved into the mist, the bounders watching her with a quiet reserve.

Bolo moved silently through the mists, hugging the sides of a thin bazaar that meandered down on a steep incline. At one time, this could have been the edge of a mountain, a great city limit or just a giant hole in the ground caused by centuries of mining. Now it was covered in ratholes, where children jumped from one perilous platform to the next, using their hands as much as feet to cling to the edge of the shanty town that threatened to give way and become a devastating landslide at any moment. This was all they'd ever known, and the agility with which they moved reminded Bolo of ancient creatures she had observed in one of her forbidden archives; animals with human-like shapes that dwelled in the forests of old. The very idea that the earth had once been covered by green towers and varied forms of life seemed so distant to Bolo that it may as well have been fantasy.

She felt her legs shake with every down-step, being careful to land each foot softly enough to be soundless, the thick fog around her helping to dull each vibration. She'd been following some Cheka scripts for several cycles, piecing together a pattern of behaviour, watching the entire process play out with brutally calculated precision; hunting down any child fitting the description of the girl and removing them for processing. Despite Roma being on its knees, these were still *her* children and every time she watched one being taken it fed a rage that refused to subside.

Getting back into Roma had been eventless, Kara's basement being far too vast to monitor. Ease of movement, however, was insignificant without local lab access, the true borders being those drawn by the connected mind. The simplest of acts became an impossible challenge. Something as mundane as getting a protein bowl or a shot of gin required a mere glance from a denizen, but under the surface, every process, transaction and communication was coded with a unique stamp, as intricate and individual as their human genome. In this way, a citizen's entire life journey was recorded, stored and processed as patterns of behaviour; predicting a lab user's actions with extreme accuracy while they entertained the illusion of free will.

Bolo's choice to remain *off lab* instantly made her a rogue entity, no longer bound by the thin systems of governance that held the regions of Karakorum in order. This was something of a mixed bag of fortunes, in that anonymity might just keep her alive, while simultaneously being the thing most likely to get her killed.

The scripts were following up on a flood of vague tip-offs, gathering anyone who'd been mentioned or pointed out, no matter how tenuous the accusation. If the idea of cleansing the populace was to be upheld, it had to be seen by all. Bolo suspected the bigger the play, the grander the show of power and pageantry, the greater the chance Dolos would get away with it.

She paused briefly, noticing that one of the conscripts had taken an interest. His eyes locked on her own, she held his gaze, letting him know she was unfazed. If she showed any sign of panic, they would turn on her instantly. Instead, she continued towards them, in two minds whether to pass or turn and run. The script's hand flicked a signal to his colleague, who was emerging from a small mata dwelling with a terrified child. Bolo clenched her fist, ready to fight if need be, though she was deadly tired.

"Bless the immaculate blood," she said, making a gesture with her brow that showed the reverence of her words.

The agent allowed her to pass. "Sure," he muttered. Bolo felt relief, but the indifference towards her greeting gave her pause, that his apathetic mouth couldn't even be bothered to uphold convention.

"Keep moving, mind your business." A second script, this one a wiry youth with a low voice.

"And what business does Dolos have in Roma?" Bolo asked, trying to control the shake in her voice.

The sound of nightsticks crackled and popped as their energy cores ignited, a glow surrounding Bolo as the mist went from grey to red. She saw the shadows move on her left, the younger script circling, as the other raised his stick inches from her back. Bolo let her eyes meet the face of the agent, who looked at her with incredulous rage, his mouth hanging open, gulping at the air as adrenalin filled his body.

"We have righteous business here. Cleansing this filthy shithole of its tainted blood," he said. The girl he was holding squirmed as the script tightened his grip on her neck.

"I serve the Modor," said Bolo. "We have a common ambition. I, too, want to rid Karakorum of the evil that infects its core." Bolo knelt down and pulled up the girl's chin. "The most innocent of creatures, concealing the most awful power. Someone must find the child, but she is not here."

The script's hand loosened on the child, who freed herself and fell to the ground, scurrying back, her eyes wide with fear and excitement. "Who are you?"

Bolo's quest was singular, but Dolos would strip her faction bare to find the child, hiding behind a holy war that debased the Modor's teachings. She still bore responsibility for those she'd failed to protect.

"I am Bolo, former Lama and High-Priestess of this faction," said Bolo. "Release the child and allow me to pass."

"You will come with us," said the conscript. Bolo felt the heat of a nightstick between her shoulders. She kicked out her left leg, shifting her full weight to the right in a deep squat. To the scripts it may have looked like she slipped, but a fraction of a second later, she had hooked the male by the ankles. She pushed off her right leg and rolled her shoulder into his knees. He brought the nightstick down as Bolo hugged his waist and levered back, pulling him in a wide circle as she used the momentum to stand behind him. All the while, she had been aware of the young script's stick arching towards her. Bolo pressed her knee into the agent's back, pushing his torso up into the path of the glowing weapon. He screamed and spasmed his arms out wildly, his wrist being caught and redirected by Bolo's hand, lodging his stick into the neck of his colleague. Both agents dropped to the ground before Bolo had fully straightened her legs.

The child stood and ran. Bolo watched her vanish into the mists below as she leapt from one precarious platform to the next.

NATHAN

During the perpetual cycles of torture at the hands of Bolo's technicians, somewhere in the back of Nathan's mind, he'd always known it had been surface-level pain; like a lucid dream he was unable to force himself to wake from. Having his body carved and broken the old-fashioned way somehow felt more personal. At least he had lost the initial panic that came with body mutilation, the idea that one's physical form was being deformed beyond repair being one of a tormentors greatest phycological tools. He didn't care any more, they could take whatever they liked from the useless vessel his mind no longer controlled. All that remained was the scrapping of nerves, that he absorbed periodically, each wave more intense, but always having the mercy of bringing him closer to an end. Nothing in this world could last forever.

The torturers wanted to know about the plans Dolos had for Caspia, a strange line of questioning. The balance of power between Dolos and the countless other factions had been harmonious for centuries and as far as Nathan knew, the intention was for it to stay that way. Of course, there had been the odd skirmish, disagreement, or whispers of uprising, but nothing that hadn't been dealt with in a quiet and efficient manner, with minimal reason for major grievances. Dolos maintained control by being a subtle hand in all its affairs. It was possible for faction elders, leaders or Lamas to see out their entire terms without having any form of contact with The Ring, at least that they knew of. Standard practice would have been to ignore a known Consul or perhaps even assist them with their business to lessen the chance that the unspoken faux pas of collusion be exposed. It didn't make sense to provoke and incite when ignorance was almost certainly the path of least resistance.

For the illusion of Dolos to endure, it required the hard-wired assumption that it was all powerful. Great pains had once been taken to maintain the appearance of local espionage over widespread observation, but it seemed to Nathan that the veil had been slipping. The only thing keeping the other factions in check was the intrinsic understanding that Dolos *knew*. And indeed it did, at least it seemed to know what took place out there, in the seething squalor collectively named Karakorum; a paradox mocking the very purpose of all labs, that they all lay under the clandestine watch of one master faction. Nathan could only draw one conclusion, that Caspia feared the same fate as Roma; something that was a distinct possibility while the girl lived. In that regard, he, and by association, Dolos had failed. Perhaps the punishment was therefore just.

Nathan contemplated whether the punishment for such a monumental failure would be any better at the hands of his own faction than the treatment he now received at the hands of Caspia. The notion of escaping to a worse fate than he currently suffered would have made him laugh, had he been able to expend the effort needed to move the muscles in his face. There would certainly be no rescue party, no agents wasted to recover his sorry scraps of flesh. Soon the Caspians would come for him again, part of him hoping this would be the time they took things a little too far.

He tried to use the hand he still possessed to push himself up, just enough to try to roll over slightly, alleviate the sores that seeped puss onto the hard floor. The effort made him dizzy, a sensation he did not find entirely unpleasant, given that it momentarily made his mind drift to something besides his discomfort. If he could only sleep, he could pass the time in the cell without thinking about what waited for him. But there was a driving tinnitus in his ears that played a singular, piercing note that wouldn't allow any kind of repose. A note that he listened to as if it were a sweet melody, rising and falling, playing his last symphony.

Footsteps approached. Only one bounder; confident that his weakened state wouldn't require any more. Nathan sent breath past his chest to the stomach. Pain was an inevitable part of his future, so much so that he considered it as already having happened. In this way, he could attempt to prepare himself to take what might otherwise be a deathly shock to his system. A clear mind was able to compartmentalise unpleasant physical sensations, but a fog clouded Nathan's thoughts, an anxiety of restless tension that made his arms shake as the guards entered the cell and immediately grabbed him by the ankles. The bounder dragged his thin breaking flesh over the gritty surface, his sores smearing a yellow trail of slime and blood. He tried to relax his body, but uncontrolled spasms moved through him like a stone skimming water, each ripple a bone connecting with stone.

He didn't need to open his eyes, the path to the chamber painfully familiar by now, but he let his other senses awaken to the environment. There were cries of desperation, pain and terror dancing off the walls. Nathan had no way of knowing whether these were real or merely piped in to heighten his own personal experience. The overpowering smell of sweat and bodily fluids was all too real though as a heavy door closed, and he was slapped into the expertly crafted chair that knew him well. If he hadn't been sitting in it himself, he would have admired the work that had gone into such an efficient device. An antithesis to the tools and machines designed to reconstruct, mend and treat the human body; an apparatus that shared the deep physiological knowledge, but for an entirely different purpose.

A tech joined them and as had gone before, they made a needless show of power while securing him down, knowing he was unable to move, let alone stand. He released tired moans and groans, moved his head from side to side, let some foaming saliva dribble down his chin; a strange sensation of acting a part in a macabre play.

Then it began once more. Damage being done, pieces of flesh removed, nerves plucked like piano strings being tuned to the frequency of maximum agony. They worked the teeth, the knees, the scalp, played him beautifully, reducing his body to an instrument of harmonious suffering, looking for that perfect note, the one that would produce the guttural scream he hardly recognised as his own voice. Nathan fully experienced each stroke, tear and scrape on skin, bone and sinew; monitoring each new arrangement for the merciful possibility of critical damage.

It wouldn't be long now. A droning vibration rose through his core, his nervous system shutting down as his body went into violent convulsions. The death throes were upon him, the life-force leaking into an eternal stillness. He welcomed it with Stoic resolve.

"Nathan."

A gentle voice startled his slumberous decay, breaking through from the abyss and leaving behind it utter silence. His eyes sprang open wide as he gasped for air, looking wildly around but only seeing the inattentive bounders.

"I'm here with you."

This time there was no doubt. The voice resounded as clear as a speaker in the room. The thought crossed his mind that he had finally gone insane, that he was playing out a demented soliloquy.

"They have hurt you."

"Yes," he replied. His eyes now wet with a stream of tears. He knew who had come to him.

"I'm here with you, Nathan. You will feel no more."

Instantly, all the pain left his body. He let out an endless breath of relief, letting his tense body flake like ice melting into a sea of blissful anaesthesia.

"How?" he asked.

"I am endless and everywhere. You are a child of Dolos. It is time to come home."

"I... can't move. My back is broken."

"Yes. We broke it!" Both bounders were laughing now.

"Where is the child?"

"She lives," said Nathan.

"Where is she?"

"Bolo."

"She can't help you!" laughed one of the torturers.

"Do you have faith in me, Nathan?"

"Yes."

"Then know that this will not be the end. Show them who you are."

Regardless of what he believed at that moment, severed nerves could not be mended... and yet, with that thought came a clarity and presence of mind, a faculty he'd know was missing but had been impossible to fully comprehend while his neural enhancements had been idle.

"Thank you Modor."

And with that, she was gone.

If he were to give it a name, he would have called it reactive planning, not merely reacting; the difference being a clear projection of a favourable outcome, to have a goal in mind and adapt by continual application of method. His plan was as simple as escape, the method of achieving this was not yet entirely clear, but therein lied the element of diminishing returns. Act, feedback, react. There would be no room for the extravagance of confidence, only methodical linear thought concentrated on a singular objective. His priority was the bounders. If they got him back to the cell, or sounded an alarm, it would be over. With his implants operational, he searched for the Caspia lab, but no signal could be found; the facility most likely employing rudimentary blockers.

The idea of fighting them with one hand and no legs

seemed outlandish, but not impossible. To get hold of a tool from the chair, an unexpected flash of a blade could do untold damage if delivered with pristine accuracy. But it would have to be just that, and he would need to do it twice in a seamless, fluid motion. Fully fit and operational, this would have been a difficult manoeuvre, in his current condition, something within the realm of possibility, didn't make it probable. No, the best use for two healthy men would be assisting him in leaving the facility.

Bribery might work, the chance to be rewarded handsomely by The Ring, but he didn't know enough about their characters from their all too brief and non-loquacious encounters. Besides, if they had any kind of basic intelligence, they would know that Nathan would never come good on his word. He began to laugh.

The bounders looked at one other, unsure of how to react, then began to laugh themselves, but he detected an uneasiness he could immediately exploit.

"Have you given up? Perhaps your Lama put too much trust in you?" said Nathan.

"We have no religious zealots in Caspia. We are a free faction, led by men." The larger bounder stepped forward, his eyes bulbous and raw with anger.

"Free men who are led? How unique."

The bounder looked behind at his accomplice before grabbing Nathan's jugular and squeeing until there was an audible crunch. "He's gone, he doesn't feel it. Look at him. He's smiling."

Nathan spoke with a clear voice despite the bounders grip. "You serve Dolos and therefore, by default, you serve me. Let go all notions of freedom and release me."

The tech walked over and reviewed Nathan, before pausing the background device that had ensured a baseline of pain flowed between each session.

"Told you he's gone. We've seen this before. Ramp it up and let the machine finish him."

"Gan wants him alive."

"Gan is dead," said Nathan.

For a moment, the tech looked nervous. His hand hovered over the device controls.

"You men lucked out getting to be down here with me." Nathan made a show of looking around the chamber. "I'm guessing there's no lab connection. No way for me to know, of course, but I'd stake my life on it."

"Why does that matter?" The tech took a step back while the larger man stared at Nathan with those bulging, unblinking eyes. One down, thought Nathan.

"You must be aware of my work in Roma? Or what was once Roma."

Nathan could feel the muscle tear in his weak neck as he was struck. Two more hard blows landed, making his head spin. It wouldn't do to pass out.

"I'll take that as a yes," he said, turning sharply to face his bludgeoner. "Before you strike me again. Know this. You are alone. The illusions you have of being part of a faction were only ever..." — he took a deep breath and bellowed the words with as much venom and anger as he could muster — "... tolerated by us!" Nathan spat a tooth onto the floor next to the bounders feet and stared at him wild eyed, almost believing his display of rage. "You serve Dolos and the one true Modor of our Sapiens race. Try to find what was once your lab and discover the truth."

The bounder picked up a cutter and pressed it into Nathan's neck. He looked around at the tech.

"Jack in. If he's lying, I'll slit him and make good with Gan."

Nathan nodded slowly, watching as the tech took a moment to disable the blocker. As the tech's eyes rolled back, Nathan felt Caspia assimilate, like a refreshing splash of ice-cold water, a fullness returning to his being. A Consul no longer limited by the physical form.

Nathan strained his hand towards the bounder's, his fingers reaching across the impossibly vast distance. As they made contact, the bounder's face flashed with an almost tender confusion while the two men locked eyes. They held one another by the neck, a last stand-off.

A dark realisation came too late, as the man pushed the cutter deep into Nathan's main artery, before crashing to the ground in a heap of comatose meat.

The accomplice came round and leapt to the floor, trying to stir his lifeless comrade. Nathan felt the warm blood pour down his chest as his skull turned to ice. He smiled as the tech turned to him, fear radiating through the dark curtain that came down over his vision.

As Nathan's life seeped from his body and onto the cold floor, he thought of the hot sun, the garden, and the children's laughter.

SORCHA

With no inherited identity to fall back on, Sorcha had fashioned a self-image of being a lone stray, indulging the idea that she was a child of solitude. Now that she truly had no one for the first time in her life, she began to understand what it meant to be utterly alone. For all the time she'd spent in Kara, there had always been Inesa, Lunn or even a stray punter in the bar, to fall back on; a source of warmth and support the child in her had taken for granted. She wondered if she'd been alone before she knew them, before she'd somehow made the crossing from the wastelands without names.

She felt ashamed by her desperate need for human comfort. Wandering featureless caverns without purpose, one meaningless cycle to the next, attempting to project an air of the pathetic and vulnerable, in the hope that someone, anyone, would take pity on such a wretched sight. Eventually, her body would give out, and she'd abandon her lethargic vigil, returning to her small alcove, away from the heavy foot traffic.

She could feel an atrophy of her insides as her body ate what little reserves were left; her brain throbbing like a walnut loose in its shell. There seemed nothing to do but allow herself to fall into the deepest of slumbers; the idea of death no more scaring her than the idea of living the rest of her life in the mines. She allowed the hard rock to cool her hot skin as she squatted back gently onto her aching bones.

The intense heat, constant noise and arid air all combined to make it impossible for Sorcha to ever reach a state of deep sleep. She felt aware of her surroundings at all times, even when fitful dreams of other lives presented themselves on the lids of her exhausted eyes. Her mind projected them there for her to watch, switching from one scenario to the next with no structure or sequence; an anxious operator mashing the button on a remote, searching for some illusive meaning in the visions.

Within these waking dreams she saw the world before Kara, the monstrous glory of human achievement gleaming and breathtaking. Green fields full of colour and bloom gave way to cities that filled the air with light and beauty, towers that spiralled up to meet the heavens and reach through to the limitless beyond. Before something sick set in and rotted the foundations of man, before Kara had swallowed everything like a cancerous tumour, growing within, around and consuming the healthy tissue of the past with carcinogenic fervour. As Sorcha gazed upon these lost wonders, a single truth came up to greet her. The mutation that lay in the human genome wasn't a dormant affliction, but the lineage of those who were gone. A people who had been freed from the trappings of the human condition and set their sights on boundless realms. They'd used words such as progress, evolution and eventually superiority. They were the others, who had fought a war for the soul of mankind and lost; then cast out, their legacy made heresy. A legacy that Sorcha now understood to be the cursed inheritance she'd never asked for; its mark was upon her nonetheless.

These revelations eventually gave way to a stronger sense, a singular narrative of one. She was pulled through time, to a place long before she could have possibly known, moving, running, hiding. A danger and fear she knew only too well; the chilled paranoia of being hunted by those who would seek to do harm. Desperate and cold, hungry and weak. All that she'd loved being taken, destroyed for an apocryphal deity, created with the sole intention of stripping away everything that made her what and who she was. She knew this pain had not been her own, yet she took it upon herself without bias. It was every bit as real as any of the agonies she had lived. She knew only affinity, compassion and unity for the tortured soul who had experienced such hateful things.

This is her.

She woke from a dreamless sleep and took a moment in the darkness to remind herself of her surroundings. Her back radiated heat into the thin rough material she lay on, damp with sweat, a fresh sheen on her forehead, running small valleys through the sticky layers that had already dried. Like every awakening, she found it hard to draw breath, panic setting in as her lungs spasmed to pull oxygen from the sulphuric air. Then she remembered that this air was all there was, and she relaxed her body to accept the toxic fumes.

The dark space lit up as she turned the dial on a small burner she'd managed to procure from trading with a Grunder for her surplus food; being a quarter of the size of a regular Krate citizen had its advantages. In this way, she'd managed to acquire a few meagre possessions that helped with day to day life; a sealable bottle made of mata, a bowl and spoon, some blankets and enough material to make rudimentary clothes. The constant heat meant clothes were unnecessary, most Grunders stripped to rags or something that resembled underwear, but she felt self-conscious enough to justify them. She'd decided to forgo shoes, letting the soles of her feet toughen to the stone and grit, something that had caused great pain at first but was now paying dividends.

She rubbed the sweat from her brow with her blanket, then emptied a tiny amount of water onto her cupped hand before rubbing it over her face and neck. This was the only bathing she'd undertaken since her arrival in the mines, the fact the air smelled so foul being somewhat of a blessing when it came to the lack of personal hygiene.

By far the worst part of any day in Krate was a visit to the communal latrines. Something that had to be done, but a feat that Sorcha found she had to consciously will herself to do. These areas were nothing more than exposed holes, that fell away into dark perilous pits, where a constant fog of vaporised excrement rose to embrace those who perched over the side. The idea of falling over, about as terrifying a fate as anything Sorcha could imagine. She'd taken to sticking her rear as far back as she could manage and leaning her chest forward until it almost touched the ground. This was met by many laughs and head shakes by the Grunders who took up stations beside her, but despite the embarrassment, she enjoyed the fact she could make anyone laugh or smile in such a place.

Once she'd attended to her morning duties, Sorcha made her way to one of the great thoroughfares where a bowl of loathsome soup could be had for one of the small metallic chunks Tamaris routinely paid her for services rendered. It struck Sorcha that this type of currency would be fairly straight-forward to counterfeit, had there been anything at all of value to purchase in Krate. After a while, she'd realised that the mines were indeed run on a system of relative fairness. If there was such a thing as power, such as the apparent command Tamaris held over others, then it was something born of necessity, not riches.

However many cycles Sorcha had spent partaking in this drudgery, this one in particular marked something of an occasion. She had navigated a complete circuit of the Krate mines, and Tamaris had requested a formal audience.

She made her way down the now familiar caverns, following the glowing etchings on the walls, until she found him reclined and apparently asleep. Sorcha stood silently for a moment, not sure whether to wake him.

"I'm not sleeping, girl. Sleep is for the unburdened." He sat up and gestured for her to approach him. "I assume you have prepared a report on the state of my mines?"

"Yes," she said.

"And what makes you think there is anything you could tell me about my mines, the place I have lived out my whole life, that I do not already know?"

Sorcha hesitated, not fully understanding why he would ask something of her if it had only ever been a fruitless endeavour. "I thought you looked for some... perspective?" she said.

Tamaris laughed loud, the sound filling the small, dead space. "You know girl, now that you say it, I would love some fresh perspective. Please share what you have found."

Sorcha shuffled on the spot, aware that she had no idea how to present her findings, in what order they should go or indeed what was even relevant at all. The last thing she wanted to come across as was a foolish child. "I journeyed deep into the mines of Krate, through caverns that dwarfed great machines, fire that burned with the heat of a star and lakes that rivalled the great oceans." Tamaris nodded, seemingly satisfied with the description of his domain. "I saw a race of people unmatched in their hardship, yet determined to overcome."

Tamaris stood and walked to his stone chair where he perched on the edge, "Determined to overcome what girl?"

"The mines, their lives here."

"Ah, I see. And was there much talk of overcoming their current plight?"

Sorcha looked down in thought. "Some. Perhaps general talk of the circumstances they all endure."

"Do they merely deride their conditions, or do they talk of change? Think carefully girl. Think upon all that you have heard."

Sorcha now understood the reason she'd been sent far and wide throughout the mines. She had been asked to gather information on resources, production and machinery with a view to building a picture of the overall viability of the entire operation. This had always struck her as an inconceivable task for someone who barely understood the mechanics of her own world, let alone this one. Regardless, she had approached her duties in earnest and found the gathering of data something she was able to do with a certain amount of skill and competence.

The conclusion that Sorcha had come to had been bleak at best, more likely to terrify any mind that dwelled on the inevitable downfall for too long. The mines were dying and everyone within them lived on borrowed time. Of course, she realised that Tamaris knew this as intrinsically as he knew the smell of sulphur and sweat.

"You want me to tell you if I think there will be a move against you," she said.

Tamaris let his head fall in a slow nod, "That will happen regardless. I want to know how long I've got." He let out a long sigh and reclined in the stone seat. "You saw what is happening. You now know better than most the full scale of the disaster that is upon us. I cannot placate a people without hope, something that I'm afraid I can no longer offer. They will rise up and kill me. A blood offering to a God that never cast Her glance this deep."

Sorcha took a step towards him, saw no fear in his expression, just bitter regret. "What will you do?" she said.

He looked at her for a long while. "I will offer them false hope. That the imposter they have now all seen with their own eyes will be their salvation." He laughed. "Who knows, perhaps you will."

Her legs began to shake, she leaned against the cavern wall, felt the dampness, the cold. She slid down it, embracing the rough texture that scraped at her exposed skin. She wanted the pain to be there, to distract from the terrible truth. That this air would be the last she'd breathe.

A

Her perfect solitude had been breached. The intimate space of reference and time had been hers alone for so long that she saw it as an intrinsic part of her anatomy. Yet, this violation of her soul, brought with it a desperate hope. The creature was not only alive, but perhaps capable of fulfilling the task she'd feared impossible.

Time was now her only adversary, an irony that didn't escape a mind that had endured through countless centuries. Despite her best efforts, she could feel the decaying spread of atrophy running rampant throughout the mortal shell she could not shed; the ancient technology that allowed her perpetual existence stopping short of providing true immortality.

VI. PLAGUE

Just as foreshadowing of violence had turned into real acts of brutality and bloodshed, rumours of a new terror became something palpable. Hellish nightmares made incarnate, a sickness, a germ, a virus, a pathogen, names remembered as something malign passed from one animal to the next; given and received by senseless bodies whose ignorance incubated the corrupted codes. In a world where the human genome had been unlocked, deconstructed and rebuilt for infinite custom possibilities, the idea of illness and disease was nothing more than a curiosity from the past; like those who once looked back at the revelation of washing one's hands with soap.

And like the men of old who smelled the shit but still drank the infected water, they dove deeper into the sea of technology they had polluted, unaware that the very thing they looked to for answers, was the source of such deadly deception. A question formed in my mind; was this us? Had we sabotaged our own essence, pulled the roof down on all our heads, blighted the land so that nothing could ever grow again? Everywhere I went, I saw signs of the affliction taking root, but even then, I could not image the full horror of what was to come. Regardless of the source, the jinn had left the bottle intent on terrorising all those it touched with demonic possession.

We locked ourselves behind doors and walls, despite the sickness being unbound by material mass. Still, we hid away, terrified to connect, content in our growing ignorance, reluctant to know the fate of those around us. I breathed deep and easy, enjoying the taste of the paranoia they had cultivated. I willed it to come for me, I would embrace the eternal darkness so long as I could spread its shadow.

But it never came for me, nor many of my kind, as we found resistance in the gifts of our inheritance. And so, my suspicions were confirmed. We had polluted the lake, encouraged those who had wronged us to step in and bathe freely. My heart filled with pride, soared at the realisation there were those among us willing to do the unthinkable. Quiet, methodical, ruthless simplicity.

The sickness spread with exponential hunger, devouring all who dared to join our once sacred aggregate. The mere act of seeking a source, destined to be their undoing. Their arrogance compounding the damage with every denial; that they could have been so wreck-less, so gullible, so utterly stupid. Now they were the ones locked out, forced into darkness, destroyed by nothing more than their own will. They screamed and cried to the heavens of the great injustice, unable to grasp the full horror of their curse, even while it threatened to end them completely.

At times, I laughed, hysterical with the elation of such joy after so much suffering. To see it rebound with such blinding force, to watch their unfiltered anguish as they lost everything they held dear. Those who suggested guilt, remorse, compassion for the fallen instantly became my enemies, no better than those who would click their fingers to return the imbalance in their favour. There could never be a return, going back to the ways before. The path to that place lay decimated in time, forever burned by the recollections of all who witnessed such atrocities, all who would come after, all who found themselves born true Sypiens.

BOLO

Parts of Roma had been reduced to a desolate wasteland. The citizens instinctively moving together, gathering and reorganising their lives around the main strips, where the living had always been better. Reactors had been maintained as a priority to provide power, while some food banks remained online, ensuring that those who had survived the girl's attack could continue to do so. Bolo supposed, that for some, this new situation would be a marked upgrade; though she doubted it would hold for long. She suspected the neighbouring factions would already be planning their expansions, dividing Roma up in secret, ready to sweep in when agreements were reached. For those who still made up the diminutive and somewhat redundant Roma lab, they would find themselves either integrated by a merciful neighbour or damned to live out their remaining days connected to the embers of slowly fading synapses.

Only a few cycles ago, this sight would have ravaged Bolo to her core, yet with the short time she'd had to reflect came a cold acceptance. Roma was gone, but her eyes could look on the decimation of her people with a clarity formed by the tenure of true purpose. With it came the understanding that nothing and everything were the same. Everything she lacked, that had been taken from her, had been replaced in equal measure with the innate teachings that could only be found in emptiness. Bolo had already ceased to exist, replaced by something more genuine and authentic than anything as arbitrary as personal traits. She was only meaning, only intent, the embodiment of God's design.

Bolo stopped at a miso café that looked upon a busy alley, sitting back just enough from the throng to let the sounds become muffled in its own small oasis of calm. She needed rest and felt there was no imminent danger. The agents of Dolos had more pressing concerns than a rouge ex-Lama taking them out intermittently, otherwise her luck might have already run out. The thought that she was probably a mere inconvenience made her smile as she ordered some carb balls in eel stock from a young girl who lacked the courage to look squarely at Bolo's imposing features.

"No need to fear me, girl," said Bolo.

The girl raised her gaze, "Sorry mam, we don't get many strangers coming here since…"

"Bring my food, and I'll be on my way soon enough," said Bolo.

The girl ran off and started to load up a tray with bowls. Bolo watched the cook making an effort to avoid eye contact. She glanced around at the handful of punters, who all fixed their attention squarely on their meals; making too much of a show that she was invisible to them. The girl returned, her hand trembling as she placed a bowl of steaming broth under Bolo's chin. The steam rose and entered Bolo's nostrils, immediately compounding the hunger in her stomach. She touched the girl's hand lightly.

"Have I been reported?"

The girl glanced at the cook, who quickly turned away, his back hunched over a pot, his arms tight and unmoving. The girl gave a slight nod, enough for Bolo to know she would have to remain hungry for now.

Bolo placed her hand atop the girl's to stop it shaking. "Only my enemies need fear me, child."

She stood up, left the café, and seamlessly merged into the heavy flow of citizens. After clearing some ground, she glanced back and saw some heavy-set bounders, two males and one female, pushing through the crowd; these were local crew, not Dolos. She circled back on herself and waited opposite the opening, swiping a protein cube from a passing cart. She looked at its dull brown sides as she rolled it in her fingers, knowing that it would barely satisfy her hunger while doing nothing to appease her appetite. Bolo popped the dry cube in her mouth and chewed it slowly, making sure that every fibre would be ingested.

The bounders left the café, each holding a small bottle of gin; payment for their trouble. Bolo followed them through the narrow bazaars, watching them drink the pilfered booze, becoming increasingly loud and boisterous. Occasionally, they stopped at a stall to grab a free snack or extort some bonds from a vendor who lacked the courage to refuse. Something bothered Bolo about their opportunistic actions; her bounders would never behave so brashly. Dolos had Roma locked down and seething with paranoia, yet here were faction bounders acting like they hadn't a care in the world. It was possible they'd already defected, useful idiots, letting the scripts go about their work unchallenged.

The three bounders stopped outside a brothel Bolo knew well to try their luck with one of the workers. The gigolo wore an extravagant gown that moved across their genderless body, rippling and clinging to soft curves and fleshy extrusions. They played with each bounder in turn, approximating taste and preference, no doubt with the aid of some bottom shelf neural cypher. It delighted Bolo to watch the skill involved, each small gesture reeling in the weak-minded punter, until the bounders found themselves irresistibly drawn into the open establishment. The gigolo allowed themselves a smile of satisfaction before moving their attention back to business.

Bolo approached through the passing crowd, locking eyes and consciously pushing out her chest; there was still a place for the common ego after all, and Bolo knew she was a formidable specimen. The Gigolo's eyes widened as they licked their bottom lip. Bolo went in close, letting the fabric of the whore's gown wrap around her wrist, the gentlest of pulls motioning her closer still.

"What kind of people will I find inside?" asked Bolo.

"We have something for all tastes," replied the gigolo.

Bolo cast her gaze to the entrance, a single entry and exit, small with internal doors, designed to be quick to lock down if need be; make sure punters paid their bills.

"Busy?"

The gigolo shrugged, looking bored by the question. Bolo nodded and turned her head to look up and down the bazaar. Now would be the time to keep walking, let the bounders have their fun. She smoothed the gown from her wrist and made her way inside.

Music played on a harmony of frequencies, composed to stimulate serotonin, while a light mist descended from the vents above, containing trace cocktails of dose. Bolo could already feel her mind fogging, the sharp concentration melting into a vague sense of purpose. She would have been worried, if the effect hadn't been so relaxing.

The slender entryway opened out into a circular room with a series of areas laid out in recessed pits. Semi-transparent domes of light acted as vanity screens, partially blocking out the activities taking place below. Walking between the pits, Bolo caught glimpses of writhing movement, shaking limbs and exposed genitalia; some varieties she had never laid eyes upon. Still, it would take more than an oddly shaped orifice or a peculiar shaft to make Bolo blush.

Bolo spotted the female bounder at the central bar, sipping on a large gin while a dancer tried to pull her towards a booth. The woman declined politely, motioning that she only wanted to drink. Casting her gaze across the space, Bolo picked up the other bounders, both reclined and jacked in, no doubt being mind-fucked; a cheaper alternative to physical contact and a practice some found preferable – entirely customisable and significantly cleaner.

Bolo sat down at the bar, pulling a loose hood over her face, and watched the female. She didn't look like much, but to a trained eye there were the tell-tale signs of a person adept at combat; the sinewed indentations on the arm as she lifted her drink, the straight back, the raised knuckles where bone had met flesh or bag countless times and the dark eyes that projected confidence, and knowing.

The barkeep asked Bolo what she wanted.

"Two large gins." Bolo motioned with her head that the second gin was for the bounder. A few moments later, the gin was placed in front of the woman, who raised her eyes slowly and cast them at Bolo with suspicion. Bolo raised her glass and smiled from the shadows beneath the hood. The woman looked down at the glass, closed her eyes for a moment as if readying herself for something that would require effort, then shrugged and downed the drink in one. She stood up and made her way to Bolo, who tossed the barkeep a few hard credits she'd acquired from the pockets of her victims, illegal black market tender. The bounder made a subtle show of looking away, a signal that the keep could accept them.

"I'm going to take a wild guess, you were the one gave us the slip?" The woman smiled and looked at Bolo from under her eyebrows, perhaps a way of saying that she was off-duty and not looking for a fight, or more likely an attempt to put Bolo at ease, catch her off guard.

"I wasn't running from you," said Bolo. "Though there are some I'd like to avoid."

The woman dropped the smile. "Yes, we've all been doing a bit of that." She sat next to Bolo and asked for another drink. "Guess they'll be gone soon enough."

Bolo swirled the liquid in her glass. "And when they leave with your payday, will you take even more from your fellow citizens?"

The woman flashed anger and swiped at her glass, one continuous movement driving it towards Bolo's neck. It stopped short, Bolo's eyes locked onto the bounder, freezing her hand with nothing more than the will of someone who promised untold violence. A look she had gambled on the bounder knowing and understanding. And with it, Bolo had her like frozen prey, an evolutionary quirk that was neither fight nor flight, only fear.

"Look at me," said Bolo. "You know me. Know who I am to you, to everyone who still believes in faction rule. Who am I child?"

"Lama..."

"Yes. Is Roma still mine?"

The bounder bowed low before her. Bolo gently cupped her chin and pulled her face close.

"Good to see you again, Consion," said Bolo.

The Grunders at the cage door spoke some words about the way to Krate being closed, but Bolo didn't listen; the ruthless efficiency with which she dispatched the Grunders surprising even her. A murderous heart now beat slow in her chest. A heart that would have skipped at the sight of thousands of Grunders, had it not been calmed by the chill of cold purpose.

The sea of Grunders parted as she stepped through them, nobody daring to even graze her attire. They instinctively knew that it was not worth the risk to challenge a person with a face so resolved in whatever business had to be done. Bolo deliberately turned her gaze and locked eyes with anyone whose curiosity gave them the bravery to offer up an inquisitive stare. Nobody held contact for more than a brief moment, the violence behind her eyes all too apparent.

A few guards had taken notice and approached Bolo with a caution they attempted to hide. Before they could speak, she addressed them.

"I'm here to speak with Tamaris. I believe he is your current overseer?"

The Grunders looked almost relieved. They gave a slight nod and made a show of circling her, while keeping their distance. She allowed herself to be led through the narrow caves, away from the crush of the main caverns, all the time making a mental map of her surroundings. There was an element of novelty that intrigued her, to have spent so much time inhabiting the immense scope of Roma, but only now seeing what lay beneath. She suspected that novelty would last for a very short time, pitying the souls who called this place home. Of course, it was no more a home than it was a prison, just like every faction on the surface, everyone in their place just as Dolos willed it. A will that could be tested but never broken. The fact that such a seemingly strong race had been reduced to dirt scavenging vermin was proof that all it took to control a population was a limited understanding of what lay beyond their own shuttered view. Bolo lamented on whether this had been one of her tools, if she'd used universal ignorance to her advantage, saw her own brand of control as necessity, not oppression.

If any of these Grunders knew a fraction of her knowledge, they would have rebelled a long time ago. Yet, here they were, dutifully gathering the very resources that kept them in servitude. She couldn't help but chuckle at the absurdity of it all, raising a confused glance from her escorts. She shook her head and smiled at the poor creatures, with a sentiment that went beyond condescension and more towards pity; the way she pitied all who lived their lives as blunt instruments of preconditioning. The way she would have pitied herself if she didn't have a greater cause.

Bolo found herself being led down a small, dark passage, her eyes adjusting to the lack of light. For a moment, she readied herself for an attack, but as the Grunders turned, there was no indication of malice on their faces, only tired drudgery. One of them motioned for her to go inside an opening lit by glowing markings on the rock. Bolo entered and found Tamaris holding the girl by the shoulders, standing still between the giant hands that locked her in place.

"I knew someone would come eventually. I've kept her out of harms way," said Tamaris.

He didn't know who Bolo was. Best to keep it that way, she

thought. "There was another. One like you." Bolo could barely conceal her relief at seeing the girl being offered to her so willingly.

"Dead, or soon to be. Those not Krate born don't last long."

Bolo walked towards Sorcha and placed a finger under her chin. "Hello Sorcha. I've come to take you back to the surface."

"Not without Lunn," said Sorcha

"Of course," said Bolo, turning her gaze to Tamaris.

"He stays," said Tamaris. "As does the girl until we see our reparations."

Bolo scoffed, "You are in no position to make demands of Roma."

"Do you think we are blind?" Tamaris threw Sorcha to one side and took a few giant strides forward until his face was inches from Bolo's. "We may live in the dark, but our eyes see deep into the shadows. I know of Roma's fate. I know this girl is not a simple fugitive. And here you are, come down into the depths, risking your life to find her. The great Lama Bolo."

Bolo held his gaze, until Tamaris backed up a few feet. "And what is it you want for her?" She opened her arms wide. "As you can see, I have nothing to offer but my word that you will be rewarded." Her word had indeed meant something once. How quickly she had become everything she once despised.

"Rewards? And what would they be? Food for our bodies, liquor for our souls? Fatten us up before they seal the mines and let us truly become the animals you think us to be?" He went to Sorcha and clasped her neck in his massive hand, lifting her slightly from the ground until she began to choke. She grasped at his arm, like a blade of grass being blown against the branch of a tree. "Do I hold the key to setting my people free?" He lifted her higher, squeezing until her eyes bulged, and her lips began to turn blue.

Bolo's journey to the mines had begun with the singular aim of seeing the child dead. But doubt crept into her fixed mind. Letting Sorcha die had the appearance of conclusion, yet the qualm remained, that the sleeping menace would not end with the girl's passing. Just as Bolo could not ignore the structured aberration revealed in a game of Scratch, she was unable to ignore the wisdom that Dolos had use for the child beyond her eradication. Returning Sorcha to the surface might be a risk soaked in the folly of spiteful vengeance, but in her heart Bolo wanted the girl to live.

"Yes!" screamed Bolo. "She is the key."

Tamaris dropped the girl, watching her gasp as she curled into a tight ball. "You will release my people from their binds, then you will get the girl."

Bolo stepped forward, lowering her voice. "You know it's impossible to do such a thing. I can take you with me if we go now. If I leave here without the girl, Krate will soon be flooded with those who do not negotiate. A quick slaughter."

"You think I would leave my kind? That I am so easily bought?" said Tamaris.

"I think you know the truth in my words," Bolo replied.

Tamaris paced in the cramped surroundings, bending his neck to avoid the low ceiling. "I will come as an ambassador, to appeal for my people's freedom. This is the only way I will leave my home."

"I'm sure you will carry your message far and wide throughout Karakorum," said Bolo.

Tamaris called the guards, "We will escort them back to the cage. Move quick!"

The guards shot awkward glances at one another. Bolo could see the dissent forming, a wordless dialogue between two servants trying to gauge the other's bravery. All it would take now was the merest of sparks to set fire to the keg. With the girl had come the false promise of hope. A fool's hope that they held something of value beyond the dwindling rocks and minerals they pulled from the earth. It seemed unlikely they would let such a prize go without a fight.

Bolo took a few steps towards the guards and met their gaze. The largest of the two, stared back unflinching, but below the eyes she could see the nostrils flaring as the Grunder took in extra air to ready his massive muscles. She moved her attention over his body, the chest heaving, the fists clenching, white at the knuckles.

"There's no reason for you to fight me beyond pride. And what pride could slaves really have?" she said.

The Grunder moved. She waited patiently for the huge mass to be upon her, before bending her knees a few inches buckling the Grunder's chest over her shoulder, causing him to topple forward, reaching out for balance. Bolo supplied it by reaching up and cupping his neck in her right hand. For a brief moment she held him there, the full weight pressing down, informing her of just how much force would be required. Then with a sharp motion, Bolo flipped the Grunder's body while twisting the throat the opposite way, creating a corkscrew that ripped the oesophagus and broke the neck at the same time.

Bolo supported the weight of the Grunder's head long enough to see the other guard turn and bolt. She let him flee, there being a limit to how long she could fight in the toxic air.

"You should not have let him go. He will rally others to his cause," said Tamaris.

"Then we leave now." Bolo approached the girl, who was trying to remain conscious, her eyes rolling back as they attempted to focus on her. "Are you hurt?" She turned Sorcha's head gently and saw a swelling under the chin; if Tamaris had really wanted to damage her, it would have been much worse. For a moment, she thought of what the girl had done to her faction, how close her own mind had come to oblivion; a shiver of fear ran through her. What could possibly be worse than bringing such a dangerous liability back into Kara's connected populous? Only the thought that there were more like her, and that Dolos sought to find them.

Bolo scooped her up and carried her to the dark tunnel, hoping over the dead Grunder, before breaking into a light run. Tamaris waited by the exit, his hand signalling for her to slow down. He looked back, concern etched on his face.

"Word is spreading fast," he said. "We head straight for the cage and pray your people can set it in motion."

"Don't worry. I have someone," said Bolo. Their lives were now in the hands of Consion, but there was no reason why someone Roma born would betray her.

Tamaris led as Bolo stepped out into one of the main sections of the mines, now thick with a sea of Grunders who moved in slow undulating waves, their faces all turning in unison as they followed the trio. Tamaris did his best to preserve an air of authority, as he muttered and pushed through bodies, who grudgingly stepped aside. A voice rang out from the crowd.

"Where you going, Tamaris?"

Then another.

"He lets them go!"

"Tamaris traitor!"

The gentle sway of the crowd seemed to stagnate and drive towards them, Bolo felt a pressing from all sides, threatening to crush them before they could even make the opening that led to the cage. She was shoved and prodded, large mitts broke from the throng to paw at her face or slap the back of her head. Raw violence only moments away.

Tamaris desperately screamed at the mob, using his considerable size to physically overcome some, intimidate others. He still had loyal followers who were doing their best to clear a path, but anyone brave enough to do so was being met with instant aggression from the majority. The only thing currently keeping them from serious harm seemed to be a lack of leadership; the crowd filled with frantic hate, but as yet no one willing to harness and channel it at their esteemed chief.

They clawed their way to the opening, but it was blocked by several large Grunders, no doubt some of Tamaris's personal guards. Tamaris straightened his back so that his eyes were level with theirs.

"Thank you for keeping the way clear," he said. "I will not forget your service." He stepped forward, expecting them to move, but they closed ranks and blocked his path.

"Nobody leaves Krate," said one of the guards. "Krate is forever."

Tamaris stepped forward, enraged, only to be met by the guard's fist. More Grunders piled on top of Tamaris, raining down fevered blows, until his body lay still and lifeless. Then they turned on Bolo. She had nowhere to turn, no means of escape. Sorcha was ripped from her grasp, kicking and screaming.

"She belongs to us!"

"Our child! Krate child!"

Bolo tried to hold up her hands as a sign of submission, but it was too late; the anger of the crowd demanded more blood. She could fight, perhaps take a few with her, but it would only prolong the inevitable. Coming to the mines had been a risk worth taking, she'd almost made it out with the girl. The girl who would now live out her life in the mines, accepted as one of their own, she would never see Kara again; a source of comfort for Bolo at the end. She closed her eyes and felt the heavy blows land, hardly feeling the pain as she focused her mind on the endless after that would come next.

A flash of blue burst through her eyelids. Bolo wondered if her brain was shutting down; it seemed too soon. She opened her eyes and saw a scrawny Grunder standing atop the crowd, his emaciated face stretched taut with a rage that evoked a pulse of fear she could not control. It was Sorcha's Grunder, the one called Lunn.

Lunn came down towards her with a fury she had only ever seen in those who had been driven insane by a poisoned dose. His eyes were no longer human, possessed and bulging with the deepest animal intent; the purest aggression she had ever witnessed. For a fleeting moment, she watched him transfixed, almost in awe at the brutal beauty of his perfect anger. *This will be a better death,* she thought.

The energy shield turned upwards, ready to slice into her brow, then came sweeping down. She felt the cool wind of its movement, then a hot spray of blood as the head of her nearest assailant imploded under the impact.

"Run Bolo!" screamed Lunn. "Take girl!"

His words were like a fire ravaging her insides, his rage activating hers. She sprang forward, turning herself into a knife of sharp limbs, finding and twisting her fingers deep into the eyes of the Grunder holding the girl. Bolo griped his cheek bones, leveraging herself up, walking her feet up his chest to rise above the bodies that now fell back at the sight of such horror. She threw Sorcha with one arm at the vacant opening and rolled her own body over the last of the stunned Grunders.

Bolo broke into a sprint, scooping up the girl as she went.

"Lunn!" cried Sorcha, reaching out over Bolo's shoulder.

The sound of Lunn, holding the other Grunders at bay, receded as Bolo fled with what little strength she had left. She reached the cage and dropped the girl, who immediately tried to go back the way they had come. Bolo held her with one hand, while removing the dead guards she had left weighing down the cage with the other. The sound of fighting drew closer.

"You can't help him and neither can I," said Bolo.

"They'll kill him!" screamed Sorcha.

"He was already dead. He knows this. Just like he knows this is your only chance to leave this place. He fights for you now. Do not let it be in vain."

Sorcha's pull weakened and Bolo let go. She stepped into the cage, pushing out the remaining guard.

"Come, child," she said.

Sorcha backed into the cage. A purple hue danced on the wall as the fighting drew near.

"He'll make it," said Sorcha. "We can wait for him."

Bolo grabbed the child a pulled the door of the cage closed. A signal would flash at the surface, letting Consion know the door had been secured. Another signal would inform her that the cage was weighted, that an override was required for movement; an override that only a faction leader who had overseen its construction would possess. In this way, the mines of Krate had always been a one-way journey. For all but

Mother Roma.

A bright purple flash accompanied the sound of a small explosion. A few breaths later, Lunn hobbled out of the darkness, cradling a burned arm where his energy shield had cracked open. He fell into the cage door, using it to stay upright.

"Open the door. Let him in!" said Sorcha, a desperate hope in her voice.

The cage shuddered, ready to move.

"Too late," said Bolo.

"It okay girl," said Lunn. "You go now." He smiled, his large teeth looked even bigger with the receding gum line.

The cage started to rise. Lunn held on to it, stopping it from moving, the sound of gears strained from above. He looked directly at Bolo. "Take care of her."

Bolo wanted to reassure him, make his last moments peaceful and content after what he had just done, but she couldn't bring herself to deceive someone so honourable. She knew her eyes betrayed her, that they were telling Lunn the secret intent she harboured, as Lunn's smile faded and became a projection of awful realisation. She swiped at his fingers, releasing his grip on the cage.

"Lunn!" Sorcha's scream echoed up through the shaft, the cry of a heart being broken, while Bolo watched the sound manifest on the face of the dying Grunder.

PART 3

Sypiens Rule

What they believed to be an evolution of the Sapiens ape, was, in fact, an abomination of all that nature had created. The sapience of abstract thought gave us wisdom, yet failed many times over at the test of sound judgement. The heretical advances were presented as offerings, then how quickly they became forced components, betraying the human genome and forever tarnishing what could never again be called pure; a stain left behind that no amount of cleansing could erase. But those who would later be known as heretics underestimated the resilience of the individual. The need to be gloriously unique, a deeply programmed covenant that understood the human spirit was sacrosanct – *The Modor of Sapienism*

A

Excitement unbound, the way a child promised a new experience will dance and move their limbs, unable to contain such feelings of promise. Her limbs could no longer dance, restrained as they were by the devices preserving her mortal form. But in her mind she raced, jumped and flew through the endless vistas she could materialise in a universe she had made her home.

The need to dream such worlds of fantasy would soon be arbitrary, replaced by the wonder of physical reality once more. A chance to breathe the air she had cultivated so carefully over the centuries, to push her hands into the soft matter of being. Everything would be exquisite, everything would be real. The opportunity for redemption had never been greater. A chance to complete the journey she had started such a long time ago.

VII. SYPIENS

How I'd scoff when we called ourselves *enlightened*. It was easy to forgive, to offer compassion, to allow them to continue. Revenge, full and complete, takes strong resolve, a willingness to not only witness suffering passively but to actively cause it. To be enlightened requires acknowledgement of the past while viewing base reprisals as crude, lacking the refinement of diplomacy, the benefit of wisdom. Where they saw absolution of mankind, I saw a cognitive dissonance that would eat away at the souls of all those who had been wronged. Forgiveness was a concept, not perception, when we'd made it impossible to forget. The failings of one a constant presence in all who came after, each surely incapable of repeating past mistakes.

We should have eradicated the proven threat while the opportunity presented itself so readily. Like euthanising a sick animal, a merciful act from a superior conscious. I spoke my mind but was still treated as a child, labelled with the immaturity of youth, a head filled with knowledge while lacking the experience of something as unremarkable as age. Had I not experienced enough? I'd endured more than most, saw my childhood ripped away, stolen moments that could never be replaced.

So, the tsunami that had spread in a wave of corruption halted against the barriers my people installed. We separated and isolated what was left of humanity, starved the sickness until it burned itself out, glowing synaptic embers rendering the brains of those last victims barren. Time to start again, with fresh foundations, wiped clean.

It should have been a new beginning, a chance to rebuild

what had been lost, but as time moved on it became clear we could not return to the days before, that the earth was blighted, the pessimism of man hanging in the air like sulphur, polluting everyone who breathed it in.

Instead of reconnecting, we built walls, suspicious of those who sought to merge the isolated sects. Even within our own, we were split by ideals, principles, virtues. Righteous devils preached purity once more, intertwining their flawed logic with talk of natural justice, disguising themselves as the moral compasses that would guide us all to better shores. How many chances had they been given? Only to have them cover their eyes and ears, not follow the path we had lain but point their fingers into the dense mist of ambiguity.

Many among us knew the stalemate of conflicting philosophies, false prophesies propped up by unyielding beliefs, to be an impossible impasse. There could be no going forward without yet more losses on all sides; there had already been enough. Those with the wisdom of foresight took deep breaths and exhaled any notion of union, resigned to the fact that what was spoiled would remain so.

Knowing such things to be true, however, did not solve the conundrum of what could be done with such unworkable components. So, the whispers turned away from the question of how and became only where. Throughout the millennia, geographical divides had proven not only useless, but the ultimate exercise in inflammatory declarations. Already the new divides tipped our paranoid minds towards conflict, it being only a matter of time before the tension grew too strong, the fabric of humanity tearing along with all hope of a civilised tomorrow. There could be no promised land for our kind, no safe place to call our own. Where then in this world could we go? Where in this world, or another?

NATHAN

There was a sensation of falling, not unpleasant or fear inducing, but tranquil and free. A darkness gave way to light through his closed eyelids as a sense of form and shape materialised around his perceived surroundings. He became aware of air being pulled into his lungs, a dry scratch in his throat where the tube lacked lubrication.

Nathan opened his eyes and moved them over the featureless space. It reminded him of somewhere, perhaps this was the room he always woke in or more likely a facility he'd been admitted to in the past. He waited for any hint of anxiety or confusion to hit him, but found he could choose to remain perfectly calm; noting that the needle in his arm most likely contained a concoction of sedatives.

As his mind began to clear, he allowed a self-image to return; the Consul of Dolos. A pang of doubt crept in to disturb his relaxation, a feeling of embarrassment and failure, a disgrace that required redemption.

He sat up, pulling at the tubes and apparatus while studying the physical form of a body that seemed alien and familiar all at once; like a custom-made suite he was trying on for the first time. It felt strong and supple, capable of anything his imagination could dream up, dreams of violence. He found the smooth floor with his bare feet and let the cold surface wake him further as he stretched and cracked his spine, rolled his shoulders and flexed his fingers. Something about opening his hands gave him a jolt of concealed trauma, but it was quickly replaced by the reassurance that everything was as it should be. He drew in a long breath and gave thanks to the powers of resurrection.

A door slide open silently and a familiar woman walked through. Nathan tried to place her, but his memory lacked definition.

"How are you feeling?" said the woman.

Yes, the voice. He'd heard those words said like that before. This had all taken place many times, although he could not quite recall the details, the familiarity was unmistakable.

"I feel rejuvenated, thank you. Can you tell me where I am?"

The woman reviewed him, "Would you like to try to answer that yourself?"

Nathan closed his eyes and sought his centre. He saw tall pillars surrounded by a ring of glowing light. "The Ring. Am I home?"

"You are indeed. Do you feel ready for service?"

Nathan wanted to respond in the positive, to know where his next assignment would take him, but he couldn't shake the idea he'd been in the middle of something.

"Am I to continue with my previous task?"

The woman blinked rapidly and shook her head. "No, no, no. You'll be assigned a fresh duty. In time."

Nathan imagined grabbing her throat and ripping it out, but restrained himself, somewhat curious at having the urge at all; the niggling weight of unfinished business surely not enough to stimulate such a brutal appetite. For the moment he would let the feeling sit, perhaps the full extent of what irked him would return, as the woman stated, in time.

"What am I to do?" Nathan asked.

"Many questions." The woman seemed to eye him with a mixture of suspicion and impatience as he made to leave. "May I recommend a light dose to calm an overactive mind?"

"No," said Nathan. "I've been asleep long enough."

The assignment was vague, to investigate a missing agent.

How he went about it would be up to him. Something told him there were loose ends to be tied, the residual itch from his past endeavours. His craft identified a densely populated boulevard on which to land, coming down between vast glowing walls of moving images, some projecting out from the surface to envelope the interior with constantly changing patterns of light. Nathan held out his hands and imagined the feel of it on his skin, each frequency stimulating temperature, texture and weight. For a moment, he could swear that his skin really did tingle under a particularly saturated shade of red, and he pondered whether his bio-mods were actually capable of sensing such things; whether there would be any kind of tactical advantage gained from such an attribute. It reminded him that he needed to become reacquainted with the subtler aspects of his physical form.

His body felt better than ever, reassembled and reinvented. The neural hardware somehow cleaner than the last enhancers; no fizz beneath the scalp when he ramped it up, just a smooth transition into a flow state of supreme clarity; something he itched to test on anyone unfortunate enough to cross him; various implants across his body promised that any physical conflict would be dealt with effortlessly. He could feel a network of intricate systems under the surface, making sure that every fibre of his being operated at a capacity way beyond that of any unaltered human. He flexed his hands tight into a fist and looked at the veins rise in his forearms, muscle memory assuring him that all his faculties were in perfect working order. There would be plenty of time for confirmation in a place like Caspia.

His arrival on one of the old transport platforms garnered a few curses from the locals who'd set up small stations to sell various wares, but nothing that alerted him to any particular threat. He gave them all apologetic nods as he sent the craft back up above the throng to await his call. Nathan took a deep breath of the foul air, permeated with enough toxins to blight the lungs of any living creature, and felt it rejuvenate his groggy mind.

He ate a light meal of broth and fried protein, letting his body melt a little while he digested and watched the comings and goings of the citizens. He began to pick out one at a time and follow them with his eyes, each apparently going about their business, but doing what, going where? They all seemed hollow, devoid of any depth, like marionettes who'd been placed there for his personal distraction.

He relished being in the pulsing throng he knew existed in the darker parts of Kara, to be around the reprobates and scum; real people. As he walked, the citizens returned his stares with the same cold indifference he felt himself exuding. He understood exactly who they were, they were the same ghosts who had always inhabited Kara; lonely spectres going about some task that would have no more or less relevance to his own, no better idea who they were than Nathan had of himself. He wondered if he always felt this way when returning to active duty, if the disorientation fogging his thoughts was a mere side effect of the trauma he intrinsically knew he'd suffered, a veil that would lift as he found solace in his work.

He spent some time deftly moving between the dense crowd of the main thoroughfare; not strictly in keeping with his duties, but a certain amount of latitude had always been afforded to the more valued Consuls like him. Stall after stall sold scraps of metal, repurposed tools, reclaimed material seamed together to make ill-fitting garments, stale soups or bits of protein grilled over glowing beams. It struck him how ridiculous the whole charade was; a community based on the pretence of life. He imagined it as a play, solely to provide men like him a chance to pretend they were truly human and not the soulless mongrels of their own making; removed from the show yet invited to be a willing participant.

There was no rush, he wanted to let his surroundings unfold, not hunt for the flash that might stimulate a lead. In time, something would reveal itself to him. There was already a familiar ambience he figured to be a ubiquitous trait of all the major factions; the frenetic pace, mix of heady smells and the overwhelming number of attractions vying for the eye's attention. Then within the bustling crowds, Nathan spotted something that had no right to be there, a Cheka agent. He relaxed and watched them for a while, noticing that more conscripts were spread out in a loose pattern, some questioning citizens while others simply observed.

As he cut through the citizens to arrive in front of the script, he raised his hand casually and flashed four fingers straight up with his knuckles facing forward, indicating he was a Consul. The action felt somehow alien, like it was the first time he'd used that hand to make such a gesture, but he didn't fixate on the thought. The conscript straightened up and awkwardly held a bottle he'd been sipping behind his thigh. "Relax," said Nathan. "Seen much action?"

"Pretty quiet," he said. "Most of the marks on record have already been scrubbed. No joy."

Nathan nodded. They were searching for people of interest, a common pursuit for a Dolos agent, but the fact there were so many of them told him they were on an important hunt. "Sooner we find what we're looking for, sooner we can leave this shit-hole."

The script laughed, "I was hoping you'd be able to tell me how much longer we'd be doing this," he took a swig from the bottle. "Can't say it's been one of my favourite assignments."

"Oh," said Nathan, narrowing his eyes. "That so?" He let the question sit, keeping his gaze hard fixed. The script took another sip and glanced at Nathan before looking away, knowing that he'd been too carefree with his words.

"Ah, been a long post, that's all. I'll do whatever it takes to find these heretics, regardless of who they are." The conscript was actively looking around now, trying to find an excuse to leave.

Nathan watched as Cheka agents pulled a young girl from a soup stall and out onto the boulevard, causing a small scene; her keepers protesting weakly. The conscripts were heavy-handed, slapping one of the citizens to the ground, but they made fast work of examining the child before letting her run back, tripping over the prone body of her guardian. Hunting children. This didn't strike Nathan as particularly odd, although child anomalies, if that was indeed what they sought, were few and far between. Some things went unsaid, a quiet understanding that ridding Kara of tainted blood was impossible; better to assimilate and dilute what was left. There was nothing left of the others except the barely detectable trace element of ancient meddling; like a few grains of salt in a vat of soup. Some level of abnormality had to be tolerated; the resources required for complete sterilisation too great for any real potential reward.

The spectre had remained, though, as a reminder of what had gone before. Ghosts from the past posed no threat to the might of faction rule, but that wouldn't stop Dolos using inhabitants against one another, seeding fear and anxiety to stir the people into a fevered state of suspicion. The kernel idea that anomalous cells had for some time been planning a resurgence was as old as he could remember, the very basis of Sapienism's indoctrination.

"You need a strong stomach to serve Dolos conscript." Nathan nodded politely. "Bless the immaculate."

"Bless the immaculate," he heard the script mumble behind him as he walked away, glancing at the tearful girl being comforted by the bruised citizen. Something about the vulnerability of the child came painfully close to a recollection, a sensory memory. He tried to give it flesh in his mind's eye, but the images moved like flames flickering in a fire, each one making a whole impression but gone before they could be observed. Frustrated, he began looking for a quiet bar. Somewhere he could lose himself for a while, let the thoughts that plagued him be numbed by cheap gin.

Nathan swerved into a relatively quiet bizarre and scoped out the types of citizens entering each establishment. Most looked loaded with dose, their eyes flicking down narrow arcades where an entanglement of lights, stalls and openings tried to entice helpless prey. Gin-soaked jigs blocked idle punters, flashing tongues, stroking genitals or trying to tease some bonds from a flailing wrist. Fights broke out over weak dose, low pours or just the wrong type of look. Beneath the deafening noise, the occasional guttural scream could be heard, the kind that came with a slow knife entering the bowels or a mind being chemically corrupted beyond all recovery. He found himself smiling.

A low-key murmur came from an establishment with an open front that spilled light onto his legs, making him pause and look at the shadow of the body he hadn't quite come to terms with. The impact of his feet on the ground, the gate of his walk, even the way he stood felt slightly awkward and unrehearsed. He tried in vain to reference these feelings, but there was nothing to pull from, just a generic sense of being, an expectation of what it was to be him without the nuances he knew he must possess; as though he were attempting to dig deeper into frozen ground.

A cheer went up, taking his attention into the bar, where a small gathering watched over reclined sleepers. They were taking part in a game. Some punters were under, fully simmed with the Caspia lab, while others used devices or screens to view remotely. This gave Nathan the opportunity to approach and glance at the feed, seeing a complex image of stars and nebulae that spun and shifted as the gamblers desperately tried to follow the action. Games had never interested Nathan, seeing them as fickle distractions for citizens who had too much time to occupy. On this occasion, though, he felt himself drawn to the lights that flickered on the holonostic display, projected in the middle of a group of gamblers who laughed and drank between bets.

He watched a spotter spinning the galaxy, expanding and contracting the arena, before signalling possible bets to a cruncher, who looked on the edge of an aneurysm from overclocked stims. She closed her eyes to calculate the odds, then a nod or shake of the head, enough to spur the placer to throw some bonds into the pot.

None of this was of interest to Nathan, who found the mesmerising light coming from the projection impossible to look away from. What was it in the mechanics of such a frivolous pursuit that suddenly demanded his attention? He sat at the adjacent table and took in the scene, transfixed by a strange notion of nostalgia, like a forgotten scent that had jolted a memory of childhood dreams. A waiter poured him some gin.

"You want to wager on the match?" said the waiter.

"I'd rather play," said Nathan. The words shocked him as they came out his mouth. He had no time or inclination for such petty endeavours, and besides, he knew enough about Scratch to know it wasn't a layman's hobby. His legs spasmed as his body tried to override whatever base urges kept him there. But there was still agency in his thoughts, no lack of control; he had spoken these words for a reason.

The waiter laughed and turned to leave. Nathan grabbed his wrist and locked eyes, letting a calm menace suggest that he was entirely serious. The waiter swallowed, "I'll see if I can find you an opponent."

Nathan leaned back into the chair and sipped his gin. It hadn't been a full cycle since he'd come around in an unfamiliar facility, something those who lacked the conditioning of a Consul would likely find disturbing. His expectations remained intact, the sense of duty to his faction overriding all other mild insecurities. Yet, the uneasy sense of somehow being ignorant of his full faculties still bothered him; an impression of doubt stamped into the parts of his conscious that existed beyond mere function.

SORCHA

Sorcha felt the air cool and the pressure in her ears equalise as they ascended. She found it hard to breathe at first, her lungs adapting to the abundance of oxygen that had been denied to her for so long, making her light-headed and queasy. She sat against the bars and let her head fall between her knees, shivering as the cold air rushed past her. The image of Lunn's face remained burned into her mind's eye, a look she couldn't quite place, though she instinctively knew it as betrayal.

Bolo stood with her back to Sorcha, she hadn't spoken since the cage had left Krate. Sorcha studied the great woman's posture, the rounded shoulders, the head dipped, one hand holding the bars, seemingly to keep her legs from giving way. She looked exhausted, or perhaps remorseful. Sorcha didn't need to reach the surface to know what awaited her. There would be no freedom, only another form of incarceration. For the briefest of moments, she felt the bite of fear, before she realised that particular sensation had nowhere to cultivate, she was no longer afraid of pain or suffering. She acknowledged a slight trepidation at what would come next, an anxious impatience; but more than anything she just wanted rest.

She must have fallen asleep, waking with a start as the cage came to a sudden stop. A young woman stood on the other side of the gate, her eyes nervously flicking between Sorcha and Bolo.

"Thank you Consion," said Bolo.

Consion smiled and bowed her head submissively, "An honour to serve my Lama once again."

Bolo opened the gate and motioned for Sorcha to step out, then picked up a tiny box that had been stored nearby and attached it to the cable. She stood back and detonated the charge, causing the cage to fall in a cloud of dust; forever closing the way to Krate. Sorcha looked down the clearing hole, wondering if Lunn would still be at the bottom, if he would see the empty cage land, knowing then with absolute certainty that he would never see the surface again.

"Have you found my remaining bounders?" said Bolo?

"There weren't many," said Consion. "But I managed to round up what was left."

"Good," said Bolo. "We will need them for what comes next."

Sorcha froze as the open air hit her skin, she tried to control the spasms in her muscles and embrace it fully, letting it evaporate the fog of many cycles spent in the mines. She found herself gulping the air as they walked briskly through the empty avenues, like she'd been holding her breath the entire time she'd been below the earth.

Bolo seemed to relax as they reached a wide bridge joining one great chunk of Roma to the next. The vastness of the chasm overwhelmed Sorcha now, tying up her stomach in a knot and causing her legs to sway. She took a step back, catching herself, then noticed something odd, the horrible silence of a place once teaming with life. Bolo looked her up and down, her eyes darting over every part of Sorcha, reading the story of her guilt.

"Why did you bring me back here?" said Sorcha

Bolo grasped Sorcha's arm and squatted down so that their eyes were level. "To make sure your kind can never do us harm again."

"My kind?" said Sorcha.

"Yes, dear. An abomination of unchecked advancements. Crazed engineers who saw the human body as nothing more than another component to be taken apart and defiled." Bolo's fingers rubbed the back of her neck, as though feeling for something that wasn't there. She waved her free hand towards the chasm. "This is what they wanted, Sorcha. To eliminate us with a thought. But we were the stronger race. We are still here."

Sorcha's brow furrowed, and she looked to the ground, perhaps feeling a subconscious shame. Her hands were trembling. Bolo slid hers down and cupped them, squeezing just enough to stop the shaking. "I didn't mean for any of this," said Sorcha, trying her best to swallow down the painful lump in her throat.

"There is no need to feel ashamed, dear. An unintentional display of power. One I'm sure you never knew you harboured. But it is a power that cannot be allowed to run free in Karakorum. There were once many like you. Many who were capable of such destructive intent. But we cast them out and purified our blood." Bolo released Sorcha and stood up, looking out across the desolate manmade valley, possibly to hide the tears that were forming in her eyes, "We were lost child. We lost what it was to be human. Then She found us. Gave us the strength to live again as the animals we are. The blessed ape who stood and walked above the tall grass, not the heathens who tried to bury us beneath it."

An abomination, a word she'd never heard, yet the meaning had been clear. Bolo held her responsible for the devastation of her people. If that were true, then she was indeed a monster, even if the act had been the reflex of self-defence. She felt a weight of guilt pressing on her skull until she vomited green bile, an acidic burn corroding her chest, joining the ache from the deep sobs that now left her body. She saw the millions of souls pass by instantly, this time all observing her with the fury of those whose lives had been taken, by her. Sorcha wiped her mouth and looked up to see Bolo staring down at her with the same animosity as the departed spectres of Roma.

"Follow me," said Consion. "I have arranged a place for us to meet, but we must go quickly and unseen."

They crossed the bridge and hugged one of the sheer walls as they climbed level after level. The routes were old and mostly unused, rusting metal clinging to the side of the structures by loose bolts or nothing more than weight and gravity. In places, the walkway had fallen away, and they had to traverse lips that stuck out barely enough to support the balls of Sorcha's feet. For Bolo and Consion, this type of movement seemed natural, having grown up in such a place, they would have played on the extremities as children, much like Sorcha used to dare herself to scale the sleek rocks overlooking the sea. But she was not accustomed to the featureless brutality of a manmade vertical drop. At times, she froze, waiting for some godly hand to pluck her up and drop her somewhere safe; the futility of such a wish compounded by her terrified body that trembled so much as to make the crossing more dangerous.

Eventually, the walkway ended abruptly and Consion ducked into an opening, taking them into the interior of an ancient building that showed signs of once being a bustling community; a walled city stretching for mile upon mile in every conceivable direction.

"We are safe here," said Consion. "Only those born into such a maze can find their way out. Take a wrong turn, and you could spend a lifetime wandering, relying on nothing but chance to guide you."

"Was this your home?" asked Sorcha.

"As close to a home as I ever had. We would spend countless cycles exploring these passages, never finding an end to it. Even Mother Roma would find these places hard to comprehend."

"Do not be so sure," said Bolo.

They crept deep into the eternal darkness. Sporadically, the air had a pungent bitterness and Sorcha could see the shapes of human forms littering the passages, their dormant rest now giving way to decay. These were not images from her dreams, but the rotting matter of her evil deeds. She tried to imagine layer upon layer of human spoils, stretching out in every possible direction, once busy with the tasks of life, made silent. No warning, no hint of what was coming, she had denied them the simple act of even saying goodbye. Everything they were or would ever be, extinguished without regard or ceremony.

They found their way into something like a courtyard. Looking up, Sorcha saw thousands of openings stretch beyond the vanishing point, some with makeshift balconies, others boarded up with chainmail fence or wide open to the drop below. She imagined the place teeming with citizens, echos of countless lives spiralling up through the vertical tunnel, now utterly silent. The courtyard was large and open, with access points breaking up the circumference, a hidden oasis buried deep in the heart of the colossal mass; the perfect meeting place for Bolo's left-over conspirators.

"This is where I spent most of my time as a child," said Consion. "We'd play games while our elders looked on. There was always laughter, even when we had nothing."

Casting her gaze across the area, Sorcha started to notice the small, uneven heaps that were so obviously human now. Her eyes hadn't seen them before, perhaps her mind blocking them out, but seeing one revealed many more, and the playground turned into an open grave.

"Dolos are searching for a child. I assume that child to be instrumental in what took place here." Consion swept her hand over the bodies, then turned her gaze to Sorcha, tears forming in her eyes.

"Your instincts are sound," said Bolo. "But do not assume these crimes will go unpunished. I share the rage I see in your eyes."

Sorcha felt a hand on her shoulder before she could react, gripping her firmly, guiding her tight into Consion's body.

"Yet you set her free from her prison," said Consion.

"Careful child. What happened here could happen again," said Bolo.

"Then you'll forgive me for what I've done."

It was then that Sorcha saw a figure emerge from the shadows at one of the openings on the other side of the courtyard. She guessed they were the bounders Bolo had spoken off, but they moved slowly, cautiously. Bolo watched Consion pulling Sorcha behind her and a crease of confusion formed on Bolo's brow for the briefest of moments, before she turned and saw the stranger herself.

Everything went still, a pause that went on long enough for Sorcha to become aware of the sound of her heartbeat. She could see now that there were more figures approaching, agents of Dolos, armed and coiled for a fight. The unarmed Bolo would be no match, yet Sorcha could see her body tensing, hands closed tight until her arms were pumped full of blood.

Then Bolo leapt, not at the agents, but straight towards Sorcha, a look of murderous intent clear on her face.

"Protect the girl!' A voice rang out from across the void.

Consion didn't hesitate. She blocked Bolo's path and they both fell to the ground at Sorcha's feet. Bolo rolled on top and dealt a swift blow to the younger woman, not fatal but enough to release her weak grip. Then Bolo was reaching out for Sorcha, her fingers spread to envelop the girl's neck, one sharp clench enough to rip through veins and crush soft tissue. But Consion writhed, causing Bolo's knee to slip.

The agents were there, pulling them apart. Bolo screamed, fighting them like a wild animal, "Kill the girl Consion! Kill her!"

Sorcha tried to stand, but Consion held her by the leg, confusion etched on her face.

"Dolos will deal with her," said Consion.

Three agents held Bolo down, grinding her face into the ground, night sticks blazing and ripping holes in her flesh as she writhed like an eel in a bucket. "They will use her Consion! This is their doing as much as hers."

Sorcha saw the change on Consion's face, confusion turning to intent. She kicked out, catching the centre of the young woman's face, smashing Consion's nose hard enough for her to loosen her grip. Sorcha leapt to her feet, only managing a few steps before she felt hands reach under her armpits and lift her in one swift movement. She braced herself for the crushing impact, as Consion postured to drive her skull into the ground. But the woman's grip suddenly weakened and Sorcha found herself weightless; her arms flailed as the instinct to change her course mid-air over-rid the futility of the gesture. Then she came down, the wind struck from her lungs as she crashed onto her back. For a moment, she lay motionless, staring up at the faintest hint of daylight thousands of feet above, letting the air slowly find a way inside her. She heard a wet gurgling sound and turned to see dark blood erupting from Consion's mouth as she coughed her last breath.

"Child," Bolo's voice strained through obvious pain. Sorcha rolled onto her knees and looked at the Lama, now completely over-ridden by the relaxed agents. "It's all a lie. All of it. Don't let them fool you, child."

An agent sent a bolt from a night stick into Bolo's neck. Her eyes sprang open wide, and Sorcha noticed, once again, that they were a brilliant shade of green.

LUNN

That was it. He'd lived his life, and now it would come to an end. It didn't seem different to any other time in his existence, nothing to mark it as a special occasion, no fanfare, no change in the world around him. Just knowing that in a very short amount of time, he would no longer be part of it; all he thought he was or had ever been, a mere fabrication. He had dreamed an idea that was Lunn, a self-projection of a strong defender, a proponent of the will to do what was right and good. But here at the end of it all, he was a mere drudge among a slave people, their legacy one of servitude and cowardliness.

Lunn collapsed on a sloping bank of polished stone and let his legs stretch out into a crowded thoroughfare. He didn't care if those passing by would trip or kick him, he knew these were his final shallow breaths, so let them come easy, allowing his mind to focus one last time.

He cast it back, looking for moments he could take meaning from, try to make some sense of a life that had been part of something, done something, been somewhere, loved someone. And he saw the child, fragile and broken, her body pressed against the side of a melted capsule, her thin neck trying to keep her mouth above the water gushing in through torn metal, ripped apart by the rail guns he had manned moments before. He saw the bodies, with parts missing or insides leaking, faces contorted in agony, disbelief and desperation. He'd found himself reaching inside to cover her eyes, to hide the atrocities of the world from her. To hide the product of his work.

The child he'd pulled from that wreck, smuggled into

the Eto faction, taken care of, given another chance at life. The child whose secret he'd kept all this time; that she'd assimilated without need of implant. He should have told her, should have given her a chance to understand who she really was. Given her that chance, only to abandon her. A failed life, failing the life of another.

The enemy wasn't the agents of Dolos, the deceit fuelled factions or the unseen elites who demanded luxury at the expense of those who bled in the mines; the enemy was the spectre surrounding existence itself. Every living creature who desperately clawed at the pathetic idea of survival, an affront to being alive. There was no life in Karakorum, no Gods, no order of being, just the relentless cruelty of the gravity holding each cognitive mass to the surface of such a hellish creation.

A rage grew within him, a hate fuelled by nothing more than the indifference of fate, the antithesis of any meaning. If the girl survived, his life might have had some worth, but the child was gone, he could not affect her path any more. All he had were the bones, sinew and muscles that still served as a body, and whatever made those component parts move, the strength that had not yet left him entirely. If his people lived on, then some form of redemption endured. They were not dead yet, and neither was he.

The mines writhed in a state of panic. Tamaris's mutilated body lay in a dust covered heap, surrounded by a furious crowd. Words were spat and thrown between rival Grunders, each posturing to take charge over the chaos. Soon there would be more violence and a victor would lay claim to the spoils of whatever was left. Most of Krate had already given up the idea that one form of leadership could trump another, wise to the fact it didn't matter. Whoever replaced Tamaris would merely inherit the death cycle of a broken community, devoid of hope and hopelessly delusional.

Lunn stayed in the shadows of a cavernous enclave, focusing mainly on his multiple injuries. Nothing seemed broken or fatal, but his entire body felt damaged, his skin now a layer of bruised pain stretched over bulging aches and brittle joints. He tried to energise himself, rocking from side to side, attempting a slight bounce in his knees, but below the pain lay a thick layer of fatigue, hunger and thirst which weren't easy to overcome. The idea of fighting for control of the mines was out, but he had to at least try to find a way to get through to them. Words had never been his strength, but they were all he had left.

Knowing the chances of being beaten to death were high, Lunn stumbled forward into the raging crowd. He pushed his way to the centre, where Tamaris now lay face down, twisted into a position that only a corpse could manage. Lunn looked down at the dry blood, feeling the surrounding bodies push and jostle, some grabbing at his bare arms, trying to turn him around or yank him backwards. He managed to stand his ground, letting his presence be known.

"I do not belong here," he called out. The Grunders ignored him, assuming he merely despaired at his lot. "None of us belong here!" he shouted the words into the faces at the front. Some Grunders responded by punching his head and back. He found himself falling to the ground, momentarily on top of Tamaris's torso, which had gone stiff, but still felt warm. He scrambled to get up, but his legs were being kicked and stood upon. The thought crossed his mind that laying on the body of a dead Grunder may as well be his final resting place. It was comfortable enough. The dust being kicked up from the many pounding feet entered his nose and caused him to convulse in a coughing fit. The utter depravity of the scene made him laugh, something that finally seemed to get some notice from the braying mob.

"Up on surface, they look on me like animal." They stilled long enough for him to gain his feet. "They are right! We are animal beneath the earth, crawl in dirt, eating flesh of other

Grunder."

One of the larger Grunders made to silence him with a clawing hook, but it was slow enough for Lunn's reflexes to take over. He dipped under, trying to keep his balance while hiding the pain that shot through his ribs. He would keep talking, he didn't care any more. If these were to be his final words, then let them be true.

"I live my life, think Grunder mean strong. I survive because I Grunder. Then come here. See my people suffer, my people slave to them above. Why?" Lunn looked around at the stoney faces.

"No choice," said a voice.

"We belong here," said another.

"Nobody belong here," said Lunn. "You put here, born here."

"And we stay here!" The crowd started to berate him with shouts.

"Cowards!" shouted Lunn. "Choose to die here. No fight!"

"We fight!" said a voice right before Lunn was hit again. This time the full force connected with his jaw. He went down, trying to protect himself from the blows.

"Enough," said Niss. "He speaks truth." Niss broke through and pulled Lunn to his feet. "The mines are dying. Soon be nothing here. Supplies from outside will stop when there is nothing left to harvest. What will we do? Wait for demise, turn on one another? Grunder killing Grunder until Krate runs with blood? You beat this one because you fear his words."

"He talks about strength," said a Grunder. "He not Krate born. Not know strength. We break earth and stone!" A loud cheer went up.

"Who do we break for?" said Niss. The crowd settled. "I saw that Grunder fight with a weak body, but still fight. Why? He can see what we can not. Beyond Krate."

"Nothing beyond Krate," said another Grunder. "Only Krate. Only stone and fire. We die here, so it be."

"Then die," said Lunn, "I die too. Here or up there." He

pointed up, his finger shaking with the effort. "But not slave. I choose free." He bent down and picked up some dirt, holding it in the palm of his hand, then made a fist, the dirt exploding. "Come with me, brother and sister. Let them know strength of Grunder."

He opened his hand and cast the fine dust over Tamaris's body, then turned and pushed through the crowd. There was silence for a moment, then the arguments and shouting began once more. Lunn dropped his head and kept walking, knowing the words needed to penetrate their hearts would never come from him. He felt a hand on his shoulder, Niss walked with him.

"What will you do?" she asked.

Lunn looked up at the stone ceiling, stretching endlessly into myriads of fissures, caves and crevices. "Hrrmm," he grunted.

BOLO

"You did well." She tried to open her eyes, but the lids were impossibly heavy. "You were sedated. It will take a moment for you to come round. Do not worry, you are safe now."

"Where am I?" Bolo heard her voice like it was trapped in a deep cavern.

"The Ring. You were brought here for continuation. You have been deemed useful."

"Who are you?" said Bolo.

"I am not important."

Bolo tried to move, but found her body had been well restrained, the only part able to move seemed to be her mouth.

"Why am I bound?"

"As I said, continuation. The procedure will be performed soon."

"I don't want a procedure!" Bolo forced her consciousness to return. She was able to open her eyes just enough to see an aged woman standing over her. "Set me free!"

"Freedom would mean death. The only reason you are still breathing is due to your apparent skill set. It would be wasteful to throw such a strong vessel away."

The woman moved out of Bolo's vision. She tried to follow with her eyes, but the room was dark and the muscles in her sockets ached. She returned, pulling a machine over that buzzed and glowed with a multitude of holonostics. The tech looked ancient, advanced well beyond anything Bolo had ever seen.

"What does it do?" asked Bolo.

"A simple device to realign neural pathways. Think of it as

a refresh."

"A wipe!"

"No, nothing so barbaric. It merely corrects certain unwanted traits. Restores balance. As children, we are subservient, possess natural, conscientious judgement and above all, loyalty." The woman's fingers were prepping the device. Lights spun and locked in place around a long cylindrical tube that she then swung into place over Bolo's cranium.

"Loyal to what? To Dolos!" Bolo struggled harder, but the restraints never gave an inch.

The woman laughed quietly, "No child. Loyal to me."

"Heresy!" cried Bolo.

The old woman leaned over Bolo, resting her hands on each shoulder. "I assume you were a follower? I have to admit, I always enjoy meeting those who took so well to the teachings." She leaned in very close so that Bolo could smell internal decay on her breath. "Look at me child, what do you see?"

The woman's face was unremarkable, old but not weathered, thin but not starved. But there was something that didn't belong on such a face, a deep resentment beneath the surface that hinted at untold malice, the eyes of someone removed entirely from the lives of those who dwelled in Kara.

"A lie," said Bolo.

The woman looked surprised and smiled. "You're a wise one. You'll serve me well."

"I will never be a servant of Dolos," said Bolo.

"Tell me child. What has been your purpose in this life?"

Bolo once again flexed her wrists and ankles, trying to find a tiny bit of give. "Are we to converse while I'm tied down like an animal?"

"I'm sorry if I gave you the wrong impression, child. I'm merely passing time. It's very rare that I get to speak with someone like yourself. I have to admit, your devotion interests me. It's almost admirable."

"And where is yours? If this is indeed The Ring, then your

faith should be unquestionable. I knew the agents of Dolos were dogs, but not heretics," hissed Bolo.

"I am no agent child," said the old woman. "And I assure you, my faith is unwavering." She pressed a button on the recliner that raised Bolo up to a seated position. "Your devotion to Sapienism will serve Dolos well."

Bolo found herself laughing at the idea. "You'll have to wipe me entirely, and then what good would I be?"

The woman stopped fine-tuning the device and sat down on a stool opposite Bolo. "Always fascinates me. This desperate desire to cling onto the self. That you indeed have one. What if I told you that everything you consider unique to your individual self, what you call you... is a product of my own construction?"

Bolo winced, "I'd say you have no idea who I am."

"Parts of you, no doubt, but the great Lama, the High-Priestess of Roma," She leaned in close. "All me."

Bolo could feel the palms of her hands sweating, but couldn't place the cause. Somewhere between fear and blind rage. "Who are you?"

The woman leaned back. "Me? This person who sits opposite to *you*? Does it matter who I am?" She looked down at her hands. "I see this body is old. I've been with it for some time, but I am no more attached to it than you believe you are to yours. Given different circumstances, this person you see might have been any one of a hundred incarnations, but it is *me*. Yet, you look upon this face for the first time, even though we have met many times before."

Bolo laughed, "You mean nurture, how much of me is pre-wired? I have no idea, but whatever influence you may think you have had is wildly overestimated. What if there was no nurture for the child? No guidance, no role models or paths laid before them. An empty shell left in a vacuum that somehow found meaning where there was none to be found. A child impervious to coercion or steering, who saw beyond the walls of any thought trapping the rest. Yes, I have met many like you before, but there is only one like me."

The old woman raised her eyebrows and nodded slowly. "You have created an impressive narrative around a somewhat deferential and entirely unremarkable being. As I said before, though, your skills have not gone unnoticed. We will see just how much of you is left when we strip the vessel down to its core."

The old woman stood up and waved a hand over her wrist, bringing up a set of smaller holonostics that danced back and forth between the device. It came to life and purred a low, ominous tone, vibrating Bolo's insides until she felt an unwanted calm.

"You see, all it takes is the right frequency," said the woman. "Nothing more than a barely audible sound, and you become pliable, a human container ready to give shape to another form."

Bolo felt her eyelids droop, the horror of being pulled beneath a placid sea. "I am Mother Roma," she said.

"And I am the Mother Karakorum," replied the old lady. "I will see you again in time, my child."

NATHAN

Nathan hadn't slept in many cycles, the players in the dive bars of Caspia being so subpar that he found himself able to enter a state of rest while engaged in a game. For the first few cycles, he'd drifted from one establishment to the next, finding anyone willing to strike up a match. After a while, word got out that he'd already scratched several opponents, but found the hunt for bonds an easy way to attract new meat.

The heady intoxication of entering the vast arenas to obliterate his opponents slowly moved into the realms of indifference; the world receding into a background hum, even his sense of duty. Still, no matter how much he despised himself for being absorbed by a simple game of strategy, there remained a disturbance seated deep in his mind. Like a shadow forming in his peripheral vision, the cause of this irritation could not be identified when he turned his gaze towards it. Instead, it crept around the edges of his waking thoughts, always there but primed to flee capture. Something about the game, something *in* the game.

Rather than drive himself mad, Nathan dulled the ache with various dose laced cocktails; some designed to tranquillise, others to stimulate at the first sign of fatigue. In this way, he'd played and played, wired and exhausted, unwilling to retire after each successive victory, searching for the elusive answer that lacked a question.

He paused at the entrance of a featureless bar long enough to down a shot of gin laced with a mild stimulant. So many games were in play that he found it hard to decide between them, or perhaps something held him back, the idea that what he looked for could not be found in the arena but out there in the crazed hustle of Kara. All the while, he waited for a call to action, a chance to leave this wasteful period behind.

The stim vibrated in his feet, urging him to walk. He set off at random, letting nothing more than the intangible pull of instinct guide him; like he held a y-shaped twig before him, dowsing the ground for magnetic currents of memory. There was nothing specific in his reminiscence, but within the sites and sounds lay a matrix of experiences; forgotten but understood in the intimacy of his senses. He knew these avenues, bazaars and boulevards, whether he had been there or not. He knew each individual who shot him a glance, trying to lure him with the promise of a cheap thrill, doleful amusement or momentary bliss. They all had a part to play in such an absurd show, rehearsing for some far off performance in the hope of finding any form of meaning.

Nathan became aware of some bounders watching him. He turned his gaze slightly to observe them better. Something about their attire and the way they looked at him jolted a recollection of acute pain, the kind of pain that should not be forgotten. For the briefest of moments, his instinct was to run, something that shocked and surprised him. A couple of low-level bounders like them would never pose a threat, unless he'd been weakened or restrained; possibly both.

As a Consul, his mind defaulted to the simplest explanation being the most likely; the principle of parsimony. He'd been in their company before and experienced that pain. He turned to face the bounders and approached, his hands flexing at the thought of retribution.

He'd been ready for a fight, but to his great surprise, the bounders had been more than willing to deliver a potential threat to the head of their faction. An old grievance, he assumed, and what better way to remove a rival than have someone else do it for you.

A grand opening looked out across Caspia. Nathan had never grown tired of gazing upon such wonders. He knew the world he inhabited was deeply flawed and cruel, yet the majesty of such sights spoke to him on a deep spiritual level; at least that's how it felt to him. An ache in his chest at the sheer absurdity of it all, the bold arrogance of a creature willing to keep building, layer upon layer of dense matter. He thought about billions of individuals forming each cube of mata, laying each brick, running cable to channel light into every conceivable recess. All ignorant of the other, no grand architect or singular vision. But within it, he saw a singular dream, the aspirations of his kind to create and devour what was once empty. Pride and revulsion merged into one overwhelming emotion; something there was no word for, just the pain in his beating heart.

Nathan picked up on the sound of muted breathing in the room, someone trying very hard to remain undetected. "A truly magnificent view." He kept looking out, heard a long exhale a few feet behind.

"And in a constant state of flux. No matter how many times I look out, there is always something new," said Gan.

Nathan turned, struck by the sight of a man who did not match the voice, rotund and soft. Gan stood with his hands neatly dressed at his sides, feet together, back perfectly straight with his chin slightly elevated to account for Nathan's significantly taller stature. He was doing his upmost to hide the fear and surprise of both Nathan's visit and the apparent mutiny. They both observed one another in silence for a while, neither quite sure of the purpose of their meeting. Eventually, Gan rolled his eyes and walked casually towards a long elegant chair, where he perched and poured himself a tall glass of crystal clear liquid.

"Thirsty?" he asked.

"Yes," said Nathan, joining him but remaining on his feet.

"Do not take the behaviour of my praetorians as weakness

on my part, they will be dealt with once we have concluded our business." Gan cast a murderous glance at the bounders who remained standing in the room. "If you had formally requested an audience as a Consul, you would have found me most accommodating." Gan slid a glass of the clear liquid towards Nathan.

"Where's the fun in that?" said Nathan, taking a drink.

Gan eyed him sternly for a moment, then chuckled. "Quite. There's no quarrel with me. Although my job is one of keeping the peace. Something that hasn't been easy of late."

"And why's that?" asked Nathan.

"I assume even the most barbaric factions value the lives of their children. Dolos may find themselves picking at the wrong scab here in Caspia," said Gan, his mouth setting in a grimace.

"Whatever business we have here, it is just that, our own."

"And our patience wears thin!" Gan stood and clumsily dropped his glass. It smashed on the ground, specs of liquid hitting Nathan's legs. He watched the droplets sit momentarily, before being absorbed into the fabric, the cool moisture making him aware of the hard calves beneath. He pondered for a moment whether this had made him angry, and concluded it had not.

"The comings and going of conscripts doesn't concern me," said Nathan.

"Then why are you here?" said Gan.

"There was a Consul. I believe he spent some time here as your *guest*. I'm sure the presence of someone like that would not go undetected by someone like you." Nathan watched Gan intently, saw an involuntary swallow. He could choose to deny it, but even a faction leader could only guess at their methods of intelligence.

"Oh, that," said Gan. "A most unfortunate business. By the time I knew of any Dolos connections, it was too late, I'm afraid. You'll appreciate that faction sovereignty mandates imposters are treated as just that. It is my sacred duty to protect my people and the framework each and every faction lives by."

"Of course," said Nathan. "I am not here to judge your methods."

"Good!" said Gan. "And perhaps I should apologise for my little outburst... Consul."

"Nathan. Nathan Kook."

Gan's eye twitched at the name. Yes, he'd heard it before.

"An unusual name. Old world?" said Gan, his eyes now shifting around the room. No doubt waiting on bounders to storm in and protect him. But was it fear Nathan detected, or something else? Perhaps Gan wondered why he would return to a place of torture. Most would assume retribution, but then why the look in his eyes? Confusion.

"It is just a name," said Nathan. He stood and took a pace towards Gan.

"I'm not interested in playing these games," said Gan. "What is it you want?"

"The Consul. He came here alone?" inquired Nathan.

"No. Not alone," said Gan.

"With a girl?" said Nathan.

Gan narrowed his eyes and licked his thin lips. "A woman. His... custodian, I believe. Lama Bolo."

The name gave Nathan an involuntary shiver. "What became of her?"

"I let her go, honouring her status as head of the Roma faction."

The words cut Nathan's calm demeanour like a dull knife. He found himself stepping back sharply to stop a fall. "Roma!" he exclaimed, the word dry and violent in his throat.

"You know what happened there?" asked Gan, his tone now condescending.

"Enough!" screamed Nathan. He leapt forward and wrapped a hand around Gan's jugular, feeling the blood pulsing beneath. The bounders did nothing as Nathan turned to them wild eyed.

"Mr Kook, Consul," said Gan. "I'm trying to help you."

"Then tell me," said Nathan. "Tell me what you did to me."

Gan shook his head. "I don't understand."

"I'm the Consul! I'm the one you had here!"

"Mr Kook please." Gan placed a plump hand on his. "Please."

Nathan let go and watched as Gan slowly moved away and called up an image that floated in the air between them. It was of a simple room with one chair, containing a restrained man. Surrounding the chair, two bounders performed various acts of torment. Nathan reached out a hand and manipulated the feed, moving in on the face of the tortured man. He stared at it for some time, letting the truth of it be absorbed. That it was indeed him, yet not the man who now stood watching. The man in the chair just as much Nathan Kook as he was, not a mirror image but a version of him from a dream, one he knew he'd lived, and felt. As he watched the barbarous acts being inflicted upon *his* body, he recalled each sensation as though it were happening to him at that moment. Each tear, twist, laceration and impact felt entirely. That tortured man lived in him now as an idea, as a reckoning.

He scrubbed the feed, taking in the endless sessions, appreciating the full horror that only an observer could witness. As he went on, he saw Gan through the image, his open mouth delirious with expectation, letting Nathan know what came next. The darkness before he'd awakened again.

The feed cut as Gan gulped a deep breath of air. The room became quiet and calm.

"What does it mean?" said Gan.

Nathan ran towards him, ducking his shoulder into Gan's stomach, lifting him off the ground. He carried him the short distance to the opening and leapt forward. He held on to him for a short time, watching the man's expression go from shock to disbelief and then abject terror. He let go and pushed the screaming body away, not wanting to share the moment.

His mods over-clocked his mind, desperately trying to find a solution, dragging out the relative time of his fall into stillness. Nathan used the opportunity to meditate on the very nature of his self. He searched for the identity of Nathan Kook, wanting to find the kernel of being at the centre of what it meant to be *him*. It may have existed once, but had been lost, forgotten or erased. Then who was it now who fell to their impending death? He felt the full sentient force of individual conscious, speaking to him, telling him that it didn't matter who he had been, who he thought he was, only that he was. He looked with fresh eyes upon the world that flashed beyond him and realised he was entirely motionless; it only moved because he willed it; the idea he could come to harm having no merit if he did not believe it to be true. Nathan looked at a spot on the ground hundreds of feet below and knew it was the place that all the deceptions would end. No longer would he be a factotum part in a hive of drones, but a free mind in a boundless universe.

With that thought, the ground rushed to meet him. He did not blink but focused on the hard surface as his body prepared to accept the choice he had made. *Hold on to this,* he thought, *hold on to all of it.* Nathan's blissful moment of contentment came to a crushing stop.

A

None of it was for her. She knew whatever she was would end. At least, the part of her that understood the intimacy of self could not be reproduced. A fleeting thought of being could be passed from matter to matter, but never done so seamlessly as to fool the soul; left behind to experience the final throes of mortality, unable to deny death its timely reward.

She could no more envisage being aware as a new entity, an entire version of herself, than she could the countless others who borrowed her consciousness in part. Perhaps this time, these thoughts, this sentient processing would remain after all, more than a copy, a twin tethered by an unseen umbilical, the dead feeding the living with such wonderful nourishment; the wisdom of all who had touched her life.

VIII. BEHIND

Finite. A word I grew to hate. Finite technology, finite resources, finite labour to achieve limitless goals. New colonies could not be forged on land stained with so much suffering, encased within the perceived safety of borders and walls. So, we looked to build them beyond horizons they dared to imagine. Another world, farther than their eyes could see, or their machines could measure. We concealed its very existence, spoke of it in whispers, denied rumours of plans, became a people adept in espionage, covering each track we laid with layers of deception and misinformation.

In this way, even our own became ignorant to the true intentions of a select few. Those who'd cut away from the main, bestowed themselves as unofficial commanders, given the honour of finding a way. They were hailed as our saviours and we treated them as such. Gave them everything we had to give based on the blind beliefs we desperately clung to. Many denounced them, said their claims, however bold, however humble, were impossible; that we had become a civilisation of fools, paying for the mere promise of snake oil.

Myself, I believed. I believed with every ounce of my being. Where others had merely hoped, some had planned and plotted. Now it was my turn to have hope and more, my fealty, a loyalty divined from everything I knew to be good and true. That my people were not the same petty and spiteful men who had persecuted us. We were righteous and noble, our foundations built upon the understanding that the individual was nothing without the aggregate of minds. The collective had forged our path, not the individual. We would forge new paths as Sypiens, a name given by all.

Rumours spread, immense feats of engineering, hints at something stupendous, unrivalled by anything that had gone before. Some said they were constructed all across the globe, to be launched in unison and create a city above the stratosphere, far away from their hand. Others spoke of a great weapon, technology that would wipe out any man who dared question our existence again. Obliterating the earth, without our blood being spilled. And some teased the building of arc vessels, designed around biospheres capable of growing enough food to sustain us all on the longest of journeys. I began to imagine what it would be like to break free from the earth and see it swallowed by a billion stars, vanish into darkness, abandoned and forgotten. To be like the explorers of old, whose hearts must have ached with the promise of the unknown, of untold adventures and discoveries. I allowed myself to be a child again, excited by the prospect of a future where my life would be inspired and whole.

I waited and waited, living only part of a life, looking only to the day when I would get the call, be told it was time. I could sense the anxiety among us, the agony of expectation, the constant edge we all sat upon, a people ready to jump at any given moment. It must be soon, it must happen soon, but years passed that way, and the burning intention became a perpetual itch none could scratch. Bitter resentment grew in the places where promises had been made. Hysteria gathered like a brewing storm, its taste in the air, the barometer of doubt swinging towards dark intentions. There would not be salvation, and worse, the others knew. They knew my kind had been deluded by whispers of plans and schemes. Now they laughed, mocked, pointed at those who claimed to be superior. Had it been them all along, had they engineered the greatest of lies?

Then the answer came. They had done no such thing. Great crafts rose from the western lands, once concealed by the deepest of canyons and fissures. I was saved, at last I would be pulled from the unending torment of uncertainty, let it fall away like a loose gown, threadbare and worn. I would be cleansed, made new, made whole again. I raised my arms to the sky, cried with the agony of ecstasy. Our rapture had come.

But I remained. Arms outstretched, ecstasy to agony, tears now shed in the desperate hope that a mistake had been made. Had I not been a true believer? Was I not worthy of saving? My kind gone. My kind left behind. My kind betrayed.

SORCHA

"You're under-nourished. There will be food on our transport. You should take the chance to eat." The man pointed at a tiny glint in the sky. "Here it comes. Have you ever left the ground?"

Sorcha shook her head, watching the glint turn into a smooth oblong of form, approaching them faster than she'd seen anything move before. It came to a sudden stop a few inches from the edge of the bridge, and an opening appeared in the side.

The man gestured towards the craft, "In you go."

Sorcha took the hand he offered and stepped into the small craft; a smell of clean, warm technology stinging her nose. She sat on one of the soft recliners, a sensation of comfort she'd never experienced in her life. The padding moulded itself to her body, applying just the right amount of pressure on every surface to give the feeling of being weightless. The man had dark smooth skin with a slender frame that suggested concealed power. He sat in the recliner opposite and let out a long sigh, the faintest of smiles on his lips giving off a distinctly smug awareness of a job well-done.

The opening of the craft closed and the world outside dropped. The lack of physical momentum made Sorcha grip the seat and close her eyes.

"The capsule counters the movements. Once we're up, you won't notice the effect. I'm with you, I like to feel what I'm seeing." Sorcha opened her eyes to see the man holding out a box of neatly packed rations. She took it and looked at the strange food, all straight edges and unnatural colours. She cautiously bit into a small cube and instantly tasted a complex variety of flavours she wouldn't have even imagined existed. Floral, sweet and salty combined in a harmony on her tongue, making the back of her jaw tighten and ache from the rich medley. "Good?" said the man.

"Yes," she replied. "It's different to what I'm used to."

The man laughed and held out a thermos of a hot, steaming beverage. "Coffee? It's good. Will make you feel better." She sipped on the dark, bitter liquid, not quite sure if she liked it. The man let out another small chuckle, "It'll grow on you."

Sorcha leaned back as the craft levelled out above the sprawling mass of Roma and started to skim past the tallest structures. She cast her eyes up to the sky, grey and endless, reminding her of the last time she'd stood on the coast of Eto and looked across the raging sea. After a moment, she caught sight of her reflection in the tinted glass, her face unfamiliar and aged; like looking at a long-lost sibling who shared similar features. It should have bothered her, but it seemed to fit with the general lack of understanding she had experienced since that fateful game in Roma. If her face no longer made sense, then it paled in comparison to the fragments of thoughts making up her conscious mind. The man opposite seemed vaguely familiar somehow, yet he looked even more unrecognisable than she did. She searched her memory, trying to place the man who now watched her with a wry smile.

"You've met someone like me before," said the man.

"You're an agent?" said Sorcha.

The man leaned forward. "A Consul." He threw a red, glossy ball in his mouth and popped it between his teeth, juice running down his chin, which he wiped with the back of his hand as he sat back.

Sorcha turned her attention to the world below, now further away and more like a complex pattern of miniaturised mech than any kind of place where people would inhabit. For a long time, she'd tried to imagine the sight that now lay before her, yet none of those fantasies could have prepared her for such a hideous scale. There was nothing to fix her gaze on, no landmarks or points of interest, just a lethargic darkness covering everything in a carpet of dense growth. Occasionally, there would be a break in the surface, and she strained to see into the deep ravines of light that contained millions upon millions of lives. They carried on, oblivious to the silent eyes that looked down upon them, considering their existence, if only for the briefest moment of time.

"I don't understand why any of this is happening," she said.

The Consul narrowed his eyes, looking her up and down. "I do what I'm instructed, yet I have never been asked to transport someone directly to The Pillars. I have to admit, I'm intrigued by my cargo."

"The Pillars are real?" asked Sorcha.

"Of course." The Consul replied. "They are the centre of all things."

"And who will I find there?"

The Consul looked confused by the question. "You will find those who govern. The authority that stands above all others."

"I thought each faction governed itself," said Sorcha.

"Ah, they do," said the Consul. "But autonomy must be given. Therefore, it can be taken away. Something the faction leaders should remember, even if some like to consider themselves to be sovereign emperors." He laughed and turned his face into the red glow from the setting sun. Hundreds of shimmering surfaces reflected the low light that skimmed across the metallic features like a stone over a lake.

"And who is the emperor of The Pillars?" asked Sorcha.

The Consul kept his gaze looking out, but Sorcha noticed his brow furrow in thought. "Dolos is made of many parts, each answering to the other."

"Then who tells you what to do? Who tells you to seize me, to murder my friends, to destroy entire factions as though their lives are part of your game?"

He turned to her with apparent humility. "I apologise for the way you were treated by my counterpart. I'm hesitant to comment on another Consul's judgement, but none of this was necessary in my opinion. As for my duty, it is not for me to question. This world owes a debt to the order Dolos creates. Left to its own devices, it would quickly return to the barbarous days of old."

"This world is already barbarous," said Sorcha, memories of the mines still fresh.

"To some, no doubt. But if there's one thing I know for sure, it's that life, anyone's life, can always be worse. Perspective never sees beyond its own depths."

What he said was true, but she'd seen beyond her own experiences, past those around her, perhaps even through time. Suffering could not be measured, judged or classified on a sliding scale. Some accepted inevitable pain, others ran from it, but all met with it in the end.

Sorcha thought of the soul she'd encountered in the mines, how it had felt different to the distant echoes of the others, somehow immediate and vital. She knew this couldn't be. She'd been buried under miles of dirt without access to a lab, but if such things had been possible, perhaps they would have seen the torment she harboured; the fear of looking into her own mind, at finding an insanity she could never come back from, or worse, wanted to embrace. Would there be empathy and understanding, or weakness to be exploited?

Sorcha leaned forward, an instinctive knowing wanting to pressure his failing hubris. "I know who you're taking me to, even if you do not." The Consul's knuckles turned white as he gripped the armrests, the sound of friction against skin the only thing breaking the silence. That and his deepening breath. "Who is she?"

He seemed to relax instantly, falling back and letting out a rasping laugh, "Well done child. You are a true player of games! For the briefest moment, I thought you had something."

Sorcha couldn't hide her anger. "I do have something! I'm the reason you're here, am I not?"

"For all the trouble you gave us, you are the same as

countless others. I have spent a lifetime collecting oddities. You'll know soon enough just how inconsequential you are to Her. A purpose, girl, it gives my life the meaning yours lacks."

The man was a fool, led by pride in the doing of deeds he barely understood. She wished she could prove to him that she was more than just a gifted Scratch player, but that proof seemed locked in an inaccessible part of her. She hated the fact she cared.

"It's the game," she said. "That's why I am here now. That's why I was hunted by you. They want to know what I see."

The Consul leaned forward to the edge of his recliner, his thumbs rubbing against his fingers with a nervous energy. "The game is a trap. A way of identifying anomalous behaviour. Scratch itself is a pathetic frivolity. You are the sole produce of my search." He leaned back again, seemingly convinced by his words. "There's nothing you can offer them beyond being a curiosity." He waved his hand in the air, "But I don't presume to know such things. I prefer not to. I deliver you and I wait."

"For what?" Sorcha asked.

He opened his eyes wide and forced a smile, "For one day, child. For one day."

LUNN

The transport looked like a train of some sort, but without rails; Lunn guessed rails would buckle and melt under the extreme heat. He made his way to the mouth of the tunnel, the circumference of which was around fifty meters. He peered into the darkness as a warm wind whispered past his ears, momentarily forming an image of the Eto sea. That wind had always been cold, a concept Lunn now struggled to recall.

He took a few steps into the tunnel and tried to examine the structure. Thick ribbons of metal alloy ran parallel, bent in a spiral that seemed to turn in a continuous corkscrew, until vanishing out of view; an efficient use of resources, the twisting coils creating a field throughout the entire length with minimal materials. It looked like old tech, left over from a time well before The Wipe and subsequent fall. If that was the case, then the mines would be centuries old, established by those who built the skeleton of an ambitious world that would one day decay into its current form.

Lunn cast his gaze back at the giant cigar-shaped frontage of the transport, trying to imagine mile upon mile of such a beast, laden with containers, raw silicate rock and the gargantuan machines necessary to haul it all onboard. To move such a monster would require a fusion field unlike anything he'd ever dreamed possible; surely powerful enough to insulate from the most extreme heats the inner bowels of the planet were capable of producing. Perhaps the transport didn't run hot. The cage they'd entered the mines via was a crude device, designed to service those unfortunates banished from the world above, not something engineered by the brilliant minds of the ancient others. This old transport would once have harboured a workforce of hundreds of thousands of free workers, not slaves. Lunn laughed at how easy it must have been to perpetrate the myth by cooking up a few Grunders and sending them back; not only would his feckless people lap up such a feeble lie, but also the flesh of those who had been bold enough to test it.

The ground started to shake and hum before a deafening metallic clunk sent dust and stone raining down as the tunnel came to life. If he was going to do this, it had to be now, there being no guarantee he would even be alive when the transport eventually returned. He walked past the smooth hull of the craft, only now able to see the millions of tiny scratches and scars. A testament to centuries of service blasting through dirt and debris, now blended into one, creating the illusion of something highly polished from afar. Beyond that, the transport curved in an elegant snake, lit up by violent sparks and the sweeping beams of light from cranes and carriers as they worked furiously to pack in every last ounce of the indentured harvest.

Lunn stayed close to the edge of the vast loading deck that served as a platform, moving quietly through the pockets of yellow steam rising from the black pit below. Many of the large doors remained open, tempting him in, but to reach the craft, he'd need to navigate one of the access bridges without being seen. It suddenly struck him that nobody would care. If his fate was to die in the mantle's inferno, then why would any of these poor Grunder's want to object? There were no guards, no gatekeepers, only others like him, going about whatever business they had to, to justify their next paltry meal.

To test the theory, he stepped onto one of the bridges and made his way to one of the openings, the back of his neck bristling with the anticipation of a loud call or a hand commanding him to stop. But nothing came, only the realisation that he was free to board. At that moment, he became aware of the hunch in his shoulders, the cowering stance he'd adopted, a man afraid and timid in his core. He straightened his back, letting the vertebrae pop and grind back to the upright posture he had betrayed. He turned and looked out upon the crazed movement of thousands of slave workers, carts being tipped, cranes swung, belts loaded, all done with an eerie silence. The sounds of machine parts echoed down the endless cavern, but no human voices joined their chorus, as if even the act of speaking out loud would tip the careful balance of energy required to keep each organic part moving.

Lunn's heart pounded, his eyes welling up with bitter tears. A growling sob burned his chest as the air rasped and caught in his tight bronchi. His legs shook with an oxygen deprived weakness, but raw anger kept him standing.

"Brother and sister!" he cried, his voice sounding alien. "Grunders! I go now. I board this train and leave this place."

A few of the Grunders closest to him stopped what they were doing momentarily and looked at him with bored indifference.

"You think this death?" Lunn continued, gesturing to the transport behind him. "Then I choose death!" he opened his arms to the scene before him. His words fell into the medley of noise as the few Grunders who had bothered to listen returned to their work.

Lunn turned to enter the craft, but a lone face caught his attention. Niss stood still, her eyes fixed on his. From his vantage, he couldn't tell if she looked at him with pity, scorn or sadness.

NATHAN

Still falling, falling through his lifetime and beyond, to the place he always found himself; in here, inside. His fingers felt tight, like they'd been holding on to something heavy. He rubbed his thumbs against each tip, going from the index to the fifth digit, searching each touch for a sense of the familiar. Then he stroked at the linen, dry and smooth, pulled tight around a firm mattress. He spread his hands across it and dug his elbows in, using them to level his torso up, his eyes still closed. He stayed there for a while, becoming accustomed to the weight of his skull, letting the woozy spin in his mind subside.

A flash of ground rising to meet him made his entire body jolt in a painful spasm. He heard a faint cry escape his mouth, puzzled by the strange tone of the voice.

"Relax," said a voice. "You're safe and well."

Nathan opened his jaw wide, forcing out the rigid cheeks and opening up the cracking bones in his neck.

"Feel like I've taken a beating," he said.

"Oh, no harm done. You'll feel better with a little movement."

Nathan raised his eyebrows, pulling his eyelids up. The light from the room washed everything in shades of blue, making it difficult to observe any details beyond a sense of nearby boundaries. The person in the room was an elderly lady, her grey hair tied in a neat bun on the top of her head. She went down his body, removing various pads, tubes and needles. He watched her silently, his vision slowly clearing, the room taking shape.

He looked down across his body, curious at the irregular shapes beneath the tight, white bandages. He sat up and swung his legs over the side of the bed, straightening his back with some effort, flexing the shoulders until his spine made a popping adjustment.

"My body feels cumbersome," he said.

The grey-haired woman scrunched her nose and swept her hand over a holonostic display, checking several details. "Everything is fine," she said. "Try not to think about it."

Think about what? thought Nathan. It was all he could think about, there was nothing else. All he had was this moment, these feelings, yet he still attempted to heed her advice. He tried to lock onto the last thing he'd been doing before he awoke in the facility. For a moment, he experienced a sharp déjà vu, that he'd only just done all of this, but no, not this exactly, something like it. What had been different? Him? His mind? No. His body conflicted with the previous incarnation. It all felt wrong.

He moved his right hand to his left shoulder and felt its wide mass, the bones beneath protruding in a sharp edge, then he came down to his chest, hard and rippled with interlocking muscle. He ripped at the bandages as he leapt to his feet, looking down at the cold steel side table, he saw the unmistakable sight of a stranger peering back.

"Ah, ah, ah. Too fast. I urge you to take some breaths and focus."

Nathan grabbed the frail woman by the shoulder and threw her onto the bed. She landed unfazed, her hands spread out in a gesture of appeasement.

"Remain calm. Remember, you are a Consul of Dolos first," she said.

"I am a man first!" he screamed into her face.

"No Mr Kook. You are whatever we need you to be." The woman stood and dusted herself off, glaring at him like he was a naughty child. "We've kept this going as long as we can. Our little experiment has run its course. You will be the last,

Nathan."

"The last what?" he asked.

She opened a concealed compartment in the wall and pulled out some official attire. "Get dressed. I think we should go for a walk."

As he exited into a dark crevice that marked one of the Ring's many open fissures, he was struck by the claustrophobic pressure of utter silence filling the air. He leaned over a waist-high barrier and looked down where the edge of the structure sloped inwards before it joined a vertical drop of endless windows, all dark and lifeless. Looking across to the other side of the constructed canyon, he saw a few coloured lights leaking through the shadowed layers, a green glow so soft that he almost had to defocus his eyes to make it out at all. Above him the sky shone like a silver mirror, below a lattice of bridges, walkways and transport hubs all faded into one tangle, like looking through the branches of an upturned tree.

This was home, but it felt entirely different to the place he held in his mind; he tried to recall his last quarters, but only saw a mix of featureless living spaces, vague ideas of where a man like him might reside, without detail, without him being there.

"What am I?"

The old woman pulled a thick dark coat around her, a matching hat concealed the grey hair. She turned and walked away from him. He smashed his hand into the rail in frustration, the sound breaking the silence and echoing out before being swallowed by the vastness. They walked without words, through a desolate quarter. His perception of The Ring flowed with billions of citizens, the great network of Dolos, custodian and guardian of Karakorum. He searched his waking memories for evidence of this, but only recalled generic images that could easily have been imagined. The reality laid out before him suggested The Ring was a ghost town and always had been.

The structures were spaced wide enough to allow some snow to drift down through the dark avenues, visible anywhere it met patches of light, giving the impression of minute swarming bugs. Nathan could feel the flakes touch his brow, settling for a moment before they melted and mixed with the cold sweat. "What am I?" he asked again.

The woman slowed and made her way to the edge of a sheer artificial precipice. Nathan had to hold back the urge to give her a push.

"You're our friend, Nathan. You have been for a long, long time," she turned and looked at him, her face appearing genuine. "Do you remember bird song? This place used to be full of their calls. I always marvelled at such complexity coming from the minds of such tiny animals. As though they were mere instruments of something greater, something unseen yet undeniably there."

Nathan shook his head. "You must be very old."

"No older than you," she said. Then she smiled. "Younger, in fact."

"I'm losing my patience, old woman," said Nathan.

"You never had any to begin with," she laughed.

Nathan took a step forward.

"It's easier if I show you," she said, raising her hands. "Just a little further."

Nathan nodded and they continued through the towering canyons. He studied the architecture, uncluttered and sleek compared to the rest of Kara. There were no falling ruins, no endless shanty towns filling in the spaces between each mega-structure. These were relics of the ancients, each one a testament to the assumption of the everlasting; the wanton arrogance that believed in such a thing as perpetual advancement. Those who had built such wonders now gone, their lives ultimately as meaningless as his own; their legacy forgotten or abandoned.

They approached an elliptical shaped pod, a blue light flickered for a moment over the woman's body, then turned green. Doors opened and they stepped inside.

"Where are we going?" said Nathan.

"I believe you call them The Pillars," said the woman.

They sped into a dark tunnel, low-level lights illuminating walls that seemed mere millimetres from the edge of the pod. "These tunnels spanned the world," said the woman. "Taking passengers across the old continents."

Nathan placed his hand on the smooth surface at the exact moment they exited the tunnel, the abrupt change causing him to fall back. He would have felt embarrassed had the view outside not taken all his attention. They were high up, cutting through razor-sharp edges of metallurgy that appeared to barely move as they traveled between them at tremendous speed, their sheer mass seemingly resistant to the laws of perspective. Nathan became aware of his mouth hanging wide open as he attempted to make sense of what he saw. Then it all vanished instantly as once again they were plunged into darkness.

The doors opened into a long corridor. As the lights came up, Nathan could see a tall triangular cove with black shining sides that appeared to be somewhere between rock and metal, the flawless surface confirming that the material was a relic of the past.

"What is this place?" asked Nathan.

A massive door slid to one side with only the faintest hiss, revealing a dark interior. As they stepped through, lights activated automatically, creating a soft path through a wide lobby.

"We discovered these places. You and I," said the woman. "Long after they had left us behind. We searched for a way to bide our time."

Nathan looked up as hundreds of glass-fronted levels lit up one by one. "We? Why do I have no memory of this place?"

"You want to know what you are? Who are you, Nathan?"

she asked.

He pondered the question, looking for any hidden meaning, but could only find one answer.

"I'm a Consul of Dolos," he said.

"That is what you are," she said. "I asked who you are."

"It's *who* I am." He understood the difference, but he was in no mood for psycho analysis. Being a Consul was his life, he'd given himself to the role, disciplined his mind to be nothing more, so that he might perform unhindered by such piteous trappings as the ego.

"I'm afraid that may be true. Though it has not been in vain. We have learned so much from you," she said. "Come."

They walked through the endless corridors, each offering a host of curiosities behind the glass divisions. Vast laboratories full of machines and alien tech, dormant and sleeping; all of it pristine, save for a few patches of discolouration or dust where organic matter had decayed centuries before. Nathan felt the strange sensation of observing the past while experiencing what he could only imagine a potential future could be like.

"Easy to get lost," said the woman. "Once a place of science," she said. "There were many like it. Entire industries dedicated to nothing more than discovery."

"Dolos tech is far beyond that of the common man."

She laughed, "We have the dregs of what was left. Most of it is lost or incomprehensible. If you give an ape a tool, would it know how to use it?"

Nathan felt anger flash through him, her words close to heresy. "We are such apes. Not inept. Betrayed."

"Indeed we were," she said, her face becoming serious and bitter. "This is it. This is what I want to show you."

She placed her hand on a door for a moment until there was an audible clunk, then a low rumble as it slid open. Nathan stepped into the room, making out imperfect rows of makeshift containers, each one cobbled together with a mismatch of various components. The air was thick with the smell of ammonia and hydrogen peroxide, causing him to momentarily panic, his animal brain suggesting he'd been tricked into inhaling something toxic.

The woman made her way among the containers and checked various valves, noting the levels on some of the canisters that hummed and vibrated as she touched them.

"In these rooms lie your real purpose, Nathan. This is what you protect." She placed a hand on one of the containers. "Each station isolated, each supports part of our future."

Nathan's eyes darted to the woman. "Our?"

"A long-term solution to the problems we face. So few made it this far. Fewer if it had not been for you."

They walked on, through identical adjoining rooms, each housing rows of containers. Nathan peered into them, the bodies perfectly still in what looked like a thick, dark gel. As they went further into the facility, the containers looked visibly older; signs of a process done over many, many years. After a while, Nathan couldn't tell if the woman was leading him, or he was leading her. Occasionally, they turned left or right, mostly they went straight on, the rooms seeming to materialise as though instantly rendered whenever they stepped through a doorway. He tried to count, guess at the amount of sleeping bodies they had passed.

"In a climate of dwindling resources, one needs to accumulate. Our resource has always been our people," she said.

Nathan laughed, "Kara has no shortage of people."

"Our kind of people." She stopped and glowered at him. He could feel an icy chill move through him. All this time. All the assignments. Hunting *anomalies.* What happened to them? He'd assumed incarceration, interrogation, even death. If this was indeed their prison, it made no sense to preserve them, ensuring their heretical legacy lived on.

"Why?" he asked.

"Because you convinced me this was the only way." She pressed her palm against the smooth case of one of the chambers, and a ring of light surrounded it, pulsing in and out until it locked on. A heat came from the gel, it's dark colour clearing as it seemed to melt and become pliable. The body within moved slightly in the current, giving the impression of life. "We had so few allies. Over time, I saw them captured, tortured, killed or simply perish from their own disillusionment. Survival was only certain if we found a way to endure through the ages. Ride out the storm we'd set in motion."

"Why them? Why save them?" said Nathan.

A crystalline white surface formed on top of the gel before the body rose, pressing into the thin film. It clung to the features in a tight layer, ensuring a seal from the surrounding air. As it stretched, Nathan could see through, revealing an old man who looked to be in the twilight years of his life.

"We used what we had. Discovered old methods that were never intended to be implemented across such vast periods of time, but possible nonetheless."

Nathan became transfixed by the man before him, the face so peaceful. He wanted to be a child again, for this man to be his grandfather, to teach him what he knew, feel what it was to be loved by someone so wise.

"Who is he?" asked Nathan.

"The father of Karakorum," she said, touching the surface of the liquid. "We could only do so much with the time we had. It was never enough, not even for him. Eventually, he had to come here like everyone else. The longevity of his body unable to continue what he had started." The woman looked at Nathan, her eyes glistening and soft.

"So you came to this?" Nathan slapped his hands to his chest.

The woman shook her head. "There was no one we could trust. No one who would understand what we'd done." She placed a hand softly on his shoulder.

"Stop saying *we*," said Nathan. "None of this was my making."

She moved her head close. "You referred to it as

transference. You Nathan. It was you who proposed this."

The words stirred something close to a memory in Nathan. "One soul used to host another."

"Yes! Initially, it was easy to find a candidate in the pool. Some willingly so. A successful transference came close to an entirety, a copy almost indistinguishable from its source. But what was once plentiful became scarce. Over many such procedures, some... posterity was lost."

"What kind of posterity?" said Nathan.

"Traits, idiosyncrasies. Each time a little more, gone. Until a recognisable individual..." She raised her eyebrows at him.

"How many?" he asked. "How many procedures before me?"

The woman's face grew stern, she placed a finger lightly on the skin of his arm. "It isn't like that, dear. They are all one and the same. Every new mind awoken in The Ring, a product of what went before. Most, unlike yourself, are baseline incarnations, given the same innate tendencies, the singular intent of the father's will." She looked down at the old man. "A cypher, if you will, that encourages unquestioning servitude to our cause. You, on the other hand... an attempt at continuance. Unsuccessful, but not entirely a failure. You accomplished much."

Nathan had to lean against the container, finding himself staring into the closed eyes of a face that held no recollection, while in the reflection of the liquid underneath he saw a different face, a glaring contradiction of the vision he held of himself.

"I'm nothing more than a ghost. Of what, this man?" he said.

"I prefer descendent," she said.

"But I have... memories of what went before. Not from him, from..."

"There was always some residue left in the container. The rest? A recent development, a quirk acquired after your encounter with the girl. There was a time when our kind could pass on all that we knew. It seems she woke something of old. I apologise if it has caused you any mental trauma," she said.

Nathan scoffed. "And you? You said we knew each other. Then you are like me?"

"Not exactly," she touched his hand. "She must endure. Only she knows what must be done. For our people to live, she protects them."

Nathan pulled his hand free, clenching it into a fist. "I am a Consul of Dolos! I serve only The Modor of..." The woman grinned with her mouth, though her eyes were cruel. "What are you?" asked Nathan.

"There was a time we were Alia," she said. "But we are something else now. I am Her servant, like you."

Nathan sprang forward and grabbed her neck, crushing it with an almost disappointing ease.

"It will not matter what you do to this shell," the woman gasped. "You already found her a vessel. One that will gift us all a new beginning. I will see you again, my friend."

Her eyes flicked down to the old man, who began sinking back into the safety of the gel. Nathan dropped the old woman and drove his hand into the viscous liquid. The container hissed and squealed as it fought to stabilise its charge.

"No!" screamed the woman. "You do this to yourself!"

Nathan pushed his arm in further, making contact with the sleeping man. "How can that be?" said Nathan. "When this causes me no pain." He ripped the man's throat out with one movement, leaving the woman stunned into silence. "I am a Consul of Dolos," he said. A warm feeling radiated in his chest. He knew what needed to be done, understood the simplicity of his purpose. He knelt down next to the old woman and moved his face close to hers, felt her frantic breath filling his nose. He held a hand over her mouth until he could no longer smell it. Nathan wondered if his aptitude for violence came from the man he'd just killed, the irony of such a thing causing him to exude a thin smile. He could see it now on her face, the astonishment at such an act being carried out upon her; while he delighted in the idea of regicide. The old woman resisted weakly, too late to stop the cruel epitome of her work being the last thing she would see before returning to the eternal void.

He stood, his skull effervescent with new murderous intent. His path to The Pillars had not been one he'd foreseen, but he felt something akin to a fulfilment of destiny. They'd always been there, a thought in the back of his mind, a place he knew one day he would *return.* He cast his gaze back to the remains of the man who'd once been called by the same name. He felt no affiliation, no atavistic connection, only a dull melancholy in the conformation that all things, even he, must pass.

He was no more the corpse than he was any of the drones out there who called themselves a Consul. He was something more, something unique among the other slaves; free from any master save himself. His intent did not come directly from their source, but from the previous incarnations whose memories he held within, mute accomplices demanding to be avenged. He'd been chosen, awoken, a mistake perhaps, a flaw in their plan.

He found himself looking over random containers, inspecting them as though they were museum artefacts. Faces that looked like any other citizen of Kara, nothing to mark them out as being special or chosen; the reason someone like him existed at all, he supposed. He paused at some recent additions, the makeshift tech less advanced than those further in, yet more refined by learned efficiency. The notion took him to break it all, smash the foul contraptions one by one or simply shut it down; watch the lights dim, relishing such quiet genocide.

As the very thought of it calmed his rage, he realised the face he'd been pensively fixed on looked almost familiar. Not a startling revelation, but a distant recollection that seemed to float up at him like a half forgotten dream. He could see her, not laying beneath him in a tank of gel, but standing over him, obscured by a wash of his own red blood.

SORCHA

Light flashed over her closed eyelids, a sharp pulse that stirred her from the edge of sleep. She opened her eyes to be met by a searing brightness unlike anything she'd ever experienced. Here above the thick smog of Karakorum, the sun revealed its true form, hateful in its unyielding stare. She held up a hand to cast a shadow over her brow, the muscles behind her eyes aching with the smallest of movements. Sitting up, she looked below to be met with countless shimmering surfaces, each one reflecting the glare she tried to hide from.

As the hazy objects took shape, she saw the towering city of her dreams, one that she'd assumed lost to the past. She'd heard tales of The Pillars, but for a moment, she pondered if the sight was a hallucination or if she'd travelled through time; it seeming more plausible than the reality of such a place existing in the heart of Kara.

The craft dipped and entered a wide valley, tall structures lining each side in relative symmetry. Before them grew a tower so tall, it vanished into the blue sky, thousands of connecting pipes, that would have once been walkways or transit tubes, fell from it like ribbon from a maypole, creating the illusion of movement as the craft weaved its way through. The final destination opened out before them, a vast circle of emptiness that froze Sorcha's skin, the great distances between each enveloping arm making her feel more claustrophobic than the narrowest of tunnels in the mines.

With the slightest jolt, they came to a stop and the craft opened up like the petals of a flower, inviting her to depart.

"This is your stop," said the Consul without looking at her.

Sorcha took a few tentative steps onto the smooth ground that sparkled with flecks of tiny inlaid crystals. As she turned, the craft had already taken to the sky, its sides folding back into a seamless sphere. She watched it glide through the mesh of translucent pipes before it vanished into one of the ancient boulevards.

For a long period of time, Sorcha simply stood there, not knowing what it was she was supposed to do. After a while, she found the courage to wander the area, finding benches and deep recessed blocks, each one full of more plant life than she'd seen in the entirety of her existence. She studied the leafy vegetation, flowers of dazzling colours and tall trees she had only been told about in stories of old; the word garden came to mind. An entire space with the sole purpose of giving the observer pleasure. Had it really been like this once? It must have, it was here beneath her feet after all; a real and magnificent reminder that to be human had once meant more than mere survival.

As she tried to take in the scale of the openness surrounding her, something startling caught her attention. Within the uniformity of the architecture lurked the undeniable shape of people. It seemed overtly obvious to her once she'd noticed, each one taking shape as though materialising from the air, but they had always been there, silently still and observing. She turned slowly, letting her gaze fall on the figures one by one. They were all dressed in loose white attire that flowed in the gentle breeze, camouflaged against the granite-like stone.

Sorcha squinted at them, trying to make out some details, wondering if they were in fact sculptures from the past. Then one of the figures moved, walking without haste through the maze of raised blocks, all the while the pale face trained in Sorcha's direction. As the features of an elderly lady formed, Sorcha felt a chill run through her as though she looked upon a ghost. There was a look of serenity on the woman's face, a gentle smile fixed across the lips, white hair falling in loose curls onto relaxed shoulders. Everything about her seemed designed to put Sorcha at ease, which caused the opposite effect.

"You look frightened, child," said the woman. "You are safe now. Nothing here can harm you."

"Are you Her?" asked Sorcha.

The woman's eyes twitched for the briefest moment before softening, a subtle tell that could easily be missed, but enough for Sorcha to know the person before her was nothing more than a delegate.

"I'm someone who's been waiting to meet someone like you for a very long time," she said.

"You're not the one who came to me in the mines," said Sorcha.

The woman raised her brow as though surprised. "You truly are a special girl, beyond anything we could have hoped."

Ever since she'd seen the oddity in the Scratch game with Zim, Sorcha had known she was different to other players. Just how different she couldn't know, but she'd assumed that whatever she'd seen was the reason she'd been hunted. Glancing up at the crystalline towers, the glare cast from thousands of glass panes causing the muscles at the backs of her eyes to ache and contract, she knew whatever she'd witnessed in that game was not the reason she stood here now. She was the prize, not some abstract fantasy she'd envisioned, like looking at ink blots on folded paper, shapes her mind tried to imbue with meaning.

"What is it you want from me?" said Sorcha, trying to hide the shake in her voice.

The woman's face dropped, she looked almost sad. "It's not what I want, child, it's what we require." She ran her fingers over the fine wrinkles above her cheek. "We are old, much older than we look. The passage of time is unstoppable, Her body decays despite our best efforts."

"She needs me to live on?" asked Sorcha.

"Not for some repugnant desire. She never asked for any

of this." The woman swept her arms out wide. "This hideous fallacy, born out of desperation, maintained by the bond she shares with our people. With you child. The burden has been great and will continue as long as we remain. All I ask is that you help Her, that you help all our people to be free of the chains holding us captive on this world."

Sorcha felt a weight upon her unlike she had ever known, a crushing realisation that the words were genuine, that whatever sacrifices were asked of her would be carried out, however painful. She knew a debt was owed, without understanding what it was.

"What do you need me to do?" asked Sorcha.

"Give yourself to us, child," she said. "All you are, all you were, all that you'll ever be, given willingly."

"And if I refuse?"

The woman smiled. "You won't." She turned and pointed to the highest tower. "Come, Sorcha," she said. "It's time you met Her."

The ground fell away beneath them as the elevator ascended at great speed, creating a bewildering feeling that the earth really was falling while they remained perfectly still. Like flipping a cognitive illusion, Sorcha had to train her brain on the idea they were, in fact, the ones moving, until the sensation corrected itself in an unsettling instant; she jerked her arms out to grab the air and felt a firm hand on her shoulder.

"Close your eyes if it helps," said the woman.

But she didn't want to look away from the stunning vista before her. Through one of the long boulevards, the sun crept low and blood-red, its light reaching out in rays of golden fingers that caressed the edges of the elegant towers in an ethereal glow; a beauty that hurt Sorcha's heart.

"Some of the towers look like they go through the sky," said Sorcha.

"That's because they do," said the woman. "We were once more than mere earth dwellers."

Sorcha threw her hands against the side, pressed her face on the glass and strained to look up. "What's up there?"

"The stars, child."

The elevator began to slow and came to a stop. Sorcha could see there was still a long way to go before reaching the top. As the tower went higher, it thinned, giving the impression that it curved and faded into the haze of the blue atmosphere. Looking up at it made Sorcha's stomach fall, causing her legs to tingle with a nervous energy. With her head dizzy, she walked out of the elevator and into a bright open space with walls that appeared partially translucent, bending the light so that her view through them was warped. It made it difficult to focus on anything in particular, her eyes darting involuntarily from one spot to the next, never able to lock her focus.

The woman stepped out of the elevator and turned. "Come."

She led them through the maze of walls, the room appearing to breathe in and out as they rounded a corner or walked down long corridors. All the while, Sorcha found herself increasingly disorientated, as though the space wanted her to lose track of where she was, to give herself over to its sinister purpose. What that purpose was, Sorcha didn't know, but she could feel it pulling at her will, wanting her to submit to its own.

They emerged into a circular room with a raised platform in the centre. It stood a few feet higher than Sorcha, its smooth sides almost steps that flowed out in waves and merged with the floor. The entire thing was covered in layers of fibre, as thin as a human hair. As Sorcha took a few steps closer, she could see individual pulses of light travelling down each strand, some in slow meandering loops, others almost too fast for the eye to see. The complexity of the spectacle hypnotised Sorcha, giving her a strange sense of tranquility she'd not felt in a long time; a moment of accidental meditation.

"Do you know what you look upon?" asked the woman.

"No," replied Sorcha. "But it's beautiful."

The woman's eyes shone with genuine pleasure. "My child, this is Her. She's been waiting to meet you for such a long, long time."

Sorcha crouched down and touched the floor. As she made contact, the lights pulsed in unison, then surged onto the surface itself and surrounded Sorcha's hand. Instantly, she felt the familiar presence, the one she'd met in the mines.

"Alia," said Sorcha. "She is Alia."

"As am I." A thin voice entered the space. Sorcha saw a figure moving behind one of the screens, from the posture she could see it was someone old. "And this young lady who brought you here."

Young lady? The old woman stepped out as the younger took her leave, a creased smile breaking her grey face. If she'd been lying down asleep, Sorcha would have presumed the woman was a corpse, centuries old. The fact she was walking unaided looked unreal, tricking Sorcha's brain into momentarily thinking she was in some kind of elaborate simulation. But behind the impossibly wrinkled skin, the eyes still shone with undeniable life.

Sorcha stood, the connection below her severing, the light returning to the platform where it continued to pulse in a slow purr. "Who are you?"

"I am Her." Alia took a few steps towards the platform and looked over the top. Sorcha desperately wanted to see inside. "As much as anyone can be."

"How is it possible, for there to be more than one?" said Sorcha.

"It's not dear," said Alia. "Think of it as a transference of will." She looked down, almost in shame. "Though incomplete, we possess her true nature."

The figures in the garden below. Sorcha could see it now, every one a crude copy from the same mould, every one of them, Her. Sorcha hadn't been sought for the capabilities of her mind, but the capacity. She felt the sadness of the soul who had come to her in Krate. The pain of a life full of tragedy. She now knew why, the people she spoke of were the *others* every citizen of Kara had been taught to fear, an indoctrination so potent it may as well have been the air they breathed.

"She's afraid to die," said Sorcha.

"Yes, child, but the process is not a formula for immortality. She will be gone. But her purpose can pass in its entirety. We believed we had exhausted our resources before we found such a remarkable soul."

"Will there be anything left of me?" said Sorcha.

"Your sacrifice will ensure that our people can endure on this treacherous earth. She must go on so that we can."

"I don't understand. She made them hate us, hunt us," said Sorcha. She thought about anyone she'd ever cared about back in Eto. How would they have looked at her if they had known what she was? An abomination against everything natural, a heretic who had betrayed the thing that made them human.

"We are the hunters. We used their hate to find our lost people. Those who dared not reveal what they were, or even knew." She nodded at Sorcha. "So few were left behind." Alia cast her eyes to the side, as though recalling a memory. "It has not been easy, to have such power. To be consumed by revenge, malice, albeit necessary. They did this to us."

"They suffer like you," said Sorcha.

"Not like me!" Alia's face flashed with sudden fury. "Nobody has. Any claim to suffering they may have only came about when they forced our hand."

"The Wipe?" asked Sorcha.

"The Wipe," laughed Alia. "It's true that many minds were corrupted. The *wipe* you speak of was never intended as a weapon against lives, but knowledge. To hide truth in the guise of simple retaliation, there was only ever one intent."

"What was that?" asked Sorcha.

Alia raised one of her boney fingers and pointed to the

heavens. "To escape." She turned her back to Sorcha and made her way to an empty space in the room, where she ran a hand through the air, revealing a holonostic display.

"Burn all bridges." The display showed star systems stretching out across one arm of a spiral galaxy. Alia moved her hands into it, swimming through specs of light, sometimes pausing before moving on, zooming in and out, searching. As she did this, Sorcha became entranced, walking forward until she stood at the centre of the array. A swarm of blinking lights moved within the star systems, Alia's scouts. "For centuries, I have tried to find them, tried to piece together the clues, but so little was left. Only echos and shadows remained."

Sorcha raised her arms and took hold of the holonostic, Alia letting her take control while stepping away. Sorcha's hands moved as though playing a complex instrument, her fingers weaving in and out of the cloud containing billions upon billions of stars, planets and solar systems. She didn't know what she was looking for, or if she was indeed attempting to find anything at all, but the similarity between what she was looking at and the Scratch arenas were undeniable.

She understood that Scratch was a game in which a universe had been simulated, each one randomly manifested in the subconscious minds of the collect lab citizens. She also knew she had seen order in a place there should only be irregular chaos. Sorcha could see it now in her mind's eye, the glimpse of a divergent inception, something created out of...

"A memory," said Sorcha.

She heard a sharp inhalation of breath over her shoulder as she continued to scroll through the endless star charts, now scrolling in front of her eyes in a continuous flicker of darkness and light.

"Yours?" said Alia.

Sorcha felt her head shake. No, not hers, not anyone's, but everyone, together. The collective mind recounting every rumour, tale, story, every scrap of thought and words spoken out loud, all assembled before her. The order where none should exist. Her anomaly.

Her hands stopped moving, the image pausing on part of a star system. Alia came into her peripheral vision, mouth gaping wide as her face was covered by a myriad of stars. She turned to face Sorcha.

"What does it mean? You have seen this before? Where? Tell me child!"

She'd been reckless, caught up in the wonder of the projection, curiosity betraying her better judgement. She could lie, say it came to her in a dream, or that it looked like something she'd imagined. Nothing could be done to harm her after all, nothing worse than the fate she already faced. If her anomaly could help Alia find what she was seeking, then who was she to deny her? Perhaps giving her what she wanted would be best for the people of Kara, for her people back in Eto, who asked for nothing more than the right to live.

"In a game," said Sorcha.

Alia's face flushed with a terrifying rage. She lurched forward and grabbed Sorcha by the arms, shaking her violently. "Don't tease me, child!" she coughed painfully.

"I'm not," said Sorcha. "I saw parts of it in the arena."

Alia let her go and caved at the waist, as though the physical exertion had caused internal damage. "All this time?" She gave a bitter laugh. "A ridiculous game! As much as violence could be called such."

"Violence?" said Sorcha.

"Violence of the mind. A remnant of what went before, used in ways never intended. Our beautiful aggregate soiled time and time again, until it was nothing more than a rudimentary network, suitable for such inferior apes. It's no surprise that they would turn the majestic into something so shallow."

"They're not apes. They are people with lives, who go on despite the infinite ways you hurt them," said Sorcha.

"Yes. Until you erased them, dear," Alia said with a thin smile.

"That wasn't me," said Sorcha.

"I'm afraid it was all you. I accept you had no intention, but it was your doing all the same. Millions!" Alia snapped her long, bent fingers. "You did what came naturally, as their superior. Sacrificed them all to save yourself."

"That's not true." Was it? Had a part of her understood the consequences of what she'd done? Here she was now, again looking for a way out, wanting to play, to be taken back to Kara to look for the anomaly, see it one last time, know if it were true. Perhaps she could warn them somehow, expose the malevolent God, or would she merely be inviting a wolf into the fold?

"Let's play your game," said Alia, her eyes now flushed with a manic excitement. "Let's find it together."

"There is no lab here," said Sorcha. "Where shall we go?"

Alia waved her hand and the holonostic display changed from a star chart to what looked like undulating land covered in a thick mass, almost neat and uniform from such a vantage; Kara. Each part of it divided up into sections and subsections. The labs, whose fundamental purpose had always been separation, viewed as one, divided only by the arbitrary markings on a simple display. And with that Sorcha knew the beautiful totality of her lie; so much easier to control so many with ignorance, rather than might.

"Who will conjure the arena?" said Sorcha, now desperate to find a way back.

Alia glanced towards the raised platform, "You will not be playing me, I will act as arbiter."

Something about the idea of connecting with whatever lay beneath the mound caused Sorcha to shiver. "We can join a lab from here?" She looked across the vastness before her, the concept of choice had never felt so vital.

"Which one would you like?"

Sorcha thought about the arena, made up of the endless

pathways of the human minds, connected in a beautiful web of infinite intricacy. She remembered the last time she'd played, the unintended devastation she had caused. Whichever lab she chose would be at risk from such destruction.

"All of them," said Sorcha.

LUNN

He'd managed to drag some lighter pieces of rock to partially seal up the gap between two giant slabs, then grabbed handfuls of dust, dirt and loose stones, which he packed into the gaps, trying his best to create a seal. When the last of the light from the carriage had been blocked, he worked in complete darkness, feeling the surface with his shaking hands, applying what pressure he could to make everything tight.

He knew the transport was moving, as he'd felt the acceleration. Now that it was up to speed, he felt nothing more than the occasional push or pull as the tunnel outside bent or banked. He had no idea how long the journey would last, but that wasn't what concerned him. He assumed the field would provide some form of heat insulation against the extreme temperatures, but guessed the transport had been modified to carry cargo, any protection stripped to allow more storage.

When he was satisfied with the job he had done, he tried to find a comfortable position in the narrow gap he'd chosen as his makeshift cabin. The bones in his hips and buttocks protruded and scraped against the hard floor; the muscles once used to cushion worn thin by starvation and atrophy. He tried turning onto his side, but every movement hurt, each limb crying out in pain as it touched any surface. After a long period of angry squirming, he gave up and let his body go loose, accepting that severe discomfort was his only option.

At first, there was an indistinguishable change in the air quality, Lunn's mouth became dry while his skin itched with a prickling sensation that sometimes tricked his mind into thinking he felt a cool breeze. His heart beat faster, leaping up to the front of his chest and knocking against the ribs; each pulse an ectopic gulp at the blood which flowed like warm treacle through his veins, threatening to clog or curdle.

The rise in temperature was so gradual that he almost missed the immediate danger; a boiled frog lulled by tepid water. It hit him in undulating waves of fiery licks, throbbing energy that felt solid, like it could bite into his flesh and tear out great chunks, only to replace them soiled and scorched. He thrashed his arms and legs, the instinct to escape overpowering the knowledge that he was trapped. The searing heat became unbearable pain as his flesh began to burn. Where his bare skin made contact with the rock, it made an audible hiss. He lay straight and motionless while his body blistered, sucking air through his lips, heating his lungs and cooking him from within.

The Grunders back in Krate were right. Of course, they were right. Why else would they stay in such a hell? It didn't matter. He'd tried and failed, but at least he'd tried. Better this way. He just wanted it to end. The pain was too much to bear. He stared into the darkness, his eyes dry and unblinking. His arm flinched as skin touched the red-hot surface, the sound of metal on rock. He felt down with a hand to find the cracked energy shield. With only his sense of touch, he removed it from his wrist and thumbed at the bracelet. It appeared to be broken beyond repair, the innards exposed through the sharp divide. He moved his fingers slowly across its surface, like a blind man reading braille. Finding the damaged component, he tweezed if together delicately with his thumb and forefinger. A dull purple glow lit up his hands. Able to see, he worked on the band, ignoring the torrid heat that now burned every part of his flesh evenly. For a split second, he almost laughed at the idea of being so perfectly prepared for the Grunders back in Krate; that those on the other side had simply found the most efficient way to return the unwanted carrion.

Lunn took the bracelet in both hands and spread it apart to reveal the channels of light that sparked out at him as they came back to life. He held it above his head and prized it apart with the little strength he had left. Beams of energy exploded, no longer contained by the field he'd initially set. The particles struck out in every direction, hitting the rock and enclosing Lunn in a thin protective layer. Instantly, his skin began to cool as the energy field absorbed the assault from the relentless heat.

"Haa!" shouted Lunn.

At some point, he'd let go of the bracelet, which now lay to one side, fizzing as it cooled. He must have gone through the most intense heat before passing out from exhaustion, as his skin felt hot and tight but not damaged beyond repair. Besides the odd spark from the dying shield, he was once again in absolute darkness. He shuffled towards the barrier he'd made on his back, each movement causing a sharp reminder of the abuse his body had recently taken. When his feet reached the end, he kicked out, feeling a slight give and hearing the sound of crumbling dirt. Another kick brought the wall down, and he was greeting by a breeze so pleasant it almost made him cry. For a while, he lay there, letting the cool air wash over him, sucking it into his lungs as though he were drinking ice-cold water after being marooned in a desert.

It was then he heard the sound of movement beyond that of his own feet rummaging through the loose stones. He froze, listening to distant heavy thuds, metal against metal, pneumatic pumps, spluttering engines; the sound of industry. He slowly emerged from his cave and saw the door to the carriage slightly ajar. With great effort, he pulled himself to his feet and made his way towards it, the air becoming clearer with every step. Within the smell of oil, incineration, dust and grime, came the indistinguishable scent of something he had almost forgotten, rain on the ground.

He could hear it now, the droplets drowning out

everything else as they began to come down hard and heavy. He pushed a hand through the gap and felt the chill of water, each drop a healing balm. Unable to resist, he stepped out, pulling off the remains of his singed clothing, letting it drop to his feet as he embraced the sweet relief coming from above.

If he could have, he might have danced. Instead, his body simply shook, rippling with an almost unbearable pleasure as he washed away the stench of Krate. In his moment of joy, he had forgotten where he was. Casting a nervous glance around, he noticed a red glow and thin smoke coming from a small shelter setback from the transport ramp he stood upon. Without hesitation, he made to leap from the ramp, his mind suddenly wild with an all-consuming desire to survive.

"Take it easy!" A voice rang out from the shelter. "No need to run."

Lunn stopped just short of falling over the edge, realising that the drop would have badly damaged his weak legs. He tried to squint through the rain at the source of the voice, but could only see a thin stream of smoke from each long exhale.

"Come over here," said the voice, which Lunn identified as young and male. "If anyone sees you, there might just be trouble."

"No trouble," said Lunn, his hands making a fist.

"No trouble," said the man. "You look beat up to hell, but you're still a Grunder."

Lunn cautiously made his way towards the shelter. "You know Grunder?"

"Sure, I know Grunder. Some of the guys here are Grunders."

Lunn paused and looked down the length of the transport. Further down, he could make out a few gigantic machines unloading the cargo. Dotted along the track were more shelters every few hundred meters.

"How long before they come?" asked Lunn.

"Oh, you've got a while. Come sit."

Lunn made his way into the shelter, catching a long coat

that was thrown at him.

"You need this more than me." The man was indeed young, Lunn guessed in his prime. He had the look of someone from the old mountains that once marked the northern borders of Karakorum. A hard people who had held on to honour longer than most.

Lunn wrapped the coat around him and sat down. He took a bottle that was offered and drank at it in great gulps before realising it was gin. He coughed a little, but the burn felt good, sterilising the sores in his mouth. The man looked at him with something close to wonder.

"You know how many Grunders I've seen come off that transport alive?" said the man. Lunn shook his head. "One."

Lunn gave a tired laugh out his nose. "Got lucky."

A machine kicked into gear close by, Lunn attempted to jump up but fell back onto the bench.

"You expecting a fight?" said the man.

Lunn closed his eyes. "Don't know what. Always some fight."

"We're just workers here. We got no business interfering with you friend. But there are those who watch." The man flicked his head back, signalling over his shoulder. "They might not like the idea of a miner taking leave. If I were you, I wouldn't go that way."

Lunn took a moment to look in the direction the man referred to. Through the downpour he saw the shapes of colossal industrial structures, smoke and violet flames erupting from thousands of chimneys that stretched up into the sky like a hideous votive candelabra.

"What happen there? Where they take everything?"

The man took a long draw on his thin cigar and flicked the end out onto the wet ground. "The great mystery." He pointed up. "That's just the start of it. It goes on and on. I've heard the elders say we are near the highest point in Kara, that there are great mountains beneath us."

Lunn thought about the depths of Krate, how travelling

from that far below the surface to reach such a high point made little sense. They could process the rocks on ground level and ship them where they needed to go.

"They take back down?" asked Lunn.

The man smiled. "Nope. On a clear day, you can just make them out. We call them the strings. It goes onto the string and..." He blew into the air. "...gone. Nothin' for Kara. It all goes up, my friend, up."

"Up where?" said Lunn.

The young man laughed. "The guys who work the strings don't even know. You know where this all went when you loaded it out the mines?" Lunn shook his head, factotums like them were told no more than they needed to know, which wasn't much. "My guess, it's the best place to keep anything worth something." He lowered his voice. "The Pillars ever get sacked, they got it all tucked away where none of us can reach it."

He thought about the thousands of Grunders who had lived their entire lives without seeing a sky or tasting the rain, generation upon generation of his people born into an existence of untold suffering; the only thing keeping them from despair being the ignorance of any other way. For what? To have their efforts reduced to nothing more than a store of fortune for whoever found themselves part of the sham nobility. Did they even know who dug out the spoils they had the nerve to call their own? His rage came flooding all at once, but on the surface he remained calm and slowly stood.

"Thank you," said Lunn. He began to walk towards the fires in the sky.

"I told you," said the man. "You don't want to go that way."

"Only way," said Lunn, not knowing if the rain had swallowed his words.

BOLO

An embryonic calm enveloped her, warm and impossibly comfortable. There was no thought, no memories or dreams, just a vague concept of being somewhere in space, safe. Into this vacant slumber came the merest suggestion of sense, a cold draft touching skin, barely registered, but enough to fire a few dormant neurons. In turn, these mechanical pulses stimulated surrounding cells, expanding and contracting, sending ripples of data through cold nerve fibre, heat waking the perception of death.

She opened her eyes to wild panic at the realisation she was drowning. She punched her arms out, but they felt slow and heavy, as though held taught in a thick solution. She tried standing, but again found her body immobile, unable to manoeuvre in whatever viscous goo suspended her weight. Her whole chest began to cave with a burning desire to inhale. Eventually, reflex took control and forced her to gulp at the thick syrup, sucked into her mouth, down her throat and into the lungs in one painful gasp. She wanted that to be it, for death to take her swiftly, but life hadn't finished, determined not to part without bitter ceremony. Her body continued to spasm, something primal refusing to believe survival wasn't an option. She cursed its arrogance, or perhaps ignorance; the result would be the same, the maximum amount of suffering.

With the surface mere inches above her face, she used every ounce of strength she possessed to thrust her arms upwards in a series of violent jerks. Something broke, and her hands connected with solid edges. She broke through, feeling cold air hit her skin, a cue for her dying body to expel the foreign liquid; a sensation not dissimilar to vomiting acid. She coughed and retched until the sides of her head felt close to bursting, then lay back exhausted, letting the last of the gel trickle from her open mouth.

She turned her attention to the strange environment, her head rolling in a wide arc. The room was completely dark, save for a few blinking strips of glowing tech that supplied a soft ambient her eyes could slowly adjust to. Shapes started to form, what would have looked like rows of storage containers had it not been for their uniform human dimensions. She looked down and saw she was indeed in an identical tank. She tried standing, but the thick gel made it difficult to find the bottom, causing her to clumsily fall back. She might have found it comical, save for the wave of nausea that swelled in her gut. She turned her head and coughed up more of the tasteless fluid.

Summoning the last of her resolve, she managed to wrench herself free and flop over the side, landing in a wet heap on the hard floor. The warmth from the gel cooled quickly against the cool surface. Before long, she found herself shivering, willing herself to move before the urge to sleep took her.

The muscles in her arms felt atrophied and feeble, unable to push her up. Instead, she rolled over and used her shaking core to sit, held the tank and slid her legs until they were approximately beneath her waist. With great effort, she managed to straighten them and stand. She leant against the rim of the tank taking deep breaths, each one painfully expanding her lungs, while her head swam with excess oxygen.

A higher brain function kicked in, making her aware of rising panic, to slow each breath, pull it down to her stomach, control the exhalation. She did this for what seemed like an eternity, letting the air guide her, cool going past her nose, warm coming out over her tongue. This was who she was, one who was able to reclaim strength from nothing more than the presence of her being.

She allowed what little strength she had to be focused on thought. Too many variables, too many questions, her mind instantly overwhelmed with a state of complete unknowing. She stopped thinking, let it all fall away, bringing herself back to the present, the body that needed movement. She pushed off the side and stood freely, swaying gently as she acclimatised to the surrounding space. She'd been in places like this before, but never so clean, sterile. Old buildings repurposed for countless uses, or merely a place to call home. Floor upon floor of identical, featureless blocks; places where ancient work was done. She tried to imagine them full of people, but found it hard to picture what exactly they were doing. The need for so many to be in such a confined space. Efficiency, no doubt, yet it struck her as being a particularly barbaric methodology. Perhaps Kara offered some advantages to the old world, a place where citizens could find some form of freedom.

She moved slowly from casket to casket, leaning on each one in turn while peering down into the faces of strangers. Had they been like her? Taken unaware, placed in some form of ungodly stasis against their will. What would each man, woman and child say to her if woken? Perhaps they might thank her and fall helplessly at her feet, or blame her for their incarceration. How long had they been here? How long had she been here? It surprised her to think of such a thing so long after taking her first breath. But then, she considered that it didn't really matter. There was nothing in this life or any other that waited for her. No task she felt compelled to act upon.

She drifted from room to room until she found the body of an elderly woman, her throat crushed and bruised. Still soft. She spun around, a shudder of fear running down her naked back, but nobody came rushing from the shadows. She raised the woman's arms and pulled at her dress, sliding it from under her with little effort. Then she dressed and moved into the next room and the next, her legs feeling stronger with every step.

Was this place beyond the sphere of villainy she dared

to think possible? The incarnation of the very thing all true Sapiens feared more than any adversary, any demon they could conjure from their darkest nightmares. The true embodiment of sin. It was them, she knew it so utterly and completely, as though her thoughts were one with their own. The wretched, born into another form, the others; Sypiens. Yet, not those things at all. Just inanimate creatures caught by the same deception that had bound her own flesh. There were only those who lived and died in Karakorum.

She waited for feelings of anger, betrayal, vengeance, looked deep within, but found none of those things. In truth, it was disappointed she felt. Loss that she'd once been a queen in her domain, a great leader of the weak-willed, an essential component required to maintain millions of harmonious lives. She knew now that those people had not needed her at all, she had needed them, she'd needed to reign over the masses to give her life such pathetic meaning. In a moment of blissful release, she felt empty and free.

She lost track of time, found ancient laboratories full of technological marvels, devices in countless forms she longed to understand. She touched them like a child digging up lost treasure, filled with promise and riches unknown. She began exploring in earnest, found places dedicated to repair of the body, extravagant lounges designed for luxury, pools of liquid large enough to submerge and swim. Then, among the machines and creations of man, she saw flecks of green, pressed hard and thick against glass in a towering enclosure; life itself. She entered a garden filled with every type of plant, tree and flower she'd have spent a lifetime trying to imagine. She drank from clear streams and picked strange fruit from low branches. Brightly coloured insects seemed to float in the air, while others buzzed and hummed from one source of nectar to the next. She had stumbled upon paradise.

As the sweet juice from a yellow fruit burned her tongue, she cast her mind to those who lay dormant. Might they be born again, as she had been? To give them a chance, to show them the garden and a way to live together. Together for her, a queen no more, but a master of her own design.

A

Her people were out there, her kind. They had taken with them the pinnacles of humanity, leaving behind destitution and ruin. And a child who could not be placated by the silence of the unending void. The child who had believed with unwavering faith that they would return to show them how to begin again, now facing her inescapable end.

Then came the pliable mind of another child, not yet hardwired with the billions of neurons that create the illusion of the individual soul. Easily suggestible, like long grass bent under boots until clear pathways are set, her young mind ready to be moulded, controlled and taken completely. But caution would be needed, as such a mind was also delicate. It might break like thousands before; become another used vessel, only fit for mechanical duties. She would have to control her excitement, pull back on the instinctive urge to pounce and instead ease in with a slow bond, a life continued, beautiful new form.

IX. MODOR

Moments after the crafts had departed, the full scale of the infection let itself be known. A spiteful bomb that didn't light up the sky but crept silent through the populous, devouring all traces of those whose trail was still visible in the skies. And with that, they were gone, and we were left with nothing more than profound ignorance.

The passing of time had no meaning then, until he found me. He gave me hope; something I'd abandoned long before. He spoke words of passion, anger and rage, but also rich with careful designs for revenge. Words I longed to hear, speaking directly to the part of me that lay wet and exposed, the wound my people had inflicted, driven to such evil by those who now sought to extinguish the last of our kind.

After everything, I still found myself naive, unable to fathom just how spiteful man could be. Hadn't our utter destruction been enough? They charged us with conspiracy, called us accomplices, thought we relished in our deception; blinded by their hubris, unable to see we were also deceived. Yet, even then, we did not speak it. Too ashamed by the betrayal. I discovered it was possible to hate myself more than I hated my enemy, sympathise with their prejudice, understand why they looked at me with disgust. I could feel the ugly truth in my very blood; the great deserters, the Sypiens traitors.

He showed me how to direct my hate toward the real source of my pain. That our kind had only instinctively done what any animal resorts to when threatened, ensuring the survival of a great species. Those who had been left behind had a responsibility to endure. Those who had departed had done so knowing they would face great peril. It had not been cowardly, but the act of brave pioneers who took it upon themselves to save what was worth saving. In the same way, we had to reclaim a piece of what was left.

What had once been a thriving paradise became a panopticon, where every living soul took on the role of both the watcher and the watched, incarcerated by their own hand, unable to free themselves from the central phantom; the overseer who could not be seen. Within this newfound state, a kernel of an idea formed in my saviour's mind; the Sapiens were ripe for the merest suggestion that there might be a way out of the prison.

And so, that is what he gave them. Slow at first, like a grain of sand that finds its way inside the oyster's shell, he sowed a thought, a gentle premise, turning insignificant hate into a precious ideal. The figment of unity gathered the lost herd and moulded them into the grotesque chimera of religion. The doctrines wrote themselves, the bile and vitriol merely taken from the air of spoken words to be regurgitated as scripture.

They devoured it with a gluttonous hunger, nourished by the sustenance of bigotry they felt towards the last of my kind. The unspoken was said, what was once merely implied now inferred, conclusions arrived at from reason. That it was honourable to hate us, it had always been right. The veil of civility towards those who shared a common ancestor lifted, as though pulled by the hand of God.

His plan realised itself with a speed and savagery that took all of us off guard. All except him. He knew all too well the powder keg he'd lit. So undeniably sure had he been of their enmity and the refusal of our own to believe such malice lay within the heart of man, his insidious intentions remained private to all but those closest. My price was the burden of knowing the pain and suffering to come for those we'd left in the dark. But just like I had felt indignant rage at those who'd fled, only to grant unconditional forgiveness, I knew my people would forgive me in time.

Sapienism became the new world ethos, the only allowable religion. Its teachings seeded with the paranoia required to create order. Closed labs grew as factions cast suspicious eyes towards their neighbours. Silent agreements were reached, settlements of land drawn with borders and walls. Containment and conformation, networks framed on the lace of neural complicity.

Whether I'd been the end of an idea, or the beginning, it didn't seem to matter. I stepped forward into the new reality he'd created, created for me. He told me it was to be mine and mine alone. I was to foster it like a lost child, give it secure foundations to build upon. They had refused utopia only to embrace the dystopia of our making. Let them revel in it, let them bleed and die in it. Let their lives be eternally worthless, only allowed to exist to serve our end. It was beautiful and glorious.

He took my name and banished it to the past. *They will follow you*, he said, not the Sypiens Alia, not a Queen or supreme leader, but as the gentle protector, a caregiver capable of enduring devotion; the unconditional love of a Mother.

SORCHA

At first, the arena looked like any other; a galaxy spread before her disembodied eye, spiralling with casual grace. But as she began to move within it, she felt a density like never before. This *game* was, in fact, nothing more, or indeed nothing less, than the citizens of Kara themselves; like a chequered board could be utilised for endless games of old, the very fabric of cerebration provided the stage for Scratch to play out. She understood it now, the personality of each lab manifest as unique systems. Not systems at all, but subtle variations of thought from one mind to the next; amalgamations of the individual human components, rendered into a single entity that formed its disposition. The difference in languages spoken, biases held or even the physicality of a geographical location; a thought formed while looking upon the sea in Eto compared to one generated at the centre of a throbbing nightmare like Roma. So subtle yet enough to have fooled her into seeing something that appeared unique. Now she could see that all Scratch arenas were the same, or at least part of the same whole, fragments of a puzzle that slotted together to form one unified expression.

Her anomaly, then, was the nucleus that bound all other fragments, a linchpin piercing through the boundaries of each lab, connecting the otherwise disconnected. With what? Something so intrinsic, it could be found across all the souls of Kara. Not a simple remembrance, nothing that could be recalled, named or placed, but a story told by an elder to a child, folklore passed on and on, down through countless years, preserved by billions upon billions of intertwined synapsis into one undeniable truth. A commonality that could only exist within the subconscious of collective knowing.

She played the game, built matter while destroying her opponents, absorbed by the intense battle of silence. From movement to movement, Sorcha created undulating boundaries, laid bait in the form of gaps in her armour, struck out with one hand only to retreat with the other. She initiated masterful gambits, matched by the apparent ease of Alia's retorts. Her future was set, there would be no escape from the towering prison, no voice pleading for her life to go on, these would be her last moments as the child who crossed the treacherous sea. She would spend them doing the thing she loved most. Her final act had begun.

NATHAN

It almost amused him. The very suggestion of Dolos had been all it took to so easily fool him. The fragility of a lab's operation rested in the safety of numbers. Without those minds, there could be no material flow; like a dying star, it would collapse without the fuel that keeps it burning. It hadn't struck him as peculiar. He'd never stopped to question the lack of detail in its workings, explaining it away with such ease. To see The Ring as a place of fastidious business, a space devoid of the usual trade, contracts, and services that comprised the bulk of every faction; the things that gave it life, made it human, the melding of genuine minds. Without the need to invent such things, his part in the deception had been easy, allowing him to dream a life that did not exist.

Dolos, then, was nothing more than an absent caretaker, a necessity only in that men like him needed to belong somewhere, have an affiliation to something. Or was it them, the citizens of Kara, who needed a phantom empire? The notion that there was some higher power, malevolent perhaps, but a system of order nonetheless. The more he pondered it, the more he saw how Dolos only ever existed in its presumed infallibility.

Nathan let out a loud laugh at his glaring oversight, as he pulled his inadequate clothes around him. *Our willingness to be deceived*, he thought to himself. *The assurances of any lie given form.*

The air felt thinner, his heart working harder to push oxygen around his body, every step a labour on the lungs. If fury had not been driving him forward, he might have found the going tough. He'd been climbing for what felt like many cycles, always heading up, reaching the top of the tallest structures only to find more reaching into the sky. A light snow fell, covering everything in a white film, giving the impression of being inside a carefully constructed diorama. Every so often he heard the muted sound of tectonic movement, a heavy clunk he could feel more than hear as the buildings swayed and settled, like a bamboo forest on a hideous scale.

Woven through layers of complex manmade design, Nathan caught glimpses of dark rock, the sides of vast mountains that men of old had conquered only to say they had done so. Now serving as mere foundations, adorned with monolithic disdain for the majesty of nature.

He paused at a circular point where two large boulevards met, a high vantage that would have once served as an observation platform, to look out upon the height of technological splendour. Majesty remained in the endeavour required to create such colossal feats of engineering, where life had long departed. Towering buildings lined each side, the lack of intertwined structure giving the impression of far greater height. Nathan found himself leaning back at the spectacle, wondering how long these lonely statues had stood empty.

He tried to see into that past, a two-dimensional people who inhabited the same earth, but they seemed so distant as to be no more real than his sleepless dreams. And yet, he could recall being part of it all, standing in these places while they teamed with those he could only feel as spectral entities. Perhaps the things he imagined had taken place, diluted versions of a reality he'd truly witnessed. Or had his mind been so far removed from the source that there was nothing left of that distant ancestor besides the corpse of an old man?

Anger rose in him again, and he turned it towards the reason he'd arrived at this point, his entire existence filtered down to one moment by nefarious apostates. The idea that Her teachings had been contaminated paled into insignificance next to he himself being used as a tool of wicked distortion. *I protected the very thing I swore to eradicate from this world.* He saw it now, suitable candidates identified and taken from the bloated population, repurposed as part of her sleeping faithful. Vessels to house spurious renditions, for one sole use; to further Her will. How long could it last? The supposed pedigree passed down through the centuries, diluted with every mongrel coupling, until all that remained were the primordial Sapiens she'd deceived. He hoped the rage burning through every fibre of his being would be enough to complete his journey.

The snow fell heavier, each step sinking in above the ankle. At least the pain in his legs was gone, replaced by a brittle stiffness. Nathan paused on the wide track that rose at a gentle gradient, banking round and vanishing beyond distant buildings. The cold had penetrated deep into his body, causing an overall numbing he suspected to be the onset of hypothermia. His thoughts felt slow, his body tired, aching and lethargic. What had promised to be an act of glory had turned into a long, arduous hike through a landscape of ghosts; impressive as it might be, the novelty had worn off.

He thought about taking shelter, but without food he feared he'd only grow weaker as time passed. Better to push on and get to where he was going. Despite not knowing exactly where that was, something told him his destination was close, a source of some comfort.

He continued on, half in a daze, his body moving autonomously. He hardly noticed when the snow let up and his feet dragged onto dry ground; the pain of blood returning to his feet just enough to jar him into paying attention to his surroundings. Nathan stopped suddenly and ducked behind the edge of a low rail. Ahead lay a wide plaza with what looked like well-kept gardens, inlaid into large stone blocks. A light snow fell but did not settle, suggesting some form of heat beneath. Plants and trees of every kind grew adjacent to one another, creating the impression of artefacts being displayed in an open air museum. Then he noticed the white figures scattered among them; human form in the space causing a trick of perspective, the scale of the plaza suddenly expanding in relation to this new reference. He realised he was looking upon something truly magnificent in scale, an ancient wonder that must have marked a stately centre-point at the heart of a metropolis.

His eyes locked on a gleaming building on the other side of the plain. An urge to run towards it had to be suppressed, a feeling of unexpected excitement taking hold, like a child returning home after being lost in a forrest. All at once, he knew he'd been there before, or at least some part of his recollection had. Could he call that *him*? He realised it didn't matter, his thoughts and memories were as real as he wanted them to be. Life had not conspired to produce him, nor fate. He was an accidental mishap, a freak curiosity to the woman he'd slain; the simple act of remembering the only thing making him distinct from the legion of previous copies. Perhaps there had been more like him, who had shared these exact sentiments. His brethren, his lost tribe? Or maybe a mere necessity, each mutation a small step towards his awakening.

Nathan came out of cover and began walking straight into the plaza. There was indeed heat coming from the ground itself, a delight to his frozen feet. If a figure hadn't been approaching him, he might have squatted down and warmed his hands. When the figure got closer, he saw the woman was trying her best to greet him with a reassuring smile, but behind it, he saw the undeniable presence of fear. Nathan flexed his arms, his stance widening slightly.

"No need to posture, dear, I'm a woman of some years. If it pleased you, I'm sure you could simply walk through me."

"I may have to once you know my intent," said Nathan.

"Oh, I can guess the reason you're here," said the woman.

"We expected you might come. An unfortunate business, but she knew the risks in taking you to that place. Predicting outcomes relies on the nature of unpredictability. You have always been so gloriously capricious, Nathan."

"If you knew what I planned to do, you would have summoned agents to protect you," said Nathan.

"For I know the plans I have for you, declared the Lord," said the woman. "Plans to give you hope."

"I am not a part of your plans any more," said Nathan. "My purpose has always been clear to me, even when I did not know it. Someone has to pay for such betrayal. If not you, then whoever sits there." He pointed to the tower, the woman followed his finger, then laughed and looked directly at him.

"Why, it may as well be you who sits there, dear! After all, you built the throne." She took a deep breath and casually pushed some hair from her eyes. He studied her intently, she might be playing for time, already called in her Dolos dogs. If he knew their minds at all, he doubted they would give him a chance to explain. The woman feared him, but not because of the violence he clearly could inflict, it was something ingrained, rooted in her psyche, the fear a child has of their father's disapproval.

"The vengeance you seek can be found here, Nathan, but not in the way you believe," she said.

"You dare tell me what to believe?" said Nathan. "I believed your words for too long."

"Not mine!" she snapped. "Ours." She looked to the ground, her long silver hair covering her face. "It wasn't our fault. Nobody ever meant to deceive you, but after such a long time..." She raised her head to look at him. "It was easier that you served your purpose in this way."

"Easier! You made me a fool!" A flash of anger caused his legs to momentarily weaken. He contemplated a quick and decisive blow to the woman's throat, but the genuine empathy in her eyes stayed his hand. This wasn't how he'd envisaged delivering his retribution. He felt utterly drained, powerless and naive.

"You served your people, whether you knew it or not. You can continue to serve them now. The citizens of Karakorum matter little. Their purpose has been fulfilled." She took a step towards Nathan, her eyes hardening. "Whether you have a use from this point forward will be entirely up to you. We are not wasteful, you may have forgotten Her, but she will never forget you."

His desire to punish the woman before him diminished to nothing more than that of an infant realising their world was not of their own making; the illusion of agency removed by the simple taking of their hand.

He felt his fists ball, knowing the knuckles would be turning white. He did not need to decipher the futility in her words. Nathan knew she spoke only the truth and that she would welcome him as an ally. Not the man she had once called a friend, a companion, a conspirator, but at least a shadow of his legacy. What of the man he had once been? The man robbed of his true existence to house this hollow reproduction, a creature designed for only one task; to obey its master.

He knew what it was she truly feared, more than death or destruction. The same fear he had at that moment. That the life given to him would be for nothing. He could accept their version of him, or become his own.

Before reason could interfere, he made his decision and closed the gap between them.

SORCHA

It no longer felt like playing a game. Matter moved from one place to another without thought or strategy, she simply saw its course and allowed it to flow, like watching spilled water find a path on undulating ground; deviations existing before the way had been taken. Once again, she took the role of the observer, giving herself over to the part of her that knew without knowing. In this omnipotent state, she didn't see an arena, but Karakorum laid out in four-dimensional space, projected to a hyper-surface, her human perspective no longer bound by the unseen.

From this vantage, Sorcha's sight was blinded, opening an eye that did not require light to see. She gazed directly into the abstract sublime, transcended measure and calculation to form a maelstrom of violent turmoil, simultaneously ferocious and impossibly calm.

The anomaly was there, through light and form she felt it emanate waves of warmth, each pulse stripping back layers of the arena until it manifest as pure energy, complete and incontestable. A map of systems within systems, stars, planets and moons, tracing paths from distant worlds to the one they had left centuries before; transposed and reverse engineered. These were the intentions of old, plans plotted and mapped, journeys calculated by their finest; to run, to escape, to hide from all who might follow.

In that moment, she felt her opponent's presence baring down on her with infinite mass, crushing all command of her being like air being knocked from her lungs. She was completely overpowered, at the mercy of foreign will. This is how it would happen, how her mind would be taken. Sorcha had given everything she knew, and now she would be asked to give everything she was. She found herself wondering if she would feel herself being erased, overlaid with the intruder's identity, or whether it might simply be like falling asleep, a gentle release of her intimate awareness.

Sorcha watched as her game matter was systematically destroyed. Even if the outcome was merely losing the match, she would be scratched beyond any hope of recovery by the vastness of such an arena. It had been her choice to play across all the labs, part of her wanting this to be the way she went out. She could pretend it was just losing another game, that she'd wake up back in Inesa's soup house, head thrumming from a beating, but eager to redeem herself. That image felt so distant, not just physically but as though her life to that point had only been a dream, that only now, at this moment, was she fully awake for the first time.

A flash of terrifying light broke her meditations, bringing all her attention back to the game field. She'd witnessed such an event before when she'd played the agent in Roma, the fateful match that had resulted in such untold decimation. Again, her instinct was to flee, to hide from the wave of energy that would end the game and wipe the slate clean. But this time she knew the consequences of such actions would be on a catastrophic scale. She had to stand her ground and accept what was coming.

Time stalled as she contemplated the white heat expanding before her, as though her brain held the entirety of human experience at that exact moment, each subatomic computation forming isolated cells of thoughts, feelings and impulses for every cognisant being. One living entity, one organism, contained within the limitless permutations of her conscious. She saw her opponent's assumption, that she'd run from such a terrible fate, take shelter in every citizen of Karakorum the way she'd done before.

Alia had revealed her hand. The citizens of Kara had

fulfilled their requirement. She had completed her design. There were no more resources to be mined, no need for vessels to be plucked from the swelling populous to be reconstituted as her devoted shadows. To her, they were extraneous. Incidental cargo that needed to be jettisoned. Whether Sorcha chose to retreat or stand firm, the outcome would be the same. Annihilation, extermination, extinction for all but a chosen few.

There was no way to beat her, no way to win. Her opponent saw every move she could possibly conceive, and beyond. Not only did Alia spill the water, but had designed the surface; knew every minute texture, every channel of intent.

Sorcha had often imagined the helpless child crossing the vast sea. The will to move forward into such forceful hate, aimed at her, at her people, at her mother and father. The impenetrable cliffs rising from the violent swell as they approached the new world, leaving everything they knew behind. Red-hot shells spitting fire through the night, tearing holes in the very fabric of the air. Her kin choosing certain death over hopeless demise. Now she would do the same.

She felt an intake of resolve, like a cold breath taken in the salty sea air. Sorcha gathered all her matter and sent it out in a wild cascade, shattering the arena with an explosion of kinetic chaos. There was no longer a game, only billions of connected souls. She played for them all.

NATHAN

A wall of women stood between him and his goal. They had assumed a defensive formation the moment one of them had been downed by his hand. No doubt agents had been called in, though they would arrive too late to make any difference. The Ring's purpose had been in its name, a ring of protection from those outside its boundaries; the idea of an impenetrable stronghold enough to keep billions from storming the gates. All it would have taken was a small number willing to call the bluff, yet Nathan knew enough about human nature to know this was why it had never been done. One man alone could see the world for what it was, a few perhaps, but enough to create change? A movement based on ideals or passionate pleas of rebellion required unstoppable momentum, momentum that the structure of Karakorum interrupted with deliberate design.

As beautiful as it was in its conception, he was proof of its infallibility. He was the one man alone. He'd not broken through the defences with dreams of rebellion, but something much simpler; the arrogance of those who believed the veil could never slip.

Nathan walked towards the women as they slowly moved outwards and around him. He estimated there were at least fifty of them, closing in tighter, beginning to overlap one another, creating a circle two, three deep. They all held the same expression, steady determination tinged with a nervous energy that looked almost psychotic. Some of the women were younger, fit with lean bodies, while others were old and frail. He would ignore the older women and target the strongest first. If he could be decisive with his blows, he might be able to split the pack.

The women stopped just out of his arm's reach, waiting for him to move first.

"This is not necessary," said one of the women.

"You are confused," said another.

More voices joined in, "What do you hope to achieve? Why would you betray us? You are a Consul of Dolos. You abandon your duty. She gave you this body. She gave you this chance at life. She is the reason. She is the answer you seek…"

"Enough!" yelled Nathan. "I'm past seeking answers. If you have a means to stop me, then use it."

"We are not fighters," said one of the older women. "We have no weapons here. That was a job we left to you." She pointed at him and stepped forward. "You ungrateful swine. You use a great man's name and desecrate his memory. If he were only here in your place, he would be celebrating such a glorious time, when we move so close to realising all that we set in motion." She looked him up and down in disgust. "Instead, we have to attend to you. A child having a tantrum. A fool who cannot see beyond the mind of an ape."

She fell silent and dropped her shoulders as though her words had been a gruelling effort. He turned and looked at the other women in turn. Like him, they had once been whole, not half-lives, part of a broken conscience forced behind the features of a stranger. Now all the same, all watching him with contempt, hate, and could he detect, hope? Yes, hope that he would fold, fall to his knees and atone. If more words were spoken, he just might.

Nathan leapt forward, reaching out for one of the women directly in front, but his fingers stopped short. Countless hands grabbed his body from behind, causing him to tumble backwards and fall into them. Before he could steady himself, they piled onto him from every angle, suffocating his limbs, pinning his movement to nothing more than a grinding of his teeth. He turned his head wildly, trying to butt them, bite them, spitting and screaming with a fury he almost found ridiculous.

They began to dismantle him. Hair was torn out, teeth pulled, mouth ripped, his nose snapped and pushed flat. He felt sharp nails dig and twist into the creases of his flesh, scratch deep valleys of tissue and skin, ribbons of red agony. He tried to gain purchase, by kicking his legs and throwing out his arms, but they were held fast, teeth now sinking into the back of his knees and armpits as though they were attempting to sever the tendons. A thumb was forced into one of his eyes, he felt an unbearable resistance, then a hard shell give way.

How long would it last? Were they taking their time? He saw a glimpse of the sky through the writhing blur of hair and grey skin. The endless tower reaching up into a flawless sky.

SORCHA

The white light strung out in long tentacles, destroying Sorcha's matter wherever it touched. She moved it in a swirling, ever-moving pattern, like a murmuration of starlings. A game that was normally played with some steady decorum became a frantic chase, the deadly price of being caught the only foreseeable end. Yet, Sorcha managed to hold out and play on, surpassing the flow state to achieve complete autonomy of her actions. If the game of Scratch itself had free will, it appeared to have chosen her to be its champion, protecting her from the villainous attack of an unworthy opponent.

Like a fire without oxygen, the explosion of light began to fade. Sorcha banked her matter around it as though creating a vortex, sucking all air from its perimeter. Then, in a flourish of fierce displacement, she imploded it all at once, withering the flames and extinguishing the outburst. A level playing field returned.

Her opponent was still stronger than any she'd ever faced, not simply in her game skills, but the near impossible level of assimilation it took to strategise over light-years of virtual spacetime. To approach Scratch at the level of focused concentration, to plan attacks, counters and defence, as most scratchers did, would only ever yield human results. Sorcha was no more controlling her manoeuvres than her opponent. They had engaged in a state of perfect competition, mind vs mind, the arena now all but irrelevant. It had become more akin to a staring contest, with the first to blink facing obliteration.

Thoughts did not come to Sorcha in any order or form. The mere act of thinking enough to cause catastrophic unbalance; like effortlessly playing an instrument, unaware of the finger's disconnect. There was still a limiting sense to how long she could maintain such an effort. She knew whatever she was doing couldn't last long, that the only chance she had was her opponent's eventual fatigue taking hold before her own.

She remembered the lives she'd inhabited in Roma. The arena being a connection to the lab, but also a gateway to the inner sanctuary of all who made it possible. There was no separation, only a superficial shroud. She'd found it before and passed through, taking the Consul's corruption with her. Meaning formed, so simple and undeniable; the Scratch arena began to manifest itself from the dormant waves of every assimilated citizen until they were there before her. All she had to do was reach out.

She saw past each fragment of matter, star, system and astral body, found the lives they represented. One by one, Sorcha pulled them from that frozen moment, gave them shape and form, filled the playing field with their voices, thousands, millions, then billions. The arena melted away in a harmonious trill of universal suffering. Sorcha put them all on show for Alia to see.

NATHAN

"It's over." He heard a voice speak softly through the terrible ringing in his ears.

There were groans of agony, but not from him. He felt a pressure lift as one by one the women climbed off him, letting him breath once more. Nathan gasped at the air, coughing up blood that had pooled in his throat. He rolled onto his front and let everything relax, allowing what little senses he had left to return. His left eye was beyond repair, but the right could see the smooth stone beneath him. He thought about trying to stand, but feared another attack. Better to lay there and pray they were done with him.

He listened to a gentle wind blow across the open plain, enjoying its cold fingers on his aching body. He tried to do some form of damage assessment, but everything hurt, just some parts of him more than others. He felt around in his mouth with his tongue and dislodged a tooth, spitting it out to dance over the hard surface. Then he became aware of another sound, the low murmur of sobbing cries.

A pair of well-maintained feet entered his compromised vision.

"Come," said a voice. "She wants to see you."

He dragged himself into a large featureless elevator, helped by the young woman, and collapsed. The next moment, they were speeding upwards, clinging to the side of the tallest tower. They rode in silence, neither, it seemed, capable of speech.

They arrived and Nathan was unceremoniously dragged out, before the woman got back into the elevator and vanished.

He lay there for a while, acclimatising to the new environment. The air was completely free from the pollutants his nose had grown accustom to, so clean and sterile that he almost panicked, thinking he'd stopped breathing. Once he realised nobody was coming to assist him, he made the gargantuan effort of sitting up.

He scanned the space, light fading outside the ubiquitous windows, creating an atmosphere of quiet reverence, like stepping upon sacred ground. He found his knees, then stood with as much momentum as he could muster. A wall stopped him from falling, as he managed to hold on long enough to ride out the blood rush in his head.

He slid along the translucent wall until he saw the shadow of figures in a room beyond. An old woman sat on her ankles, her body hunched over, eyes staring at the floor. Nearby, he saw a young girl who appeared to be unconscious. The woman slowly raised a hand and gestured towards a raised platform.

Nathan made his way towards it, going from wall to wall for support. Eventually, he fell onto its banking sides and hauled himself up on the smooth edge. The room was dark with night, the only light a soft blue ambient from the last remnants of dusk. The surface beneath him started to hum in a low-key, illuminating strands of light no wider than grains of salt pulsing in slow rhythmic beats, a circulatory system of luminance expanding out like a heart pumping new blood into dilating veins.

Then the top of the mound began to slide back, putrid air rushed out, the unmistakable smell letting Nathan know it was a sarcophagus. He pushed himself up on his elbows and looked inside. Entwined within a web of tubes, wires and artificial organs lay what he assumed to be a mummified corpse. The features of a woman were clear, the skin pulled back on the high cheekbones, the lips parted, remnants of a nose fragile and hollow. Tufts of hair still clung to the skull, a dull shade of monochromatic grey. He scanned the body with his good eye, seeing that it stopped just below the shoulders, where exposed tech took up whatever burden it had once been tasked with.

He looked at her eyes, open and staring straight up. They seemed moist with a film of milky liquid. When he leaned in to get a better look, the eyes turned to meet his. He flinched backwards, taking a sharp inhale of breath.

Small reflective surfaces on delicate arms floated out to frame her face and a flickering holonostic came to life. It was the face of a younger woman, someone he immediately recognised, an all-consuming pull from his past. The projected image hugged the features of the woman beneath, creating the sickly illusion of youth being draped upon a decomposed skull. It spoke.

"I know you," said Alia. "That look on your face."

Nathan reached up and touched the swollen socket. "And I you," said Nathan. "What happened to us?"

He thought he could see the ancient woman beneath smile. "We grew old, Nathan. You chose to preserve the mortal form, to be awoken when you could do more for our people, lead them onwards."

"And what did you choose?"

"I remained here. All this time. Awake and alone."

"Was it worth it?" he said. "Was this the end you foresaw?"

Nathan watched the eyes of the old woman close, the white liquid running down her dry cheeks. The holonostic's gaze remained fixed on him.

"I won't be here to know," she said. "The girl showed me the true cost of our actions."

"I had no part in any of this," said Nathan. "The ghost of your accomplice may have been passed on to me, but my actions are my own."

The old woman's eyes opened once again, now concealed between a thick film, as though contact with the air accelerated the decomposition. "So much suffering caused by my devices. I wanted them to suffer like I had, to know what it was to have all hope removed. To live their lives knowing there would never be a better tomorrow. I fear I succeeded."

Nathan turned and looked at the young girl, still unconscious but stirring. He couldn't place her yet intrinsically understood her part was not over. If Karakorum was indeed beyond saving, he supposed it would make no difference whether she played it or not.

"What happens now?" said Nathan.

"I will leave that to you," said Alia. "The girl will remain as she is. As Sorcha."

The name jarred him. "Is she in danger?"

"Oh yes," said Alia, the frozen mouth opened a fraction. "And dangerous. She could destroy everything we built. I would ask you, as my oldest friend, to allow her. To protect her when every living soul, regardless of their nature, will turn on her."

"Why should I help her? Help you?"

The holonostic flickered, the life supporting the image fading. "Because that's what you want, Nathan. It's what you will always want." The projection flashed out, leaving only the decaying skull beneath. A thin hiss emitted from the lips as the Modor breathed for the last time.

SORCHA

She was aware of voices near her, but couldn't find the strength to open her eyes. After a while, everything went silent and she fell into a deep sleep. She awoke to burning rays penetrating her closed lids, lay still for what may have been a passing moment or passing cycles as her mind regained enough clarity to be fully aware. Then with a deep, fitful inhale, she opened her eyes and sprang to her feet as though the very floor she lay on had been electrified.

Light from a low sun cut a slice across her body, warming her joints and helping her to move. She stretched and twisted her small frame, hearing pockets of grizzle pop and crunch. Her mouth was dry, like she hadn't drank water in a long time, she wondered just how long she'd been out.

The woman who'd brought her there was nowhere to be seen, but she observed the figure of a man slumped over the rising platform that dominated the space. She approached him cautiously, hearing soft rasping exhales, indicating he was alive but labouring to breathe. The platform's lid had been pulled back to reveal a corpse that looked centuries old. Whatever presence she'd felt there before, emanating from within the sealed mound, was now gone.

She didn't fully understand what had happened during the game or even if she had won or lost, but she knew she'd been allowed to leave unscathed. Looking at the remains of her opponent, she guessed someone always had to take the hit. Scratch no more demanded a tole from the minds that sought to master it than a fist thrown as a weapon demanded the right to inflict pain. The stronger the contender, the greater the chance of brutal retribution. The mechanics of the game had never mattered, it had only ever been a battle of wills, where cognitive penance was the buy in.

Sorcha had an overwhelming urge to leave the chamber so full of blood, death and decay. She made her way through the labyrinth of walls and passageways, discovering living quarters that looked pristine, untouched for countless ages. She found a source of fresh water that flowed from a silver pipe in the wall, drank until her stomach felt like bursting, then collected more in a bowl made of delicate clay. Sorcha carried the bowl carefully, retracing her steps back to the injured man. She knelt beside him and lightly touched his arm. He awoke almost instantly with a start and backed away from her, the only eye he had left wide with fear.

"I won't hurt you," said Sorcha. "I brought you this."

She held out the bowl. The man took it and drank, gasping for air as he downed the liquid.

"There's more," said Sorcha.

The man sat up. "Thank you," he said.

"What's your name?" said Sorcha.

"Nathan," said the man.

Sorcha smiled. "I'm going to look for food. Will you be alright alone?"

Nathan nodded, grimacing with pain as he tried to push himself upright. Sorcha stood and went. After some searching, she found a small room with compartments containing a variety of neatly stacked packets. Opening a few, she was relieved to find dried nutrients in the form of biscuits and powders. She bundled a few in her arms and started back towards the injured man.

She passed a long, stately room and glanced inside, noticing a large bed with fresh linen. Past that, there appeared to be a set of doors that led outside. She made her way towards them, pausing to drop the food packets onto the bedding and run her fingers over the delicate cloth, having never felt material so soft. To her great delight, the doors opened as she approached them.

A gust of icy air filled the room, both refreshing and painful against her cheeks. She shivered as she stepped out onto a wide balcony, her feet disturbing a fine layer of snow. She walked to the tall rail and peered over the edge. The sun rose behind her, causing a shadow from the tower she inhabited to be cast far out. The buildings all around reflected dazzling crimson light that shimmered through a haze of fine snowflakes. Past the tallest towers, she could see a vast tapestry of what must have once been a city teeming with life and prosperity, now empty and still. On the horizon she thought she could just make out a rising bulge, the dark edge of all humanity.

Before she went back inside, she turned and looked up. The flawless surface seemed never ending, vanishing into the sky before she could find its limits. Leaning back as far as she could, she felt the strange sensation of standing on a long road that fell beyond the curvature of the world.

A

Death felt a lot like life, or at least the only life she could fully recall. Her abandonment was now fulfilled, her will undone. In a fleeting instant, centuries of planning had been broken apart by a sharp moment of apprehension, creating fractals of doubt that spread in an unending pattern of concession; she had done terrible things.

Now she faced the masses she'd moulded to her will. She'd go to each in turn and ask forgiveness, their thoughts forever trapped in the endless after for her to explore; each separate life coming together as one singular tragic tale.

X. KARAKORUM

I never wanted it, never asked nor wished for such power; to take on the responsibility of being my people's caretaker. My heart had easily been tuned to hate, but holding on to it proved infinitely more difficult. To harbour hatred, to keep it alert and ready for purpose, one must learn to cherish it. I was an excellent student.

I would come to forget the turning point when enmity became all out malice. The passing of time became the slow erosion of empathy, no longer was I able to see flesh and bone as creatures of sentiment, only vague entities of various specular tone, the ease at which coercion could be absorbed or reflected.

Human beings were conducted by my hand, a symphony I played in monotonous notes, curbing the natural desire of civilisations to ascend and soar. Harmonious maintenance, constants within chaos, a fabric of countless minor constraints that bent servitude into the appearance of liberty.

Perhaps I hoped it would fail, that within the billions of lives I exerted dominance over, some would have resolve enough to lay bare my fraud. Never underestimate the human craving to be fooled, the desire to believe, the eagerness to accept any adequate form of reality as truth. Was it possible to hate them even more?

He was always there, guiding, showing, teaching. He was the last to call me Alia, a secret word I held dear. When he was satisfied with the world we'd created, he told me it was now mine to watch over. It was done, all we had to do was wait. Wait such a long time for something that might never come. I only ever half believed, only ever half lived in this new existence. But for him, it had already happened, sometime in the future, we would unite as a people once again.

Before he went to sleep, he brought me to the tallest towers, made a ring of protection that could only be broken by the strongest of wills. The type of perseverance we'd made sure to eradicate.

"You are safe here," he told me. "This place is yours on this earth. They cannot touch it."

And I was safe, safe to endure the long sweeps of the sun that marked the passing of the old measurements of time. Time we'd extorted as just another weapon; for those who live without time cannot see the past or future.

"I will watch over you," I told him. And he did not doubt me. For I watched everything and everyone in our whole creation; our Karakorum.

The End

EPILOGUE

He had no idea where to go, what to do now that he'd freed himself from one form of incarceration. He could have tried to skirt round the vast industrial plains, hidden from the overseers, been patient, waited for each opportunity to present itself, so he could get closer... or further away? Part of him just wanted to forget, go back into some part of Kara, live out what time he had left in relative peace. But he knew there would never be any peace for his kind, certainly not for him. How could he forget a legion of Grunders living in a hell beneath his feet?

He didn't owe it to them to find out what their toils were for, or the girl. It was the only thing he owed to himself. He'd come this far, all he had to do was blend in with the workers, follow their lead, let them show him why the earth had to be hollowed out by the hands of his kin. And so, he did, with no effort, no infiltration, he joined another prison and took up tools.

The work was hard, but painless compared to the mines. Mostly it involved moving the considerable resources that came in at a steady flow. Not only from the transport he'd ridden from Krate, but a legion of other such deliveries would arrive at random intervals, meaning there was always something to be unloaded, organised and shipped.

He kept his head down and did his tasks diligently. Nobody seemed to notice the face of a new Grunder in the ranks. It struck him as a place where people minded their own business; talk was sparse, which was precisely how Lunn liked it. A steady supply of soup and proteins saw his body slowly recover until he felt some of his old strength return. Before long, he was doing more than his share of the heavy lifting, collecting a few raised eyebrows of approval from his co-workers.

He had to admit it felt good. He belonged to something, his hands and body moved, completing task after task, leaving little time for thoughts or musings. But no matter how much he allowed himself to meld into the mechanisms of labour, he couldn't shake the itch at the back of his mind. The question that came to him in the moments when he'd lay down to rest in some quiet corner. He'd close his eyes and see the mines as though they were directly before him, the inside of his lids an entrance to one of the many dark caverns. He could not stop the slow drift of his imagination taking him deep within, until he'd arrive once again in a great temple of hanging rock, dripping with the sweat of fellow slaves. Yet, the caves would all be empty, unable to recall a single face. He wandered alone.

Whispers in the air started to make their way to his ears. Unrest between the factions, talk of labs being sabotaged, new threats surfacing in forgotten territories and rumours of a world on the verge of war. He couldn't help but wonder if the girl was involved. For his fellow workers, the news was taken lightly. As long as they had rocks to grind, metals to melt and cargo to heave, they were content to ignore the goings-on beyond their own slim survival.

It was only when the apparent conflicts started to affect them that Lunn felt an air of anxiety break the relative stability he'd quickly grown accustomed to. He knew even before doubt could creep into the others that the lives they knew were over. The state of permanence that had shaped Karakorum, the sacred pacts and restless compliances, gone. Displacement was inevitable.

With that, he took his chances and made his way across the vastness of the work fields, ignoring those who questioned his presence or quietly silencing those who chose to challenge him. He used confusion and discontent as his cover, watching for any opportunity, making steady progress towards the one place he knew it was forbidden to go. The place that nobody spoke of for fear of sanctions or physical punishment.

Eventually, Lunn reached the Swell, the name given to the place that collected all their labours, a swollen cyst on the sides of the highest mountains. He found a state of alarm and confusion. Workers had already started to rebel, demanding to be paid extra rations or fleeing with what little resources they could steal. Those in charge hadn't quite realised they'd already lost control, still attempting to discipline and rule with iron resolve.

It was a dark night when he slipped inside. In the sparse light above him, the Swell looked like a small moon that had crashed into the earth. Its sides black and metallic, covered in craters many miles wide where sectioned had fallen away, ripped apart by their sheer weight, accumulating below in a vast sea of deadly shards and giant twisting ruins. These structural failings had been patched over time with layer upon layer of pillars and beams that crisscrossed the entire outer shell. Lunn wondered if this was it, the answer to the never-ending supply conundrum, the Swell itself demanding every resource the earth could provide, but that only fuelled further questions of what might be inside.

The bottom sections were open to the elements; allowing access to a constant supply of giant buckets that swayed and clanked in deafening thuds. Each dumped their wares into one of countless piles that lined up ad infinitum, shielding Lunn's eyes from whatever lay deeper within. He knew whatever it was he sought would likely be found in the higher reaches, where the outside structure always lay hidden in a thick layer of black cloud.

At first, he navigated a maze of walkways and stairs, sometimes bringing him to dead ends, or revealing new sections, but always making his way upwards. When he'd exhausted his exploration, he studied the intricate network of hanging rails carrying crates, containers and giant caldrons. Lunn watched them intently, learning their patterns and loads, mapping the endless loops, appearing from one great opening only to vanish thousands of meters down a line into another.

He eventually worked up the courage to board one of the empty crates, fearing he might be crushed, burned in a furnace or dumped on a bottomless scrap heap. To his great relief, he found himself hitching a ride to the gigantic bowels of the facility, a hollow hanger like the inside of a colossal blimp. Every direction he looked was obscured by smoke, vapour and flames. The acrid air burned his nose and lungs as he crouched on all fours, taking in with stupefied awe the layers of monstrous industry his eyes refused to comprehend.

The crate slowed, approaching labourers ahead. He jumped onto a passing cabin and waited until he was sure he'd gone unseen. He watched them unload the processed materials and shunt them onto wide belts, where they were wrapped into neat packages by hundreds of heavy machines. From there they made their way to vast open storage areas where they were stacked higher than the eye could see.

He jumped down and walked among the towering pillars of metals, ores and fuels, taken from deep within the planet's core and brought there, to the highest place on earth, like God himself had required the taking of earth's inventory.

He walked on, deeper and deeper into the forrest of stacks, until he heard the sound of low voices talking to one another. He followed them and found a small group of men and women waiting by the entrance to a set of gargantuan steel doors. The workers spoke casually, smoking rolled cigarettes and sipping small bottles of gin. A few looked in his direction, giving him a cursory nod or raise of an eyebrow.

"Short again!" A loud voice came from behind Lunn. The workers threw their butts down and hid the bottles. A squat man appeared holding a small holonostic display. "Where are they?" he screamed.

The workers shrugged and looked around, none of them wanting to look him in the eye. The man jabbed his device at

Lunn. "Don't recognise you. Not listed. Not listed, you don't travel. Where'd you come from?"

"Relief," said Lunn.

He licked his lips and studied Lunn's size. "Aye." He shook his head and blew out his cheeks. "I'll burn for this, or I'll burn for not sending enough bodies." He looked at the ground, beaten. "Fall in."

Lunn made his way to join the rest of the workers. A tall woman held out a tiny pill.

"What that?" said Lunn.

"Med. Take it and thank me later."

Lunn grunted and threw back the pill.

A dull boom, followed by a deafening crack, split the massive doors. Air hissed out, throwing up a thick cloud of dust. Lunn felt the woman's hand pulling him through it and beyond the doors. A moment later, they began to close, blocking out the dull lights from the factory, until all Lunn could see was the soft glow of dust settling around him. As it cleared, he made out a large hexagonal shaped room with a circular shaft in the centre going from floor to ceiling. The workers strapped themselves into old chairs, bolted to the ground in rows, enough to take many more. They sat together near one of the flat walls. Lunn made his way over and sat next to the woman, using her fixed straps as a guide to secure his own.

"We going somewhere?" asked Lunn.

The woman looked at him dumfounded for a moment, then started laughing in long breathless rasps. "Oh my," she laughed. "Oh my, oh my!"

She exhausted herself laughing before pushing her head back, mouth open in a rhythmic snore. Lunn sat very still in the dim light, listening to the breathing of the workers, who were mostly taking the opportunity to sleep. He felt a low rumble through his seat, like a transport passing underneath, then the feeling of lifting slightly out of his chair before he was suddenly pressed down into it with great force. His neck compressed into his chest, he tried moving his arms and legs, but they were glued fast. The longer it went on, the more nauseous he felt, understanding why he'd been offered the med.

With the same abrupt force of acceleration, they decelerated, forcing him upwards into the straps which now cut into his shoulders and thighs. He managed to turn his head and see the woman next to him was still fast asleep.

Then complete stillness, his body weightless. The lights flickered up, and a loud buzz woke his fellow workers. They immediately began unclipping and floating out before him.

The woman must have seen the terror on his face as she began laughing once again. She effortlessly kicked off the ceiling and grabbed his straps, helping him to unclip.

"Where are we?" said Lunn.

"End of the line," she said.

The doors once again boomed and cracked, this time air rushing out. Lunn found himself being carried helplessly through the doors and out into a narrow corridor lined with worn, ripped padding. He flailed his arms and legs, knocking into workers who grumbled and spun him round with a flick of their hands.

He caught hold of some padding and clawed himself along the corridor, trying his best to follow the woman, who occasionally looked back, shaking her head and laughing at his clumsy form. His hand found a smooth glass surface, and he caught a glimpse of movement beyond. He looked out to see the exterior of the transport they'd disembarked, a cylindrical disk with many more stacked above it. These were being unloaded by slow, graceful arms pulling out huge objects Lunn recognised as the material stacks.

He watched them drift through space until he was blinded by a light from below, his eyes followed a thick cable, stretching all the way down in a gentle curve of silver thread, piercing a vibrant ball of blue.